Bess managed to twist free of the hand that covered her mouth and screamed again, the sound merging with the stormy night.

"Griffith, Griffith." Her piteous cries caught the wind and soared above the storm, and, in answer, a figure appeared at the edge of the clearing.

The men fell back, for indeed it was Griffith Beaufort who stood before them. Griffith—or an ancient god of war invoked by the plight of this hapless maiden. In his haste to answer the screams, Griffith had snatched up his sword and shield and, clad only in his small clothes, his cloak whipping out behind him, now stood like a god of vengeance. The wildly whipping firelight and the screams of the wind joined with his battle cry as he unleashed the fury of his mighty sword, casting men about as though they were leaves, defenseless against the storm of his anger....

Dear Reader,

Barbara Leigh's first book, *To Touch the Sun,* showed her strength as a medieval writer. This month, she returns to that era with *For Love Alone,* the story of a young commoner, just out of the convent, and the handsome nobleman who fights for the right to wed her.

Also this month, we are very pleased to have Curtiss Ann Matlock back with her new historical Western, *White Gold,* the unforgettable story of unlikely partners who must face countless dangers and their own growing attraction on the sheep trail west.

Our other titles include *Lion's Heart,* by Suzanne Barclay, the beginning of a new medieval saga featuring the Sutherlands, a clan of Scottish Highlanders, and *A Bride for Adam,* by contemporary author Muriel Jensen, the tale of a mail-order bride who is forced to keep the secret of her own sons from her new family.

We hope you will keep an eye out for all four titles, wherever Harlequin Historical novels are sold.

Sincerely,

Tracy Farrell
Senior Editor

Please address questions and book requests to:
Harlequin Reader Service
U.S.: 3010 Walden Ave., P.O. Box 1325, Buffalo, NY 14269
Canadian: P.O. Box 609, Fort Erie, Ont. L2A 5X3

BARBARA LEIGH

For Love Alone

Harlequin Books

TORONTO • NEW YORK • LONDON
AMSTERDAM • PARIS • SYDNEY • HAMBURG
STOCKHOLM • ATHENS • TOKYO • MILAN
MADRID • WARSAW • BUDAPEST • AUCKLAND

ISBN 0-373-28854-9

FOR LOVE ALONE

Books by Barbara Leigh

Harlequin Historicals

To Touch the Sun #98
Web of Loving Lies #177
For Love Alone #254

BARBARA LEIGH

discovered romance at the tender age of five, when she got chills listening to Snow White sing about Prince Charming. It was then that she realized "there was life after Dick and Jane." Unable to find the kind of stories she sought, Barbara began making up her own and never stopped.

Barbara, who has five children and six grandchildren, lives in Southern California with her husband, a large doll collection, two dogs and a cat. She writes in a loft above the family room, which is affectionately known as "fairyland."

To my agent,
Florence Feiler,
a true lady of the literary world,
with love and gratitude

Prologue

England, 1508

"Elizabeth! Elizabeth!" The imperious voice demanded immediate attention.

Bess got stiffly to her feet from the prie-dieu where she had been kneeling. "Yes, Reverend Mother," she answered. "I'm here."

The nun's face crinkled into a mass of wrinkles as she smiled at Bess. She was fond of this girl, whom she had raised from the time Bess had arrived at the convent, hardly more than a babe.

"Perhaps your prayers have been answered," the nun told her. "Your mother is here to see you."

Bess's eyes flew open in amazement. Not once, in all the years she had spent at Saint Lawrence of Blackmore Priory, had her mother come to see her. She had been allowed to visit her home occasionally, the last time being after the death of her father. It was unthinkable her mother would come here.

Bess stepped back. "What does she wish of me?"

"Perhaps she has come to arrange for you to take your vows," the prioress said hopefully. There was little enough money at the priory, and the girl's dowry would be welcome. The monies that had filtered in through the years for her board and keep had done little to support the healthy young woman who stood before the prioress. Smiling to herself, she ushered the girl toward the room where her mother waited.

Edwina Blummer was a small woman of exquisite proportions. Her natural slimness and petite figure did much to belie her age. Her smile seemed painted on her lips as she turned to face her daughter.

"Bessie, sweeting, let me look at you." She embraced the girl and then held her at arm's length, scrutinizing her closely. Yes, she would do nicely, Edwina thought as Bess squirmed under her mother's determined surveillance.

"I would speak to my daughter alone," Edwina said, dismissing the older woman.

The prioress raised her eyebrows, but took Edwina's words with good grace and left the room.

"Have you brought my dowry so I may prepare to take my holy vows?" Bess asked. She sensed something strange about her mother, something Bess, however inexperienced, thought might be the signs of a woman in love.

"No, sweeting, not quite..." Her mother turned to glance out the window. The sight of her lover leaning casually against the wall gave her the impetus she needed to continue. "Actually, since your father's death, we've been burdened with taxes and other debts. I'm afraid your dowry has gone to pay those."

Bess opened her mouth to protest. She knew that a dowry was held inviolate, and was the absolute last money to be used.

Edwina caught the girl's sharp look and was aware that her daughter suspected something, but she went on with her little speech; after all, there was no reason for Bess to know that her dowry had been spent on Sir Morris.

Edwina hesitated, thinking of the joy she had gleaned from the use of those monies. A flush of color rose to her cheeks as she remembered the impassioned lovemaking. Surely she would find a way to provide another dowry for her daughter at a later date. Now it was imperative that she hold the affections of her lover and that he not discover she had a daughter of marriageable age.

Edwina sighed to herself. It was lucky Bess had inherited not only her mother's good looks, but the illusion of youth, as well, for Bess Blummer looked very much the child. Her face was filled with the innocence of childhood. She was untouched by the world in her little haven at the priory, her body yet unripened, slim and straight, apparently shapeless beneath the robes she wore. It would be simple to pass the girl off as several years younger than she actually was.

Not only would this ploy allow Edwina to subtract several years from her own age, making her very nearly the same age as her youthful lover, but it would give her some time to acquire another dowry for Bess.

Flashing a quick smile, she returned her thoughts to the girl who stood before her. "Now, my sweeting," Edwina continued, "I have wonderful news! I have secured a place for you in the household of the Earl of Pembroke. You will serve in waiting to the earl's daughter, Mary. Does that not please you?"

It did not please Bess, but she held her counsel, allowing her mother to continue singing the praises of the house of Pembroke while she fought back tears. She had thought to spend the rest of her life at the priory, never to have to face the world, of which she knew less than nothing.

"Now, hurry and get your things," her mother was saying. "We must leave immediately to arrive at Pembroke in good time."

"Leave now?" Bess gasped in disbelief, "I cannot—"

"Of course you can!" her mother said, interrupting her. "Sir Morris is here to escort us." With these words, Edwina glanced toward the window, assuring herself that her lover did, indeed, wait without. "There can be no better time!" Looking again at her daughter, Edwina caught the promise of an amazing beauty, all but hidden beneath the voluminous robes.

Edwina's mind worked quickly. She knew that her lover was fickle. It took all her wiles to keep him interested. Now, faced with a lengthy trip in the company of a younger woman, she winced at the thought of comparison.

"Remember, Elizabeth, you must keep your face covered. I do not want Sir Morris to think you forward. I have told him that you are but a child, and I expect you to behave as such." Edwina coolly disregarded the astonished look on her daughter's face, and hurriedly continued. "You wouldn't want him to think the nuns had been remiss in their instruction, would you?"

Bess knew the nuns had not been remiss, but she would comply with her mother's wishes, as she had no other recourse. The first of the lessons she had learned was that of obedience, and she had learned it well.

After gathering her meager belongings, Bess stopped for the mother superior's blessing.

"Oh, Reverend Mother, I do not wish to go," she sobbed, and knelt for the prioress's blessing.

Placing her hand on Bess's shining head, the woman commiserated with her. "Pray do not weep, my child. Trust in God, for his will must be done."

Bess doubted that it was the will of God, so much as the will of her mother and the man, Sir Morris, that would be accomplished, but she kept her doubts to herself and asked, "Will you bid farewell to the others for me?"

"Of course," the prioress said, fighting back her own tears. "We will remember you in our prayers and in our hearts."

Her hand rested on Bess's head, as it had so many times in the past. But this time would be the last. The girl, in her innocence and beauty, was to be thrust into a world for which she had not been prepared.

"Remember all we have taught you, Bess. Be true to God and to yourself. Remain devout and chaste, and know that you are always welcome to return to the convent, should you feel the need to do so."

Unable to contain herself, Bess broke all rules of decorum and buried her face in the skirt of the woman's habit.

"Why must I leave?" she cried. "I love it here!"

The reverend mother held the girl close. "Perhaps God has an even greater love awaiting you," she said softly. "A love so great you will forget all about us."

"I will never forget you." Bess tried to dry her tears. "Never!"

"Nor I, you," the Prioress responded.

In response to Edwina's insistent rapping at the door, Bess took her leave and followed her mother down the narrow hallway.

"You certainly took your time," Edwina complained. "Sir Morris will be at the end of his patience."

She looked at her daughter, noting with envy her shining white-gold hair. "You must cover that hair," Edwina demanded. "Braid it quickly, and put it atop your head. You cannot ride with it blowing about you like a shroud."

She watched impatiently as Bess complied with her wishes. When Bess's hair was braided and secured satisfactorily, Edwina threw a traveling cloak about her daughter's shoulders, pulling the hood well over her head.

"Here we are." Edwina's voice changed to sugared sweetness as she reached the gate and her lover hurried to meet them.

"So this is the little girl," he said, trying to peer into the dark recesses of the hood.

Bess, finally realizing that she was really leaving the only home she had ever known, had reached the limit of her emotional endurance. Tears started down her cheeks. Her nose and eyes turned red as she scrubbed at them, trying to fight back the torrent of sobs that threatened to engulf her at any moment.

So it was that Sir Morris saw only a red-eyed waif in his cursory glance beneath the hood. Perhaps the child had some promise of future beauty, but for the time being, he was quite contented with the charms of the mother. He could not repress a smile as he helped Edwina mount the horse, his hands lingering about her supple body. He would be rid of the girl soon enough, he thought as he mounted his horse and led the little procession toward Pembroke.

Chapter One

Bess hurried down the cold, damp hall of Pembroke Castle. The servants were the only ones who stirred this early in the morning, and their duties kept them, for the most part, in the kitchens until the nobility awakened. It was during this time that Bess had chosen to take a few moments and go to the chapel to pray. As was customary, the chapel was in the oldest part of the castle, directly above the dungeons. She shivered from the thought, as well as from the chill of the air. She had only thought to throw a thin robe over the nightdress she wore. The mornings were cool, though the days were warm enough. During the winter, it had been difficult to pray without one's teeth chattering.

Slipping through the heavy door, Bess took her usual place at the back of the chapel. She had been at prayer for several minutes before she raised her eyes to the soaring nave. There, kneeling before the altar, was the figure of a man.

Bess stared in disbelief, never before having encountered anyone in the chapel so early in the morning. He must be a wayfarer, perhaps a pilgrim on his way to the shrine at Walsingham. She studied him curiously. He might be a man of God, perhaps a poor cleric, from the drabness of his mud-spattered clothing. And he must have been traveling some distance. Weariness was reflected in the strong lines of his body. His head was hidden by his cowl, but it, too, was bent with an air of exhaustion as he continued his prayers.

Silently Bess crossed herself and slipped into the aisle. The last thing she wanted was a confrontation with a man when she was not properly dressed. Since she had been at Pembroke, Bess had learned much, but she still hardly knew how to respond to the good-natured jests that followed her through the servants' quarters and into the upper regions of the house.

She blushed at the thought of the ribald words to which she had been subjected.

Bess genuflected, silently apologizing to God for her abrupt departure. She had hardly regained her feet when a voice echoed against the silent walls.

"Perhaps God has answered my prayers and sent an angel to give me ease."

She looked up and was stunned to see the man towering above her. His face was tanned, adding contrast to the blueness of his eyes. His red-gold hair gleamed in the candlelight like the sun on a summer day.

Bess could only gasp in surprise. He was much younger than she had thought, and in spite of the drabness of his clothing, his bearing was that of a nobleman.

"F-forgive me, m-my lord," she said. "I came only to offer my thanks for a safe night, and ask the Lord's blessing on the day. I had not meant to disturb you."

In her haste, Bess stepped in front of the huge nave window and was caught in the first rays of the sun. It reflected through her nightclothes, revealing the sweet young curves of her body.

"But you do disturb me." His eyes flickered over her before he looked away. "You disturb me greatly."

"Forgive me, my lord." The girl curtsied in confusion before she whirled around and fled from the chapel.

"I forgive you," he said as he watched the lithe figure running down the darkened hallway, the white gown flowing about her as if she were a wraith, or an angel, her white-gold hair falling veillike below her waist. "I do forgive you," he repeated, "but I doubt I will forget you."

He turned back to the altar and genuflected before leaving the chapel himself.

He had hardly taken ten steps when a voice called out, "My lord Beaufort" Walter Prigge hurried toward him. "We had all but given up finding you, and were about to conduct a full-scale search of the castle."

"And, like as not, you would never have found me!" Griffith Beaufort laughed heartily, slapping his companion on the back. "But, since you have discovered my whereabouts without tearing a sleeping castle to bits, let us break our fast and get on with the hunt. If we are to supply the tournament with game, we must be swift and lucky."

"But, my lord, we've ridden all night. Surely you must jest about participating in the hunt today. Tomorrow would do as well," Walter protested.

"Today would do as well," Griffith said, and strode down the hall, his long strides causing his companion to hurry to keep up with him.

Bess looked from the high window, barely able to peer over the edge, though she stood on a clothes chest. The men were mounting their horses in the courtyard below. Her eyes searched out the golden-haired man she had seen in the chapel.

He stood near the edge of the crowd, talking jocularly with his host, the Earl of Pembroke. Bess realized she had been mistaken in her first impression. The man must be of some importance, to be so familiar with the earl.

The young man's eyes scanned the castle, and Bess stepped back from the window, lest they find her. Then, unable to restrain her curiosity, she again leaned forward, in time to see the men mount and ride through the castle gates.

How beautiful he was, Bess thought as she watched them disappear into the forest. He was taller, and far more handsome, than the others in the hunting party. For a moment she rested her head against the coolness of the stones. This man had awakened some unknown spark within her. It seemed to grow more intense, more volatile, each time she thought of him.

Despondently she tried to tell herself there was no place for a girl of her lowly station in the life of a man who spoke so easily with the master of Pembroke. Closing her eyes, she sought to blot out his memory and determinedly uttered a silent prayer, but it did little to ease the gnawing that had begun deep inside.

"Elizabeth, whatever are you doing up there?" called Mary, the youngest daughter of the earl and his lady.

Bess whirled around, almost toppling from her perch. "I—I but watched the men go to the hunt," Bess explained.

"Then they've gone?" Mary glanced at the window, a hint of disappointment in her voice.

"Aye, m'lady, they have made the forest by now," Bess assured her.

"Well, come down from there and get dressed," Mary commanded. "There is much to do today. The castle is in a turmoil, and my lady mother is wringing her hands. So many guests to feed and bed, and so unexpected. How like

Prince Henry to descend unannounced on a household.''
Mary shook her head as she spoke.

"The prince is with them, then?" Bess asked in a small
voice. Could it be that the magnificent man she had met in
the chapel was the crown prince of England himself? But no,
it was common knowledge the man who would one day be
Henry VIII loved rich, brightly colored clothing and that his
father, Henry VII, was hard put to keep him from indulg-
ing in his wardrobe.

"Aye, the prince is indeed with them." Mary smiled a
small, secret smile. "The handsomest, most magnificent
prince in Christendom, they call him. And truly said, too,
but hardly the most thoughtful. Now hurry, we have much
to do this day."

Mary rushed out the door, leaving Bess alone in the room.
Bess was starting to obey her mistress when her eye was
taken by the reflection in the tall mirror standing against the
wall. Recently brought from Venice as a gift from the earl
to his daughter, it was one of Mary's proudest possessions.
Bess had paid it little mind, but now she paused before it.

In its depths were reflected her wide blue eyes, dark-lashed
and tilted at the edges, and her thick white-gold hair, tum-
bling about her shoulders. She pulled her bulky nightclothes from her body, diligently inspecting her youthful
figure. Sighing deeply, she turned away. No man would look
at her. It was as her mother had told her—she was too young
and immature to do anything but wait on Mary, and she
should be glad she was allowed to do that. No man would
think of looking on her childish body with anything but
distaste.

Despondently she compared herself with the rich curves
of her mistress, measured her small, firm breasts against the
round, deep orbs of which Mary was so proud. No, no man
would look at Bess, and even if he did, what use would it

be? Bess had no dower, and her blood was not good enough to attract a husband from the entourage that rode with the crown prince of England.

Hurriedly Bess girded herself to meet the challenges of the day.

The castle was abuzz with excitement. Despite the added work, everyone was eager to please the prince, who had come for the tournament. It was a singular honor.

"With His Majesty the King in doubtful health, any favor the earl might attain could place him in good stead when Henry comes to power," Wat, the steward of Pembroke, said in his most authoritative voice as a group of servants gathered about him.

He nodded his head as he spoke, his bald pate glowing in the light of the afternoon sun. "Now, off to work, all of you." He clapped his hands, and the servants scurried to do their assigned tasks.

Bess approached the man quietly. "Mistress Mary has nothing for me just now. Is there something I can do to help?" she offered.

"There are linens to be folded," he told her. "You may do it, for there should be much use of them before the prince and his party depart."

Bess smiled her assent and hurried away to begin the task. It was thus that she was summoned to take those same linens to the upper regions of the castle.

"Take a goodly supply to the bath chamber," the steward told her.

Bess was aware the hunting party had returned. The horns had sounded in triumph above the thunder of hooves as they entered the courtyard. She had longed to leave her post and again look out the turret window, but her promise to Wat that she would finish the task before her held her to the spot.

Gathering up an armful of linens, she hurried to do as she was bidden.

The bath chamber was the most unusual room in the castle. The earl had designed it himself, having seen its like on one of his journeys. It boasted two fireplaces, with a large stone basin built between them.

Water flowed from a pipe that was heated by the fireplaces. The walls and floors were covered with furs to give further protection from drafts. It was a favorite with many guests, and Wat had been heard to remark that he felt some of the travelers who came to Pembroke Castle came to visit the bath chamber, rather than the earl.

The fires were blazing when Bess knocked timidly at the door. Quickly she glanced about, assuring herself the room was empty. She had placed her burden on a small table when a sudden draft told her the door had opened.

She turned to flee, but the man stood before her, blocking her path.

"So we meet again," he said with a smile. "I had thought perhaps you were but a figment of my imagination, brought on by the long night's ride."

"No, my lord," she said, in pretty confusion. "I'm real enough, and I must hurry back to my duties."

But the man continued to block her way. "And what might your duties be?" he asked, unwilling to forgo the pleasure of her company so easily. The girl was lovely, yet seemed totally unaware of her exceptional beauty.

"I wait on Mistress Mary," Bess said, without raising her eyes. She concentrated her gaze on his feet, which were encased in hose and soft leather boots. There was nothing in his attire to indicate his rank, but his voice rang with authority. Instinctively Bess knew he was not used to being disobeyed. "I must go to Mary." Bess's eyes pleaded with him to let her pass, but he was not looking at her eyes.

His gaze swept over the simple gown she wore, noting the slim young lines of her body and comparing them to the delightful curves he had beheld as she escaped him in the chapel. He didn't intend to let her escape again. He was enchanted by her, from the fragile bloom of youth and innocence that shone from her face to the halo of lustrous hair shimmering about her. He hadn't been able to rid his thoughts of the girl all during the hunt, and now fate had sent her to him again.

"Perhaps your mistress could spare you for a short while," he suggested, and he began to unfasten his shirt. "My man is occupied, and I need someone to assist me."

Bess was well aware that in some households, women assisted the men in bathing, but the women were usually chosen from those already married. The custom was old, and had never been followed at Pembroke. Surely this man didn't really expect her to stay while he disrobed and bathed, Bess thought frantically.

"I have long overstayed my time, my lord." She tried to edge her way to the safety of the door. "I'm sure my mistress will be wondering about me. I must help her make ready for the evening."

"What sort of hospitality is practiced at Pembroke, that you refuse my request?" Griffith's eyes snapped dangerously, and the girl blanched before him.

Drawing herself up in an effort to bolster her courage, she said, "I must refuse, my lord."

She moved swiftly, but not swiftly enough. As she sought to slip past him, he reached out and caught her.

"Then you must pay a forfeit!" His eyes feasted on her soft, moist lips. He held her body tightly against his. Her lips parted to cry out, enabling him to explore more fully the honeyed sweetness of her mouth. She tried to draw back, horrified by his action, but even more horrified by the creeping weakness engulfing her body. His hand moved through her hair, holding her immobile, while his mouth plundered hers.

The moment he loosened his grip, she pushed herself away.

"You had no right—" she gasped. "You had no right!"

He brushed aside a strand of hair that fell across her cheek, but she struck his hand away.

He caught her wrist. "None of that, little wildcat—or perhaps you would like to pay yet another forfeit for the displeasure of Griffith Beaufort."

Bess pulled as far from him as his grip would allow.

"It is I who have been displeasured, sir... knight!" she declared. "Now, please allow me to pass."

He released her. There had been something about her kiss.... A hidden response of which even the girl was unaware. He would have wagered she had never been kissed before. It pleased him to think he had been the first. He would make inquiries of the earl as to her background. After all, finding favor with the cousin of the future king of England was nothing to be frowned upon, but somehow, he thought "frown" was exactly what she would do.

Bess ran down the hallway, her heart beating wildly. It was all she could do to stifle the sobs tearing at her throat.

The room she shared with Mary's other maids-in-waiting was empty when she entered, the other girls still busy with their duties. Bess crawled onto the bed and allowed the tears to come. Her limbs were still shaking from the passion-filled kiss that had threatened to consume her entire body. She huddled into the feather ticking, seeking the solace its familiar warmth brought her.

What would she have done, had he insisted she stay? How would it have felt to have touched the heated flesh of his body, slick with soapy foam? Her mouth went dry when she imagined the muscles rippling beneath her fingers as she soaped his body. The rivulets of moisture on his skin as she doused his body with pitchers of water leaving him glistening like a statue in the firelight as he rose from the water to be dried.

To be dried . . . It would have fallen to Bess to take the thick, thirsty toweling and blot the water from his body. Her hands trembled at the thought, and she sat on them to keep them still. But she could not still the trembling of her soul. Somewhere deep within her soul she wished she had dared to stay and grant his request, and she chastised herself for her shortcoming.

The nuns had warned her about sins of the flesh. They said it began when a man kissed a maiden. Then when a man begged for more favors and looked at parts of a woman's body that were usually covered by clothing and . . . and touched her there. Bess shivered at the thought, remembering the nuns' whispered embarrassment as they had warned her. The crawling feeling returned to her stomach. Her body burned despite her continued trembling. She lifted herself to her knees, drawing out her rosary as she began to pray for forgiveness.

Timidly, fearfully, she let her mind wander on to the rest of what the nuns had said. After the kisses, the looks and the touches, a man did something so horrible, so despicable, the good sisters had not been able put it into words.

Bess's heart beat madly at the thoughts that coursed through her brain, losing themselves in her throbbing bloodstream. Guiltily she tried to return to her prayers, but the memory of Beaufort's mouth against her own blotted out the sincerity of the words. She knew beyond all doubt that what she had done must have been terribly wrong, because she had enjoyed it so much.

* * *

Bess was aware of Griffith during the dinner, as was every other woman, and man, for that matter, in the hall. Tables had been set up stretching from one end of the room to the other, with the prince and his entourage in the places of honor on the dais. Bess couldn't stop her heart from turning over each time she glanced at the imposing figure above her. For indeed, Griffith Beaufort was more handsome than the prince himself. Griffith Beaufort, whose kisses still burned on her lips.

A flurry of giggles arose from the other girls.

"He's looking this way," Ann whispered behind her hand.

Without thinking, Bess glanced up, only to meet Griffith's eyes. He smiled at her, and she felt color suffuse her face, washing down her throat and disappearing beneath her neckline. Seeing her discomfort, the girls were unable to keep their minds from running to wild speculation.

"That's Griffith Beaufort, the prince's cousin. Their blood flows back to the great duke, John of Lancaster." Ann bubbled with information, and sought more. "Does he know you?"

Bess shook her head. "I saw him in the chapel," she admitted reluctantly. "He must have thought I seemed familiar and has not been able to place me."

It sounded lame even to Bess's ears, but she could think of no better ploy, and was determined not to let any of the others find out she had been alone with any man, let alone the cousin of the prince, and in the bathing chamber, at that.

"He doesn't even know my name." Bess said, looking down at her trencher.

"I'll warrant he knows it now." Ann laughed as she saw Griffith speak to the earl, motioning toward Bess as he did.

Bess swallowed hard. Surely he couldn't be asking about her.

The last thing she wanted was to draw undue attention to herself, especially attention given by someone of royal blood.

The meal dragged on, but Bess was unable to eat. Even the crusty white bread that was her favorite and was only served when there were important visitors in the castle, could not tempt her. She was relieved when the last course was finished and she could slip from the table and make her way from the crowded hall.

"Ah, and here she is..." The earl's voice boomed out, stopping her in her tracks. "Mistress Bess, is it not?"

She turned slowly, dropping into a graceful curtsy, despite the fact that her knees had turned to water.

"It seems our guest is quite smitten with your charms, my dear," the earl teased. He was obviously looking at Bess in a different light since discovering she had gained his guest's favor.

In less than no time, Griffith had learned all there was to know about Bess. She was of good blood, albeit not noble. Her father, now deceased, had been a landed knight, and her mother had been recently and frequently seen in the company of one Sir Morris of Bladacglen. From what his host had told him, the girl had little, and was hardly more than a child. Any attention Griffith might cast in her direction couldn't help but improve her lot.

And Griffith Beaufort found himself more than willing to give the girl a great deal of his most personal attention. To his utter amazement, he found himself interested in learning more about her background. She was shy and unsure of herself, yet she did not hesitate to stand up for that which she felt to be right and morally correct. A change from his usual conquests, for the lovelier the woman, he found, the more willing she was to exchange her beauty for the favors of a rich and powerful man.

It was strangely refreshing to be denied by a maiden, as long as the denial did not continue over any lengthy period of time. It would be interesting to watch her emerge from her cocoon of propriety as he instructed her in the social graces, and subsequently introduced her to the wonders of first love.

Griffith smiled down at the girl, and, taking her hand, raised her to her feet.

"And do you dance, Mistress Bess?" Griffith indicated the floor, where the musicians were tuning their instruments and singing light songs prior to taking their places in the gallery.

"I have danced but little, my lord," Bess responded, hardly able to look at him as she spoke. He seemed to shine like the sun. His tunic of gold velvet encrusted with a collar of fine jewels made him all the more magnificent to her eyes.

"Perhaps it's time you danced a little more," Griffith teased. "If you will excuse us?" He bowed to his host.

By right of propriety, Griffith should have led the daughter of the house of Pembroke to the floor for the first dance, as Henry led the earl's wife, but for once, Griffith ignored propriety, so beguiling did he find this diminutive creature.

After the first dance, Bess confessed that she knew no other dances. For a moment, Griffith seemed perplexed. He spoke briefly to Henry, who turned to the knights and ladies who filled the room and asked, "How many of you are familiar with the newest dances from France this past year?"

Although there was a sudden murmur of interest, only one or two stepped forward to indicate their knowledge of the dances.

"Then we would be happy to instruct you."

There was healthy applause in response to Henry's words. Only Bess held back. She instantly realized Griffith's purpose. She knew she would be the object of much speculation before this night was over. But her worries were swept aside as Griffith's hand closed over hers and he began to teach the intricate steps to the assembly.

Her heart skipped along with each beat of the music as she followed his steps, only to be taken off guard by the kiss that signalled the end of the dance. Flustered, she ran from the floor and tried to lose herself in the crowd, her lips still tingling from his touch.

"Oh, aye," Ann whispered as she lay beside Bess in the bed in the crowded women's quarters. "You didn't know him. You only saw him in the chapel, and then quite by accident."

There were stifled giggles from some of the other girls. Bess remained silent. Perhaps if she continued to do so, they would think her asleep and let her be. But she was not allowed this luxury. When she didn't answer, Ann reached over and pinched her.

Bess let out a little squeal.

"We know you're not asleep, Bess. Now tell us about my lord Beaufort," Ann prompted.

"There's nothing to tell," Bess protested, rubbing her hip. "Before tonight, I had hardly laid eyes on him."

"Mayhap we should all start going to chapel, if it will produce such wondrous results," Lucy Dumaine suggested from across the room. "After all, Bess has obviously reaped great rewards."

"Of course, if you don't want him, Bess, perhaps you could present me," Ann mused. "I know you're not interested in men, and it would seem Griffith's attentions have overthrown you completely. You blush every time he looks at you."

"I cannot help it. He should not look at me, nor I at him." Bess fought to hide her tears. "He is of royal blood, and someday, God willing, he will be a powerful lord of England. There is no place for me in his life."

"Oh, listen to Mistress Proper," Lucy said, and laughed again. "There is a place for a lord in any woman's life, if he so chooses, and don't you forget it, my girl."

"Oh, Bess..." Ann's eyes gleamed in the darkness as she spoke. "Just think, if Griffith Beaufort decides to show you favor, he could give you a dower portion far greater than anything your mother could ever afford."

Ann didn't bother to remind Bess that her mother would very likely never be able to give her a dowry. In Ann's opinion, any advancement Bess made would have to be done on her own, and a liaison with the cousin of the prince could hardly help but be beneficial.

"I want no favors from any man!" Bess declared.

"But if he offers, you'd be a fool not to accept. One word from him and you could have a brilliant marriage."

Bess shivered. "I don't want a brilliant marriage." Now the tears she had been fighting made themselves known, and she cried, "I want to go back to the convent."

"Lord have mercy on us!" Lucy exclaimed from the other bed. "She attracts the handsomest man in Christendom, and then moans she wants to go to a nunnery."

There was a pause, and then Bess realized Lucy was bending over her.

"There is no disgrace in being mistress of a great lord, Bess. Never forget that," Lucy whispered. "Would I could trade places with you, for I swear I would not hesitate one moment."

"But I dare not give myself to him," Bess protested. "To lie with a man outside of the marriage bed is a sin punishable by everlasting damnation. I would be lost both in this world and in the next. I could not hope for marriage, nor could I return to the convent."

Lucy chuckled knowingly. "If your maidenhead is all that keeps you from an alliance with my lord Beaufort, you need have no worry. As a knight, he is pledged, along with his cousin, the prince, that he will not indiscriminately deflower a maiden. He will, most likely, practice the ways of the troubadour, leaving your maidenhead intact."

"Do you mean he will worship me from afar?" Bess asked wonderingly. She had never heard the term, and had no idea what the ways of a troubadour might be.

Lucy made a noise that sounded almost like the purr of a cat. "He will worship you in far more ways than you have ever dreamed, unless I miss my guess," she confirmed. "But your virtue will remain intact. Prince Henry frowns on lords with royal blood in their veins who sire bastards. He well knows how successfully a bastard can challenge the throne, and gain it, too. One only has to look at his father, the king, to see that this is true."

Bess nodded in the darkness. It was common knowledge that the king had claimed his throne through the Beaufort blood and succeeded in his quest despite the blight of bastardy.

Giving Bess a little squeeze on the shoulder, Lucy scurried back across the floor.

And though Bess pondered the advice she had been given, she knew she could not take it without much prayer and contemplation. Despite Lucy's declaration, Bess did hesitate. Not because she was not attracted to the Beaufort and honored by his attentions, but rather out of respect for all she had been taught to believe during her years in the convent.

Within a few minutes, the sounds of even breathing told Bess the other girls were asleep. The first rays of the dawning were peeping through the high windows as Bess still lay awake, pondering her problem.

Chapter Two

Griffith was not accustomed to being avoided by women. In fact, since he had come to manhood, they had sought him out. Therefore, he was somewhat at a loss as to how to react to the lovely but evasive Bess. Her smiles, and the shy glances she cast his way from beneath her long, dark lashes, told him that she was interested, but whenever he sought to be with her, she seemed to melt away and could not be found.

It had been so that morning, and, not wanting to listen to the prattle of the women or the boasting of the men, Griffith walked alone about the castle yards.

He was passing a section of the kitchen gardens when he heard the murmur of a voice. Puzzled, he looked about, seeking the origin of the sound. He made his way toward a bush that looked to be a part of one of the many privet hedges that wound their way throughout the grounds. The smell of herbs rose about him as he heedlessly crushed them beneath his feet.

There, at the end of the garden, all but hidden by the hedge, was a small grotto, hollowed out to serve as a shrine. High in the wall, a niche held a small iron statue of the Virgin, and before it knelt Bess. Silently Griffith moved toward her, dropping to his knees at her side.

His voice joined hers for a moment before she gasped and jumped to her feet.

"My lord, how did you find me?" she asked, before realizing what she was inadvertently admitting.

"I came to the garden to seek out the loveliest flower, and I have found it," Griffith replied, and reached out to take her hand. "Now, as I would not interrupt your prayers, sweet Bess, we will continue."

With that, he reached inside his doublet and drew out his rosary.

"Oh, no, my lord," Bess protested. "Surely you did not come here to pray."

"And why not?" Griffith asked, glancing about, "It seems an adequate place in which to pray."

Bess hung her head as he resumed telling the beads. When he realized she was not responding, he stopped and looked at her for a long moment. "Do you not wish to pray with me?"

Bess saw the hurt in his eyes, and hastened to explain. "My lord, I would be most honored to have you join me in my devotions, but it is unseemly for us to be here, alone in the garden."

"Unseemly," Griffith repeated. "We are out in the open, and certainly praying is no sin—at least not to the best of my knowledge."

"But there are only the two of us here." Bess was aware that her heart was beating at an amazing speed. It sounded as though horses were galloping through her chest. She doubted she could count the beads, let alone remember the words.

Griffith looked at her, then got to his feet, drawing her with him. "Then perhaps we should walk back toward the rose garden, where the others idle."

Realizing there would be just as much talk if she suddenly appeared with Griffith in the rose garden, Bess hesitated before answering, "Whatever is your pleasure, my lord."

For a moment, Griffith's eyes glinted. Then, seeing the innocent candor in the girl's face, he turned back to the little shrine.

"I left the others because their idle talk held no interest for me. I think, if you don't mind, I would rather stay here and pray with you."

"As you wish, my lord." Bess again sank to her knees, and was vaguely relieved to hear Griffith begin reciting the rosary.

When they finished, it was Bess who spoke first. "You did that very well, my lord," she said. "You said the prayers as though they had some meaning, and were not just memory work to be recited before a tutor."

"I was trained to become a bishop," he confided as they walked back through the kitchen garden. "That was how Henry and I became so close. We studied under the same tutors. Then my brother died, and so did my dreams of becoming a holy man and saving souls as had no other before me."

"Had you been given the opportunity, I know you would have done just that!" Bess exclaimed. "Your prayers, the way you repeated the words, had such meaning."

"How can you understand their meaning?" Griffith asked in a chiding tone. "I recited them in Latin."

"I spent many years in the convent, my lord," Bess confided. "The mother superior felt that we should know that of which we prayed. I can speak and read Latin." She tossed her head just a bit as she spoke, bringing a smile to Griffith's lips.

"Amo, amas, amat..." Griffith laughed at her obvious discomfort in his choice of verb to conjugate. "I see you do know your Latin."

He turned toward her and placed his finger beneath her chin, drawing her face upward so that he was able to look into her eyes. "Bess, why have you been avoiding me?" he asked quietly.

"My lord, I have not been avoiding you," Bess declared staunchly. "I do not care for the constant company of the court. I need time to be alone, and so..."

"And so you come here to pray," he finished for her.

She nodded her response. "That is why you could never find me, if you did, indeed, seek me out."

They walked in silence for a while, and then Griffith asked, "What is it about the court you don't like? I think my friends are rather interesting."

"I don't... understand their jests. Some of their words have double meanings, I think, and I cannot tell how to answer them. When I do venture an answer, they laugh, and I know that somehow I have made an error."

"And was there no jesting in your parents' home?" Griffith wondered aloud.

"I was in my parents' home but little," Bess told him. "My mother sent me to the convent when I was very small, and only brought me out and put me into service after my father's death. Sir Morris was instrumental in getting a place here at Pembroke for me."

"Sir Morris?" Griffith repeated, trying to place the man.

"He's a friend of my mother's. Sir Morris of Bladacglen."

Griffith nodded: he knew of the man. A lesser knight, little more than a soldier of fortune. He probably had seduced the girl's mother, taken the girl's dower, along with any other monies the woman might have had, and was now on his way to greener pastures.

"Where is your mother now?" Griffith asked.

"I do not know, my lord," Bess admitted in a small voice. "I've not seen her since she left me here, but I'm certain she'll return for me."

"Of course," Griffith agreed, stroking the smooth skin of Bess's hand. What could the mother be thinking of, leaving a girl of such rare beauty alone and unprotected in a castle the size of Pembroke? Without anyone to watch over her, at best she would be seduced. God knew, Griffith had been thinking of seducing her himself.

At worst... Griffith couldn't bear to formulate the thoughts of the worst that could befall this lovely creature floating along beside him through the sun-filled afternoon. The delicateness of her features and the daintiness of her slim figure only enhanced the hint of sweet sensuousness that played about the corners of her mouth. Griffith realized fully that Bess was not safe here. Not safe from other men, or from himself. The only way he could ensure her safety was to make the others realize that she had his personal protection, and that was what it would be, and all it would be... protection.

"Are you waiting, then, for your mother to return and arrange a betrothal for you?" Griffith asked.

Fear sprang to Bess's eyes. "I would she would allow me to return to the convent," she said truthfully. "I do not wish to marry."

Griffith stroked his chin. "It takes a dower to be allowed to take the vows in a convent."

Bess nodded mutely. She was well aware of the truth of his words. A dowry was essential, and if her suspicions regarding her mother and Sir Morris were true, she had none.

Many an eyebrow raised as Griffith entered the garden with Bess on his arm. Then Mistress Mary was hurrying toward them.

"Bess, I've been looking for you," she said as she dropped a curtsy in Griffith's direction. "I wanted you to do something special with my hair for the masque this evening. I'm sure our guest will excuse you. There is little time left, if I am to be ready." Mary's words trailed off when she saw that Griffith continued to block their path.

"And will you be coming to the masque this evening, also?" Griffith directed his words to Bess.

"I had thought to, my lord," Bess said quietly. "That is, if there is nothing Mary wishes of me."

Now Griffith looked full into Mary's eyes. She flinched at the coldness of his gaze. "I'm sure Mistress Mary will not require your services after she has readied herself for the evening. Is that not correct, mistress?" he added, prompting her.

Mary's mouth drew into a thin line. There was nothing she could do except try to warn Bess about Griffith's advances. Although Mary might have welcomed those same advances, had they been directed her way, she knew that Bess was not fair game for Griffith's charm. The man would use her and set her aside without so much as a by-your-leave. Mary was the youngest of the earl's daughters and knew little of the world; nonetheless, she was years ahead of Bess in knowledge and maturity, having been readied from the age of five to take over the household that would be her responsibility after her marriage.

It was all Mary could do to keep her voice from trembling as she realized the anger she had incurred from their guest. The look on his face boded no good for her, but she stuck staunchly to her charge. "Do hurry, Bess," she said, fretting prettily, trying to ignore the look on Griffith's face. "There is much to be done."

Griffith took Bess's hand and raised it to his lips. Their eyes met. He knew what Mary was thinking, and well she might, because there was much truth in her thoughts, but he also knew it was beyond his power to either bid farewell to this flower of loveliness or take advantage of her innocence. "I will see you tonight," he said as he slowly released her fingers, feeling a slight quiver of response to his words.

Mary hardly waited until Bess was in her chambers before she began. "Mark my words, Bess, you'll be ruined if you don't mind your ways around Griffith Beaufort."

"But he only came upon me by accident," Bess protested. "I have avoided him in every way I could."

Now it was Mary's turn to shake her head. "I'm sure you have. Had I a brain in my head, I would send you to your room and insist that you remain there and not attend the masque tonight."

Bess fought to control her disappointment. There had never been anything as grand as the masque that was planned for this evening, at least not in the time Bess had been at Pembroke. She knew that if she missed it she would more than likely never again have the opportunity to see such a display of finery and elegance, but she swallowed and said, "If that is your wish."

For a moment, Mary was sorely tempted. Yet it would not do to bring Griffith's wrath down on the house of Pembroke for the sake of a mere girl. "No, Bess, it is better that you attend the masque as you had planned. I doubt not my lord Griffith would storm the battlements and knock down the doors to the women's quarters in an effort to find you, should you not appear." Mary sighed and sank onto a cushioned stool. "Now, do something imaginative with my hair, so the man won't think the whole afternoon has been wasted, and be more angered with me for pulling such a sham to get you from his clutches.''

Bess did as she was told. Under her quick and efficient ministrations, Mary's hair fell into place, and before either girl could credit it, Mary was ready to be dressed for the masque.

She was to wear the costume of an Egyptian queen and her ladies were to wear simple dresses depicting them as slave-girls. Mary smiled at her reflection before she turned to the others, who had come into the room shortly after Bess finished Mary's hair.

"Hurry and get ready," Mary urged, "and mind you don't leave my side during the evening. After all, a queen is entitled to her servants." She shot a quick look at the disappointment on the girls' faces, "And don't look so unhappy about it. I'm doing it for your own good."

Some of the others sniffed audibly, but Bess knew that what Mary said was true. And it was mainly for Bess's good that Mary had issued the order. Bess knew she should stay away from Griffith, but it was difficult when he was so kind and thoughtful. With the exception of that time he had kissed her, he had been the epitome of gallant deportment, seemingly content to share her companionship and asking nothing more.

The color rose in Bess's cheeks as she slipped the robe over her head. It hung from one shoulder and fell to the floor like leaves in the moonlight, silver and gossamer. Quickly she piled her hair high atop her head and twined summer roses through it. She glanced down, aware that the gown hung loose and sacklike. Then, snatching up a length of ribbon, she wrapped it about her waist, molding the cloth to the curves of her body. Taking her mask, she rushed out the door, leaving behind the other girls, suffused in clouds of fabric and scent.

Mary hardly glanced in her direction as Bess took her place, a few paces behind her mistress. It wasn't until after they all entered the great hall that Bess realized there might be anything exceptional in the way she looked. Several times she was aware of envious glances from the women and barely restrained desire in the eyes of the men. It was only the ever-present Mary that kept her from finding herself in a difficult situation.

But when the dancing began, Mary could no longer protect Bess. As though given an unseen signal, Griffith appeared at the girl's side just as Mary was led onto the floor by one of the knights.

"And will you so honor me, Mistress Bess?" Griffith asked as he took her hand.

"I doubt I remember the steps," Bess protested as she moved toward the center of the floor.

"Then I shall remind you," Griffith assured her.

Bess found the steps came to her far more easily than she had thought they might. Whether the reason was Griffith's gentle instruction or an inborn ability, her feet moved deft to the music and her body gracefully followed.

They were a delight to watch, as even the most envious had to admit. Griffith's costume of white and silver blended with the pure simplicity of Bess's tunic and contrasted with the bright colors of the other dancers.

"It seems our little Bess has made a conquest," the earl remarked to his wife.

"I would he had taken the same liking to one of our daughters," the lady of Pembroke mused softly. "He will be a powerful lord someday, and that day may likely be soon, should rumor be true."

"You must take into consideration that Mary is betrothed to one of Essex's sons," the earl responded thoughtfully. "It would be a shame to destroy such an alliance over a situation that might come to nothing more than an affair of the heart."

"Well, he certainly can't be planning on having an affair of the heart with Bess. She's hardly more than a child herself." Lady Pembroke sniffed self-righteously, seeing the sense in her husband's words but unwilling to give up her dreams so quickly.

"I'm afraid the child, as you call her, has grown up rather rapidly," the earl mused aloud. "I wondered at the time just how much of Sir Morris's tale was true when he came here with the widow and her young daughter, asking a place for the girl. I remember Bess's father. He soldiered with me during the Scottish campaign, some fifteen years ago. I stayed on his lands in Shropshire for several days and he offered me the hospitality of his home. I met his wife, the lovely Edwina, and his daughter, Elizabeth."

"It must have been another daughter, if it was that long ago." His wife dismissed the idea impatiently. "Perhaps they named all their daughters Elizabeth."

"I think not. There are very few children with hair the color of silver. But I also think it best that it remain our secret, whether or not I'm correct in assuming the girl and her mother are older than we have been led to believe." He rubbed his head under the thick turban he wore in his guise as an emir. "The girl's only protection has been her age, that and the fact she has been all but hidden in the women's quarters. Now we're for it. There is no one here who hasn't remarked on her beauty. It's only Griffith's presence that keeps the men from falling on her like hounds on a hart. I fear there will be unpleasantness once the prince and his cousin have taken their leave."

"I believe you're right," his wife said, and nodded thoughtfully, still watching the couple gracefully execute one of the more difficult dance steps. "I will do what I can to see the girl is protected . . . if Griffith leaves anything to protect."

The earl looked sharply at his wife. She was fond of Bess, despite her ambitions for her daughters.

"He will leave something," the earl said, sadly patting his wife's hand. "And we will protect it to the best of our ability."

The friendship between Bess and Griffith had, indeed, not gone unremarked. The castle buzzed. Little wonder it was the first bit of news that came to the ear of Sir Morris of Bladacglen when he arrived.

"Ah, Sir Morris," Jasper of Kent said as Sir Morris entered the crowded courtyard. "You've come, no doubt, for the tournament."

Sir Morris answered his old acquaintance, rather diffidently. "I thought to try my hand." The truth of the matter was that he needed the money, having gone through all that Edwina had managed to muster. So he had left her to her own devices and come to seek his fortune—or a woman who would share her fortune in return for his attentions.

"And where is the fair Edwina?" Jasper glanced about the courtyard, trying to pick her out.

"She remained at Kew," Sir Morris told the mercenary knight noncommittally, trying to forget the scene that had ensued when he told Edwina he did not intend to bring her along.

"I should have thought she would want to see her daughter, not to mention the prince," Jasper remarked.

Sir Morris started. He had forgotten about Bess. The girl had impressed him as being a mousy little thing, having kept her head bent and her mouth closed the whole journey.

"The scrawny brat is still here, then," he muttered. It occurred to him that when she found he had come, she would undoubtedly attempt to persuade him to take her back to her mother, and he would be forced to endure another hysterical display, much like the one that had taken place on his departure from Kew.

"The wench is here, but I'd hardly describe her either as scrawny or as a brat. At least, if I did so, I'd be most careful to see that I wasn't within earshot of my lord Beaufort, for he is most taken with her."

Sir Morris's mouth dropped open at the other man's words.

"Surely you jest," he finally managed. "Edwina's daughter is hardly more than a child. Why, it cannot be!"

"Child or no, she has taken the Beaufort's fancy," Jasper told him. "Don't take my word for it. The prince and his party are in the garden, and I doubt not that Mistress Bess is there, also."

With a curt nod, Sir Morris took his leave and hurried across the courtyard. The castle was alive with people, which was not surprising. It was common knowledge that the king held a somber and joyless court. Why then shouldn't those who wished to partake in the hunt and feasting follow the young prince, whose very presence ensured action and excitement? Perhaps even more excitement than he, Sir Morris, had foreseen. Surely it would do no harm for him to present himself to Beaufort and suggest diplomatically that the man make some form of restitution for his use of the wench. Since there could be no thought of marriage, it was Sir Morris's right—nay, his duty—to demand a stipend for the girl on her mother's behalf. After all, his relationship with Edwina made him a guardian of a sort.

What Sir Morris saw when he entered the garden from the dimness of the castle dazzled him in more ways than one. The scene before him was filled with brightly dressed courtiers, some playing at bowls, others gathered about a minstrel, enjoying his music.

Quite apart from the rest, as though in their own little world, were a young man and woman. There was no mistaking the man. Griffith Beaufort was known throughout the land. But the dainty little figure seated on the stone bench next to him ... Surely this well-bred bit of loveliness couldn't be Edwina's daughter.

"Do you not recognize her, man?" Jasper laughed. "I see you don't. It is Mistress Bess, there with the Beaufort."

"It cannot be!" Sir Morris protested in disbelief. "The girl I brought here was nothing like that."

"You were so besotted with the mother and her money you paid little attention to the daughter, I vow," Jasper responded. "Well, too late, my man. Griffith has claimed the prize for himself."

Jasper walked off, still laughing, while Sir Morris glowered after him. It was some moments before Morris returned his gaze to the couple across the garden. Griffith had taken up a dulcimer, and the girl responded with a smile that shone with admiration, and the innocence of first love.

Sir Morris did not see the innocence, but the look of adoration on Bess's face was not lost on him. If he used the situation correctly, it would mean a good deal of money in his purse, not to mention the girl herself. Surely she would need someone to turn to when Griffith's attentions waned.

Smiling to himself, Sir Morris started across the garden to make himself known to his hosts and subsequently to Griffith and Bess. He bowed effusively before the earl and his lady.

"Surely you remember me, my lord." Sir Morris smiled ingratiatingly at them, his pretty, almost girlish face alight with excitement. "I was here some time ago with Lady Edwina...Mistress Elizabeth's mother."

The earl was taken aback for a moment, as he and his wife had neither seen nor heard from Edwina since she had left Bess in their service. Now, apparently, the woman and her paramour had returned. "Where is Edwina?" the earl asked politely.

"She was unable to come, but sent me in her stead to see to the welfare of Elizabeth."

"Elizabeth needs no one to see to her welfare," Lady Margaret told him. "She is a good and obedient girl, her health is fine, and she is happy."

Sir Morris glanced across the garden. "I can attest to her happiness, even from this distance."

The earl followed Morris's gaze. So the man knew of Griffith's attentions. It took little imagination for the earl to guess Sir Morris's intent.

"If it be your pleasure, I should like to speak to Elizabeth," Sir Morris asked, and again turned to his host.

"Of course," the earl said, smiling. It would be interesting to see how Beaufort would handle this situation, and even more interesting to see Sir Morris put in his place once and for all.

Griffith looked up as the men approached.

"Will—" Griffith held out his arm, beckoning them forward "—come settle a point for us. Bess insists that—"

A little gasp from Bess stopped Griffith in midsentence. "What is it?" He leaned toward her solicitously. "Is something amiss?"

Before Bess could speak, the earl stepped in. "I would like to present Sir Morris of Bladacglen, my lord. He has come with news of Elizabeth's mother."

Sir Morris smiled prettily as he made a leg. "I am most honored, my lord."

Griffith frowned at the pretentiousness of the man's mode of address. Only foreign diplomats and peasants seeking favors spoke thus, and since this man was not foreign, he must be of the latter ilk.

"Do you have a message for the lady?" Griffith asked shortly.

Sir Morris hesitated. He could sense the impatience in Griffith's voice, and knew he had irritated him.

"Nothing in writing, my lord." He smiled at the girl, wondering that such beauty had escaped him. "The Lady Edwina prays that her little girl is well and obedient in all matters—" his eyes flicked meaningfully from Griffith to Bess as he spoke "—and that she is living a pure and moral life."

"Following the example set by her mother?" Griffith suggested quietly.

So Griffith knew. Sir Morris felt the blood rise to his face, partially from anger, partially from embarrassment. For a moment, he cursed his fair, smooth complexion. Although it attracted a number of women, it also betrayed him as though he were a simpering female himself.

When Sir Morris did not speak, it was the earl who took up the conversation. "I can assure you, Sir Morris, Elizabeth's deportment far exceeded any of the moral standards either you or Edwina might set."

"What Edwina and I do is our own business," Sir Morris said hotly. "However, what is done to this fair child is another matter."

"Are you suggesting that there is something amiss in the fact that Bess and I were conversing?" Griffith's voice rose dangerously, and heads began to turn in their direction.

Immediately Sir Morris took another tack. "Not at all, my lord! I would never have thought such a thing. As I said, I simply came to give the girl a message of her mother's love and concern. After all, the child is very innocent and untried. We brought her here directly from the convent. She knows little of the world."

"Then perhaps it would have been wise had you stayed with her for a time after you brought her here." The earl cut in, not bothering to hide the edge to his voice. This man had all but said that he, the Earl of Pembroke, was remiss in his care of the girl, and that the morals at Pembroke left something to be desired. He barely restrained himself from ordering the young upstart off his lands.

"We entrusted her to your care," Sir Morris fired back. The last thing he had wanted at the time was to have a sniveling brat underfoot, but now, as he continued to stare at the girl, he realized she far outshone her aging mother. For quite some time Morris suspected that Edwina had led him to believe her to be somewhat younger than she actually was. Now, seeing the fresh young beauty of the daughter, he felt more and more deceived.

"Perhaps I should take Bess with me, back to Kew, where her mother could watch her more closely."

Bess gave a little gasp. She was aware of the lustful look in Sir Morris's eyes as they roamed the curves of her body. Without thinking, she reached out and laid her hand on Griffith's arm in an unconscious bid for protection.

"I do not think my mother wants me, my lord," Bess began, "else she would have come herself. Please do not let him take me with him."

Griffith covered her hand with his. "The lady has been given into the care of the Earl of Pembroke," he said to Sir Morris. "She cannot be removed from his wardship unless he releases her. I don't believe he has any intentions of doing so. Am I correct, Will?" Griffith smiled at the earl, who coolly agreed.

"If the girl's mother needs her, she is duty bound to go!" Sir Morris insisted.

"You said nothing of the woman being in need," the earl pointed out.

"I did not want to alarm Mistress Bess." Then, realizing that his personal desires were about to overpower his common sense, Sir Morris retracted his words. "However, if it is your wish that Bess remain here for another few days, I will be most pleased to wait until my lord has . . . finished with her." At the look of rage that suffused Griffith's face, Sir Morris blanched and again retracted his words. "That is to say . . . after the tournament and games are over would be plenty of time to take the girl to her mother."

Bess's knuckles were white against the sleeve of Griffith's coat, and her face was drawn with instinctive fear.

"We will send for the girl's mother to come here," the earl suggested.

"I'm afraid she wouldn't do that," Sir Morris hedged, somewhat nervously. "You see, she has a place in the household at Kew, and wouldn't want to lose it."

"And just what is her 'place?'" Griffith asked. He towered above the man, stooping like a hawk about to bag its prey.

"She's . . . she's . . ." Sir Morris hesitated to lie. He knew that Griffith would have no trouble finding Edwina. "Edwina is working as a seamstress in the castle."

"Then she is not ill?" the earl prompted.

"Well, yes, she is, but she still must work. That is why she needs her daughter with her." Satisfied with his lie, Sir Morris smiled. "Of course, should you decide you want Elizabeth to remain with you—" he looked directly at Griffith "—I'm sure Edwina would be happy to allow it, for a stipend. Nothing large, you know, just enough to make her life a little easier."

It was all Griffith could do to keep from strangling the man then and there. He closed his fists as the laugh wrinkles that usually played about the corners of his eyes became lines of malevolence. "You are staying for the games, are you not?" he finally managed to say through clenched teeth.

Flattered that he should be asked, Sir Morris preened himself and bowed once again. "I should be most honored to participate in the games, if it finds favor in your eyes."

"The way you speak makes me think you might ask me to wear your favor into battle," Griffith remarked loudly.

Now it was Sir Morris's turn to feel the heat of anger, as the earl and some of the gentlemen who had made their way surreptitiously toward the little group all burst into laughter at the knight's expense.

Sir Morris bowed stiffly and left the garden, vowing silently that the man would pay for his remark.

Griffith turned his attention to the girl trembling at his side. She was so small, so delicate. His every instinct was to protect her with his very life. Indeed, to Griffith, who had grown up on the tales of chivalry and valor, the very epitome of knighthood was to save a fragile and beautiful maiden from the clutches of one such as Sir Morris. Bess gave rise to his manhood. His protectiveness and his power asserted itself on her behalf, as did his sense of chivalry.

Lifting Bess's hand to his lips, Griffith said gently, "Never fear, sweetheart, I shall let no harm come to you."

She smiled up at him, her lips trembling slightly, as much at his touch as at the fear she knew when confronted by Sir Morris. "Thank you, my lord," she answered.

Then Griffith turned back to his host. "Now, Will, as I was saying, Bess and I were wondering if you could settle a point of argument between us."

The situation relaxed, and the courtiers resumed their conversations, but they continued to cast speculative glances, not only at Griffith and Bess, but also toward the door through which Sir Morris had so recently disappeared.

Chapter Three

After the encounter with Sir Morris, there was no hope of keeping Bess and Griffith apart. She stayed near him whenever she found it possible, and when she was not with him she was in the company of either Mary or the Lady Margaret.

As far as Griffith was concerned, he couldn't have been more pleased. He enjoyed Bess's company, and found himself becoming more and more protective of her. It angered him to see the lustful desire but thinly veiled in Sir Morris's eyes when he looked at the girl. Griffith's own feelings of desire were quenched by his indignation at the other man's attitude.

As Griffith silently congratulated himself on his self-restraint in dealing with Sir Morris and his newfound platonic relationship with Bess, he still took the time to look forward to the games. Now, however, there was something more at stake than winning for the sole pleasure of defeating his opponent. In his own mind, Griffith knew that he would fight for Bess's honor, and that he would best Sir Morris and send him off in defeat, as he deserved.

The man's innuendos and lies had caused everyone at court to distrust him within the span of one day. Without so much as uttering a word to one another, the courtiers instinctively saw to it that none of the young women were ever left alone with Sir Morris, and especially not Bess, whom he seemed intent on waylaying.

Unbeknownst to the others, Griffith had sent one of his men to Kew to apprise himself of the situation with Bess's mother. It was no surprise to Griffith that Sir Morris had spoken but half the truth. Edwina was, indeed, working as a seamstress at Kew Castle, but she had sent no message to her daughter, and was far more upset that her lover had left her than she was about not seeing Bess.

Griffith listened intently to the messenger. He had been correct in assuming Sir Morris would try to bleed him for money, using the pretext of supposed liberties taken with the girl, and then make off with Bess himself, discarding her when he had done with her, as he had the mother.

Griffith knew he was well able to cope with the venomous Sir Morris, but he felt it only fair that he warn Bess, and also assure her that her mother was well and did not expect or wish her daughter's return.

So it was that Griffith sent for Bess.

At another time, the simple act would have caused no remark, but the quick eyes of Sir Morris missed nothing, and when he saw Bess follow Prigge across the great hall and disappear into the narrow passage at the top of the gallery, he asked, "Whose man escorts Mistress Bess?"

"He is Walter Prigge, one of Griffith's men, I believe," Jasper said, lifting his flagon of ale.

"And is that the way to Griffith's apartments?"

"Aye, it is." Jasper blinked his eyes, trying to focus despite his besotted brain. "You don't think—?"

Jasper didn't finish his question, for Morris nodded wisely. "Lord Beaufort has need of a woman, and has chosen the fair young Bess. I think that's obvious to all who wish to see."

"That it is," Jasper agreed soddenly. "That it is." He looked at the now-empty passage into which Bess had disappeared. "Now I, too, must go to my bed. Tomorrow will be a fine and busy day."

Jasper got to his feet, weaving carefully toward his quarters. There would be no delightfully warm young body there to greet him, but then, perhaps it was as well. Everyone knew that lying with a woman the night before a battle sapped the strength from a man. Vaguely Jasper wondered what the Beaufort might be thinking, to take such a risk.

Behind him, Sir Morris smiled. He had planted his little seed well, and Jasper would not be one to forget what he had seen this night. All he would need was to have Jasper's memory jogged a bit at the proper moment, and the man would perform admirably, in accordance with Sir Morris's plan.

Griffith was standing at the window when Prigge tapped at his door.

"I have brought the lady, my lord."

"Thank you, Walter." Griffith didn't turn his head as he spoke. He was concerned about how to tell Bess of Sir Morris's treachery and Edwina's lack of concern.

Bess dropped a deep curtsy as the door closed behind her.

He crossed the room in two strides, raising her to her feet. "Since when do you curtsy to me?" he chided as he smiled into her clear blue eyes.

"Since I learned you are a great and powerful lord, and a cousin to the prince."

"And so that little thing makes us less than friends?"

"I will always be your friend, my lord, so long as you will have me," Bess told him.

Her face was filled with the earnestness of her words, and Griffith could hardly keep from placing his lips against her warm, sweet mouth, so close to his.

"And I, yours, sweet Bess," he answered. "But sometimes friends must say things to one another that are painful to both."

Bess's eyes clouded at his words. Had she done something wrong, that he must scold her? Or must she go with Sir Morris?

Seeing the fear spring into her eyes, Griffith drew her into his arms. "No, no, sweetheart," he said soothingly. "There is nothing to fear." He felt her relax against his chest. "I am here to protect you. It was only that I sent a messenger to Kew to find news of your mother. He returned a short while ago, and I wanted to tell you what he learned."

"My mother," Bess said hesitantly. "Is she ill?"

Bess tried to picture Edwina as she had been before she had sent Bess off to the convent but could only remember the heavily powdered woman who had left her daughter at Pembroke and gone off with her lover. Bess had felt true sorrow when her father died, but now she could feel little at the thought of her mother being ill in some strange castle, with no relatives at her side. It was then Bess realized she would be duty bound to go to her, but it would be duty, not love that took her there—and, please God, not with Sir Morris as escort.

"Your mother enjoys the best of health." Griffith's hand found its way to smooth her gossamer hair.

"But you said your message was painful," Bess reminded him.

"And so it is," Griffith said as he held the girl even more firmly against him. He could feel the gentle curves molding themselves against the hardness of his body. She was so small, so fragile, like a little bird trembling beneath his hand. He would make any sacrifice to keep her from knowing even the smallest hurt.

"Bess, my messenger spoke to your mother. She sent you no message with Sir Morris. It seems she was not aware that he was coming to Pembroke. Her concern was that he had gone, not where he was going."

"Then she doesn't want me to join her at Kew?" Unseemly joy sprang into Bess's voice. "I need not leave you?"

Bess put her hand to her lips the moment the words escaped. It was all Griffith could do to keep from smiling. He had been worried the girl would be heartbroken because of her mother's indifference.

"F-forgive me, m-my lord," Bess pleaded, drawing away from him. "I meant to say I wouldn't have to leave Pembroke."

"I'm glad you find so much satisfaction here," Griffith said thoughtfully, "although you mentioned once that you had wanted to return to the convent and take the holy vows."

"That is true," Bess admitted, "but I am well treated here. And...if I were in the convent, I should never see you again."

Her open adoration almost undid him. He was used to women being overwhelmed by his presence, but this girl had stood against him and refused to conform to his wishes, and now that he must let her go, for her own good, she was admitting that she returned his affection.

Gently he held her at arm's length. He could almost taste the sweetness of her lips. Surely one last kiss would not destroy the friendship they had built. A friendship, Griffith told himself, was far more precious than all the passion in the world. His lips touched hers, so gently they scarce seemed to meet. He could feel her breath caress his lips. She raised herself on tiptoe to meet his kiss, pressing herself against the hard length of his muscular body. She sighed as she felt him take her into his arms. The intensity of their kiss caused her to gasp for breath.

He felt her lips part beneath his, and his tongue slipped into the honeyed cavern, exploring its secrets.

Bess reached out, clinging to him as though drowning. She trembled with the emotion that surged through her body.

Griffith withdrew his lips from hers and began raining kisses against her hair, and then down the long silken line of her throat, stopping again and again to feel the wild beating of her heart beneath his lips. His senses reeled, for he knew that it was his kisses, his lovemaking, his passion, that had awakened her.... Not Griffith the favored lord who would someday stand beside the king of England, but Griffith the man.

His lips found their way to the opening of her bodice, and he felt her heart lurch as he touched the sensitive satin of her breast. Her eyes widened with wonder under the gentle urging of his fingers.

Her legs would no longer hold her, and she rested in Griffith's arms, drawing her support from him as he continued his exploration of her loveliness.

"You are my rosebud, my lily," he murmured as he opened her bodice, holding her from him to behold the pink-and-white beauty that now lay beneath his ardent gaze.

She trembled as his tongue brushed against her supple nipple. Her eyes were closed now, her moist lips parted in desire, yet even in his passion for her, Griffith realized that she knew not what she desired. Her body demanded what her mind could not comprehend. Once again his mouth sought hers, feeling her instinctive response hammer its way through his body like blows on a blacksmith's anvil.

She was his to do with as he pleased. Her sweetness his to taste to the fullest. Griffith knew that she would do naught to stop him, save possibly a feeble protest when she read his intent. Still he hesitated, taking in the beauty before him. She was all the things of which dreams were made. All white and silver-gold. Her blue veins showed through the iridescent silkiness of her skin, and her high, pointed breasts yearned upward, inviting his lips to cover them, to taste their nectar.

He was filled with anticipation of promised delights. Her body stiffened for a moment as he took her breast into his mouth, drawing out the sweetness of innocence. His lips trailed down through the shallow valley and up to taste the other, while his hand moved down to know the depths of her beauty.

At his touch, her breath came in great sobs. She knew not how to cope with the intense emotion that shook her body.

Seeing her distress, Griffith abandoned his quest, holding her gently in an effort to calm the torrent of desire that threatened to undo them both. Her imminent submission warred against his need to protect her, ultimately bringing him to his senses.

Gently he drew her bodice about her again, looking one last time, with deep regret, at the delights of her lithe body.

He sighed as he cradled her against his chest. "Bess," he said softly, "you must leave me now. This thing between us will go no further, I swear it."

Bess looked at him, tears welling up in her eyes, her long black lashes holding the droplets like dew on a vine. Throughout her waking hours, Bess had agonized over her strong feelings for Griffith, her belief in that which was right and that which was sinful, and the conversation with Lucy the night of the banquet.

From Griffith's gentle demeanor toward her, Bess had come to believe that Lucy's words were true, and that although Griffith might care for her as deeply as she did him, he had taken a vow of chivalry and would not take from her what no man could return.

Indeed, until this moment, he had been the absolute model of decorum. But as their passion rose, he had gone beyond kissing and the holding of hands.

Perhaps she should have protested his liberties with her body and stemmed her rising desire, for now he thought her wanton and would send her away. She must know how she had offended him.

"Have I displeased you in some way, my lord?" she asked tremulously.

"No, never." Griffith kissed her forehead lightly, allowing his lips to savor the feel of her skin against them. "But there is no future for you with me. Someday I should be forced to leave you in much the same way Sir Morris has left your mother. It must not be, Bess. I could not bear to hurt you so."

Her heart leapt with joy. He was not angry. Perhaps it was love, rather than displeasure, that forced his restraint. "You did not feel thus when first we met," she reminded him.

"I did not believe I could fall in love when first we met," he admitted as the tears spilled down her cheeks.

The whole situation saddened her. She had denied him in mind and body for so long, and now that her overpowering emotion had demanded release within his arms, he must send her away.

"Can we still be friends?" She fought to control the sobs that threatened to overcome her.

"We are always friends, sweetheart." Griffith felt tears starting in his own eyes. "Nothing can change that. Now, go

to your room. It is late, and you should not be here alone
with me or any other man.''

She started toward the door, her eyes bright with tears,
her lips still swollen from the passion of his kisses. When she
turned, Griffith thought he had never seen anything so exquisite, so beautifully perfect. She stood there for a long
moment but did not speak. Griffith, in contemplating her
beauty, didn't notice her silence at first. Then, as it continued, he moved across the room toward her.

''Is something troubling you, Bess?'' he asked gently.

She nodded silently.

''Then can you not tell me what it is?''

Bess looked at the floor, blood rising to her cheeks. ''It is
just that I understand so little of this . . . lovemaking, my
lord.'' Her voice was hardly more than a whisper.

He lifted her chin gently until she was forced to look into
his eyes. ''Then tell me what you don't understand, and I
will right it for you,'' he assured her.

''I only wondered, my lord . . . You see, I have no way of
knowing except to ask, and I have no friend to ask, save
yourself.''

Frown lines creased her brow, and Griffith longed to kiss
them away, but he held himself in check, waiting for her to
continue. ''I will answer to the best of my ability,'' he
promised.

''Then, my lord, what I wanted to know, is . . . am I still
virgin?''

Bess drew back at the look of shock on Griffith's face. It
was almost as though she had dealt him a blow.

In his passion, Griffith had forgotten her upbringing and
her innocence. Now it was brought back to him with such
poignancy he felt humbled by the love she offered, unstintingly, without question—save this one.

"Oh, my sweet, sweet Bess." Now it was Griffith's turn to tremble as he again took the girl into his arms. "You are yet a virgin. I would not take that from you and then send you from me."

He rocked her as though she were a babe, and it was yet many minutes before he could bring himself to release her. It was not passion or lust that caused him to hold her, but a spark of feeling he had not known since his mother had passed away. A tenderness so filled with love it frightened him, for Griffith knew that a man in his position must not love for love itself. There must be a purpose behind it—the peaceful conquest of a country, the acquisition of a fortune, a political alliance, but never, never, the pleasure of love alone.

And yet, as he released Bess and watched her follow Prigge down the hall, he knew that he was on the verge of doing just that . . . loving for the sake of love alone.

The girl's trust, her innocence and her overwhelming love for him, were drawing him deeper and deeper into a quagmire of emotion that had best remain unexplored. He poured himself a goblet of wine as he waited for Prigge to return, and forced his mind to look onward to the events of the morrow.

The sun was high in the sky as the trumpets proclaimed the start of the tournament. The castle swarmed with knights, and the grounds were speckled with tents that had sprung up from the earth like a plague of mushrooms.

Griffith's tent was larger than most, and Bess found it easily from her vantage point at the tower window.

Mary was prattling on, displaying her knowledge of the champions whose pavilions spread before them. "And the dark one with the silver stripe belongs to Essex," she said, barely able to restrain a sigh. "He has promised to ask for my favor before he jousts. Can you imagine, Bess? He'll come to me and I'll wrap my scarf about his lance and he'll wear it into battle. And when he wins, it will be in my honor.''

Bess smiled indulgently. In truth, it was an exciting time in which to be alive. It seemed to Bess that never in history would these sun-bright days be matched. Never would the pageantry and color be as vibrant or the men as handsome as they were in this carefree time, when the man who would someday be Henry the Eighth was but a fun-loving, flamboyant prince of the realm.

''Should we not start toward the grounds?'' Bess suggested. ''The first knights should be about to take the field.''

''Oh, Bess, the first matches are nothing. In fact, the first days are nothing. The men take on individual challenges, most of which you could see on the practice field any day of the week. There will be wrestling, casting the bar, and other feats of strength and skill. And when they have exhausted those endeavors, they will begin the barriers, which is more exciting, probably tomorrow or the next day. When they've finished with that, they will begin the jousting, and then the melee on the final day.'' It made Mary feel very important to tell Bess of something so grand. ''But there,'' Mary conceded, ''you've never been to a tournament, and, of course, you're anxious to go.''

The girls hurried down the tower stairs, looking like displaced flowers as their brightly colored dresses lit the otherwise dim passageways.

The pavilion was a large platform shaded by a fringed canopy. Bess was to sit with Mary of Pembroke and Mary's mother, Lady Margaret. Much to Bess's disappointment, she gained her seat only to realize Griffith had just completed his wrestling match by defeating his opponent. He stood, relishing his victory, as the crowd cheered. Then, with the gallantry befitting a champion, Griffith reached down and helped the man to his feet. Bess was unable to hear their words, but she could see the smile on Griffith's face as the two men walked from the field together.

"You're so quiet, Elizabeth," Margaret of Pembroke said as she glanced at Bess. "Is something troubling you?"

"Oh, no, my lady." Bess smiled. "Everything is very much to my liking."

"It is kind of Bess to say so," Mary cut in, "but I know she is disappointed because I did not come here sooner and now she has missed seeing my lord Beaufort win his first match."

Bess blushed guiltily, but did not speak.

"That was very unkind of you, Mary," her mother said admonishingly before turning her attention again to Bess. "I will fetch you myself tomorrow, and see to it that you miss nothing. After all, a girl's first tournament is a momentous occasion, and you should not lose a moment of it."

As the matches continued, Bess took the time to view her surroundings. There were vendors with refreshing drinks of wine and ale. Men and maids were selling marchpane cleverly shaped into the figures of knights and saints. Bess could hardly contain her delight at the colorful garlands streaming with myriads of ribbons, as well as the little pomanders and nosegays made by the village women.

The jesters capered back and forth about the edge of the field. There were many of them that day—the apprentices, hoping to attract the attention of some great lord and be given a place in a noble household, and the established jesters who made certain they outdid all comers and retained their rightful places. But all in all, the crowd was the winner, for the laughter was spontaneous and continuous.

It wasn't until the field had been cleared of all opponents and the bearbaiting was about to begin that Lady Margaret decided to take her leave.

"I have no wish to watch the bearbaiting," she announced as she got to her feet, "and I suggest you young ladies return to the castle with me." She looked archly at Bess, for Mary had already risen. But Bess had hardly heard the lady's words, for Griffith had come to the edge of the field and was talking to the animal handlers. He threw back his head and laughed. His thick golden mane made him look like an untamed lion, fiercer and more dangerous than the motley bear and scurvy dogs being led onto the field. Bess was enthralled at the sight of him in his brief tunic. She blushed as she tried to drive the thoughts of their last meeting from her mind. Thoughts that rose unbidden at the sight of his body. Had she affected him as much as he was now affecting her?

She glanced about guiltily, but all eyes were on Griffith and his cousin, Henry, the future king of England. From dowager to maiden, from ancient to child, their eyes hungrily took in the youth and strength that was the hope of the realm.

It was only when Mary pinched Bess's arm that the girl pulled herself from her dreams and plunged painfully back into reality as she scrambled from the bench and followed Mary and the Lady Margaret toward the castle, where an indoor buffet had been set up for the nobility.

Bess glanced back and saw that many of the peasants had much the same idea, as the vendors were selling their meat pies and pasties at a great rate. Bess thought it would be delightful to indulge in their wares, but quickly cast the notion aside as she was hurried on.

* * *

"So you didn't watch the bearbaiting?" Griffith teased Bess as they walked together after the banquet, while the great hall was being cleared of the tables and readied for the rest of the evening's festivities.

Bess smiled shyly. "No, my lord, I doubt I would have been much enthused by it." She didn't add that had it not been for Mary and the Lady Margaret she very likely would have sat there during at least part of it, so engrossed had she been at the appearance of Griffith himself.

She cast the thought from her mind. It was unseemly that she should allow herself such thoughts and, even worse, the feelings of the flesh they invoked. They paused near the open doors leading outside.

"Come, walk with me to the walls—" Griffith took her arm as he spoke "—there is something I would show you."

Bess crossed the courtyard with him. The gates of Pembroke were open, and she could see the fields lit brightly even in the dimness of the night.

"Whatever are they doing over there?" Bess asked as she peered into the darkness, trying to make out the figures that danced about the fires in the distance.

"I imagine they are doing much the same as we do here," Griffith told her, "only they do it more freely, and with greater abandon. The common folk have their own merriment after the games. But surely you knew that."

Bess took a quick breath. Was this his way of reminding her of the difference in their stations in life?

"No, my lord, in fact I did not know. As I told you before, I went to the convent when I was very young, and this has been the first tournament I have attended since I arrived at Pembroke. When I lived with my parents, had there been a celebration such as this, I would have been too young to attend, much less remember."

Griffith paused for a moment, unsure as to the change in the girl's voice and attitude toward him. Shrugging off his doubts, he went on, "Sometimes I think they have a better time than the castle folk do with their dancing and singing and...freedom." He looked longingly at the bonfires.

"But surely there is singing and dancing enough in the castle," she ventured.

"Ah, surely there is, sweet Bess," Griffith agreed, "but it is all planned. Out there, nothing is planned. Nothing is structured. They light the fires, roast the meat and see what comes. Tomorrow there will be gypsies in the hall as part of the entertainment, but the gypsy wagons will be out there, around the fires, and their troubadours, jugglers and acrobats will perform for the common folk in a way they would never dare inside castle walls. Their women will dance as they could never dance inside a building."

"Then why don't you join the gypsies at their party tomorrow?" Bess suggested. "Surely they would welcome your presence."

"If I were to appear among them, they would instantly contain themselves, and none would act naturally. The whole evening would be spoiled for them, and for me."

They walked together in silence for a space of time. Then Griffith clutched her shoulders. "Bess, if I were to find a disguise for myself and you, would you come with me tomorrow night? Would you come dance with me to the gypsy music?"

"Oh, my lord, I shouldn't!" Bess protested. "Nor should you! Haven't you said your presence would dampen their celebration?"

Griffith laughed. "They would never think a nobleman would suddenly appear among them with a young woman on his arm. We would go as Bess and Giff, a young couple from a neighboring village, come here for the celebrations.

I could say I was in service of one of the knights. What say you? Are you with me?"

He looked at her with such anticipation, Bess knew she would be unable to deny him. In truth, his words excited her. It would be such an escapade to sneak away with him. An adventure beyond anything she'd ever dared dream of.

"But surely they would miss us in the hall."

"Not if you plead a headache, and I leave using the need to rest for the bouts the next day as my excuse. There are several peasants as tall as I, and I should be able to secure some suitable clothing without telling the need. Say you're with me!"

"I'm with you." Bess scarcely got the words out before Griffith engulfed her in his huge embrace, knocking the breath from her in his exuberance.

They walked back toward the castle while Griffith talked happily of the events of the day, explaining the rudiments of wrestling and the finer points of bearbaiting to her.

"Tomorrow I compete in barriers," Griffith told her as they neared the hall. "Will you be down to see me win?"

Bess laughed. "And are you so certain you'll win? I heard there were several knights planning on challenging you."

"And so there are, but rest assured, I shall win. And after I do, we'll leave them all and go to the celebration in yon field." He gestured dramatically as he spoke, sending Bess into gales of laughter.

"Then 'tis mandatory that you be the victor, my lord, for if you are not, I shan't go with you."

Griffith raised his eyebrows in mock surprise. "To the victor go the spoils."

"No," Bess laughed again, "to the party goes the victor."

"And his ladylove," Griffith said, and hugged her once more.

Chapter Four

Bess dressed quickly and slipped a cloak about her shoulders against the morning chill before she made her way to the chapel. It was empty this morning, and she dropped to her knees to pray for the safety of the man who had become so much a part of her life.

As though in answer to her prayers, she heard a voice behind her. Turning, she saw it was, indeed, Griffith.

"I thought I should find you here," he said as he came toward her. "Do not let me interrupt your prayers, for I have many of my own. If you'll allow me to join you."

Bess moved her skirts aside, and he knelt beside her. She wondered if he could hear the pounding of her heart. Her prayers, and any attempt to resume them, were shattered by his presence, but Bess quietly remained in her place, content to kneel there beside him, fingering her beads.

He crossed himself and, hastily, Bess followed suit, allowing him to help her to her feet. As he did, he raised her hand to his lips. Slowly, meaningfully, his eyes locked with hers.

"I go to walk the field before the games today," he told her as they left the silent chapel. "Would you come with me?"

His request took her completely by surprise, and she gasped, "Come with you?"

"Yes, you shall come with me, and I will explain to you the science of winning at barriers." He again took her hand, drawing her along beside him. Though he shortened his pace, Bess was practically running to stay with his long strides.

"Is there any reason why we must go at such a pace, my lord?" she asked, somewhat breathlessly.

Griffith slowed himself. "Forgive me—I had not meant to rush you. But in truth, I wish to get to the field before the others, so that I may take all the time I need to discover its pitfalls."

Bess looked questioningly at him, but he only smiled. "I will explain it all to you when we arrive at our destination."

The field was deserted, except for a few squires who moved about the perimeter, and some house servants who were wiping and drying the benches, removing all signs of the morning dew.

Bess and Griffith walked toward the low wall that had been set up in the middle of the field. It seemed to Bess that he essayed every clump of grass and measured every hole. When he finally reached the center of the barrier, he was even more careful, covering the territory with even greater thoroughness.

As he finished scouting the field, he began to explain his actions to Bess. "The barrier itself is waist-high, as you can see." Griffith laid his hand on the structure as he spoke. Bess glanced over the barrier and Griffith chuckled to see that it came almost to her shoulders. "It is placed there to separate the combatants and prevent wrestling or other physical confrontation. The participants wear breastplates and helmets made specifically for the game. It is a game of both skill and courage, but most of all, it is a contest of ability,'' he said proudly.

"Each man is issued a blunted spear, to be cast at his opponent. When you have cast your spear, it takes a great deal of self-control to hold yourself in place while your opponent makes ready to cast a seven-foot spear at you. Then after the spears are spent, each man is allowed twelve strokes with the two-handed sword.'' Griffith smiled at the look of admiration on the girl's face. "To win, it is mandatory that a man parry all the blows. The champion of the day may take on several opponents, usually no more than six. It is taxing, but enjoyable.''

The other knights had stirred, and were moving about the field now. Griffith took Bess's arm, leading her away.

"Have you no shield in barriers?'' she asked, glancing at the barrier itself as they moved across the field toward the castle.

"There would be no way to hold it and wield the sword,'' he explained. "There is a shield used in some cases during the spear-casting, but that, too, can become cumbersome. The swords and spears are blunted, and usually the only harm that befalls either man is some rather nasty bruises.''

Bess thought back to the day before, when she had seen Griffith talking to the handlers before the bearbaiting contest. His body had been so powerful, so perfect, his skin smooth and unblemished. It would pain her to see him hurt, no matter how slight or with what honor.

Griffith, always perceptive, immediately sensed the change in her mood. Stopping, he turned her toward him and lifted her face with his hand. "What is it, sweetheart?'' His voice was filled with concern. "Have I said something to offend thee?''

His use of the more intimate "thee'' rather than "you'' caused Bess's eyes to flutter before she was able to raise them to his. "It is only that I would not want to see you harmed, my lord," she said softly.

Bess could not know the effect her words, coupled with the look on her face, had on Griffith. Her blue eyes, tear-washed, with lashes kissed as though by droplets of dew, and her mouth, soft and vulnerable, trembling slightly in her distress at the thought of harm befalling him, melted his heart.

Without thinking, he bent, claiming her lips, savoring their warmth as the spark of passion shot between them, again renewed.

Reluctantly he let her go as he opened the postern gate and followed her into the castle yard.

"I shall not be harmed, I promise you," he vowed as he stole one last kiss before releasing her and going to his tent, where he would make ready for the day's contests.

Bess watched him disappear into the morning mist. It all seemed more a dream than reality. His interest in her, and the way he made her feel, frightened her. Still, she was not frightened enough to refuse him.

After their last encounter, he had never gone beyond the realm of propriety. He never pressed her to allow him to make love to her, although she sometimes thought she saw desire in his eyes.

Could it be that she misread him? His kisses, although touched with passion, were never insinuating enough to frighten her. Perhaps his interest was only that of friendship. If it was so, Bess would welcome it, for friendship with Griffith did not frighten her, as did the prospect of a more intimate involvement.

She knew the wild beating of her heart when he so much as looked her way portended no good for her immortal soul. The thoughts that crept insidiously into her mind were surely sinful, and she would confess them as soon... as soon as Griffith had gone and there was nothing more to confess.

The thought of Griffith's departure brought a sob to her throat. Her life would be gray and barren without him.

With insight beyond her years, she realized the plight of a lowborn maid in loving a highborn lord of the realm. Life gave them no choice of love with honor. For there could be no possibility of Griffith's marrying a girl of Bess's station, any more than there could be any question of her love for him.

The Lady Margaret was true to her word and sent for the girls long before the games were scheduled to begin, but today it was all Bess could do to keep from lagging behind. In truth, she feared Griffith would be injured during the matches that day.

"Hurry along, Bess," Mary urged as she slid into the place beside her mother. "They are about to call the first match."

One after another, the contestants came to the middle of the field, their pages and squires striding along behind them. The trumpets sounded and the colors blew bravely in the breeze as the marshal announced each combatant.

Then it began. The force of the bone-cracking blows was not lost on Bess, and she wondered if any of the contestants would survive in fit condition to participate in the jousting scheduled for the morrow.

More than once a man was carried from the field amid the cheers or jeers of the crowd, depending on their disposition toward the participants. But it took no soothsayer to realize when a champion of some note was about to take the field. Even Bess, with only a smattering of knowledge of such things, was aware that the tempo of the crowd had changed. It was then that the pages came forward bearing the banners of the house of Beaufort.

Bess felt her breath catch in her throat as the towering figure came into view.

"Ah," the Lady Margaret breathed with satisfaction, "now we shall see a contest. Griffith's opponent is to be Charles Brandon." She folded her hands on her lap and sat back with interest.

"But, my lady, I thought Lord Beaufort and Sir Charles were friends," Bess protested.

"They are friends," Lady Margaret assured the girl, "but more than that, they are knights, and they will give as good as they get to win the day. I would have thought that Griffith and Charles would do battle in the final round, but it seems that one will certainly eliminate the other here and now."

Bess stifled the urge to cover her face as the men presented themselves to the earl before taking their places on either side of the barrier.

The ordeal of the spears was almost more than Bess could bear, but it wasn't until the men began fighting with swords that she almost lost control.

The great swords came crashing down time and again. The power behind each blow seemed enough to fell a horse, but still the men blocked and parried with the skill of seasoned warriors. Finally, on the tenth blow, Sir Charles was driven to his knees, blocking Griffith's blows with his upraised sword. Unable to parry his adversary's blows, Sir Charles was forced to yield, and Griffith was awarded the match.

As the marshal stepped in to proclaim Griffith the winner, Griffith helped Sir Charles to his feet. The people applauded and shouted their approval loudly as the two men walked together from the field.

Now it was Bess's turn to sigh in relief. The next few matches didn't seem so frightening, for she knew that Griffith wasn't involved in them. The men fought on, though the sun was high in the sky and many spectators had gone to buy the tasty meat pies the vendors hawked among the crowd.

As Lady Margaret showed no signs of wishing to leave, Bess resigned herself to spending the afternoon trying to get a glimpse of Griffith in the jumble of men at the edge of the field.

With a few words from Lady Margaret, a little page was sent for food, and he soon returned with pies, pasties and ale. Even Mary, who normally had little appetite, was ravenous from the excitement of the day and the fresh air of the English countryside. The afternoon wore on for Bess until the Beaufort colors appeared again. Understanding little of the rules of elimination, Bess was surprised to find that Griffith would fight again.

"And now Lord Beaufort will fight for the championship of the barriers," Mary whispered with a nervous giggle. "If he hopes to be crowned champion of the tournament, he will have to win in this, as well as in the jousting and the melee."

Lady Margaret nodded in agreement. "He would have done well to have Sir Charles go against Sir Robert in the preliminaries. Now Griffith will have to defeat Sir Robert if he is to win, and that would be no easy matter even if he were fresh and rested."

"But surely Sir Robert will take Lord Beaufort's fatigue into consideration," Bess protested. "It's unfair that Griffith should have to fight both of the top contenders for the award."

The Lady Margaret laughed, fanning herself against the heat of the afternoon. "Griffith chose to have it this way himself. If he wins, it will be because he has beaten all com-

ers, and if he loses, it will be to one of the finest knights in
the land. There is no shame in that, certainly."

From the first blow, it was certain that neither knight intended to give quarter. The sounds of the swords crashing
together in a vicious rhythm resounded across the field, only
to be drowned out by the cheers of the crowd. From the
greatest lord to the lowest serf, each man was on his feet,
cheering his favorite.

Taking into consideration the difficulty of Griffith's previous match and the heat of the afternoon, some had chosen to place their wagers on Sir Robert. Now, as Griffith was
driven to his knees by the force of a mighty blow, those
people cheered more loudly, anticipating the winnings they
would soon receive. Griffith's followers took turns either
sinking into silence or shouting loudly for him to rise.

Bess had inadvertently gotten to her feet at the first sign
that Griffith was in trouble. She was in time to see him receive a debilitating blow across his shoulders. Such a blow
would have felled a lesser man, but Griffith twisted away
and scrambled to his feet. His legs braced apart like two
solid trunks of good English oak, he again wielded his
sword, swinging it in an arc of such magnitude and intri-
cacy that Sir Robert mistook his intent and sought to block
it before his face. At that moment, Griffith, with the speed
gained from long hours of dedicated practice, changed his
aim and dealt Sir Robert a side blow against his helmet that
knocked the man to the ground and the helmet from his
head.

A moan went up from Sir Robert's backers when they saw
that their champion could not rise to continue the match,
while the cheers of Griffith's faction resounded throughout
the crowd.

Bess could only sigh in relief as she resumed her seat and
tried to quiet her pounding heart. Surely no man could take

such punishment and still call it sport, yet it seemed that was exactly what they did.

Griffith walked the length of the field while the crowd applauded him. He paused before the pavilion where Bess sat with the other ladies. He bowed to the Lady Margaret, but his eyes sought out Bess. A slight frown crossed his brow when he saw the pallor of her skin and knew instinctively that her distress was due to his troubles on the field. Smiling reassuringly at her, he continued his rounds, allowing the adulation of the crowd to wash over him.

Even Sir Robert's greatest supporters could not have denied that Griffith had won fairly and over almost insurmountable odds. It would have been unthinkable not to cheer so great a champion.

Bess was notably nervous during the sumptuous dinner that followed the day's activities. She was able to eat but little, and saw, to her surprise, that Griffith also lacked an appetite. Once or twice he cast a smile in her direction, and she knew he hadn't forgotten their plans to go to the festivities.

As she slipped unnoticed from her place at the board, Griffith was making excuses to his hosts, declaring that he must be ready and rested for the morrow. While the earl expressed his disappointment that Griffith wouldn't be staying for the evening's entertainment, he well understood the man's desire to be rested for the events of the following day, and graciously bade Griffith a good night.

Bess was to meet Griffith at the postern gate as soon as she had changed her clothes. By taking apart one of the dresses she had worn when she was at the convent, she fashioned a simple blouse and kirtle, making a very passable copy of peasant attire. Wrapping a light shawl about her head and shoulders, she hurried down the shadowy halls to her rendezvous.

The gate was ajar when she arrived. At first she thought Griffith had not yet arrived, but then a giant figure appeared before her, causing her to cry out in fright. His hand covered her mouth, quickly followed by his lips.

"Hush, sweetheart," Griffith said, soothingly as he held her tightly. "There is no cause for alarm."

Bess could feel his heart beating, separated from her own only by the thin linen of his open shirt. She stepped back, openly admiring his choice of dress.

"You look very much the village smithy," she told him as she took in everything from his soft leather boots to his tightly fitted pants to his full-sleeved shirt, open to the waist and belted in the gypsy manner.

Laughing, he took her hand and drew her with him across the field.

"Hurry," he urged, "at least until we are out of sight of the castle. I have little desire to explain my actions this night, should we be seen by someone out for a stroll along the battlements."

"Even your closest friends would have a difficult time recognizing you," Bess assured him.

As the countryside darkened into shadows, they slowed their pace. The sounds of music and the smells of food roasting over open fires permeated the air and caused Bess's mouth to water. Her appetite had suddenly returned, and now her young stomach growled in its need for sustenance.

"I've waited all day for this," Griffith told her as they skirted the edge of the camp area.

As Griffith had promised, there was life and color to boggle one's mind. In a clearing, well-lighted by the huge fires, a band of gypsies played their instruments while others danced. Many of the people had begun to eat the food that had been provided by the castle, and the wine and ale flowed as freely here as it did in the great hall itself. Truly, the earl had spared nothing to make the festivities as grand for the commoners as he did for the nobility.

Griffith placed Bess on a tree stump where she could rest and went to secure some food for them. He returned with venison and two small game birds, a loaf of crusty dark bread and a chunk of cheese.

"There—" he smiled as he placed the food on the log "—truly a feast fit for a king."

Griffith drew a skin of wine from his shoulder, pouring it into a flagon for Bess and drinking from the skin himself.

"Thank you, my lord," Bess said, and smiled, tasting the sweet wine.

Griffith shook his head in warning. "None of that tonight. Remember, tonight we are but Giff and Bess, come for the festivities."

Bess nodded.

"Now let me hear you say it," Griffith prompted.

"Say what?" Bess stared up at him for a moment, her thoughts only of the way the red-gold hair on his chest glimmered in the firelight. The soft material of the shirt he wore molded itself against his muscular body, his biceps, developed from hours of work with the sword, stretched against the sleeves as though attempting to break through. The village girls had already noticed him and were casting covert glances in his direction, wondering who he was and what his relationship might be with her.

But it was not the village girls who posed the threat, Bess realized. It was the gypsy women, for their glances were not covert but brazen, and they swished their skirts and moved their hips seductively, hoping to gain Griffith's attention.

"Are you going to say it or not?" Griffith asked again, when Bess didn't answer him.

"What did you want me to say?" she asked in confusion.

"I wanted you to call me Giff," he told her with a laugh, "but you obviously have other things on your mind."

Bess returned his laughter before she admitted, "I was watching the way the women were looking at you. Perhaps you would have done better to have come alone. I may be a hindrance to you before the night is over."

Griffith leaned toward her, speaking softly as he looked into her eyes. "It is because of you that I have come at all, and because of you that I am enjoying myself so greatly," he assured her. "How can you think that I should have left you behind?"

"Surely you would find as much enjoyment without me," Bess protested.

"I have never known such enjoyment as I find with you." Griffith surprised even himself with his words. He longed to take the girl into his arms, but knew that, even in a gathering such as this, proprieties must be observed. Instead, he sliced off a thick portion of meat and offered it to her.

She bit into it, catching the rich juices on her bread. "You are right...Giff—" she managed to say the name after only the slightest hesitation "—it is delicious."

When she smiled up at him, her mouth was moist and luscious from the juicy meat, and the sight was more than Griffith could bear. With a groan, he found her lips, sucking the juices from them greedily.

Gently she placed her hand against his chest, and was startled at the feel of his bare flesh beneath her fingertips.

He drew a deep breath. "Forgive me," he said in an apologetic tone. "It seems I can't be near you without wanting to kiss you. I promise I shall conduct myself with the utmost propriety for the rest of the evening."

For a moment, it was on the tip of Bess's tongue to admit that she didn't want him to conduct himself with propriety, but she bit back the words and banished the thought from her mind. Soon the gypsies had struck up another tune, and both Bess and Griffith turned their attention to them.

The tempo picked up as the entertainers returned from the castle. They had been given food and drink, as well as a bag of coins, for their work, and their mood was one of merriment.

Bess applauded as Griffith joined in with a group of tumblers, lifting them easily on his shoulders as they went through an improvised routine. Then the gypsies struck up their instruments and began to dance. They asked Griffith to join them, but he refused, indicating he was not interested in dancing except with his lady.

They wagged their heads knowingly. "Then we will teach you both," one of the dancers said, pulling Griffith and Bess toward the open space around the fires.

At first the music was slow, to match the movements of their feet as the gypsies led them through the steps. Then, as the others gathered round, Griffith's feet began moving lightly in rhythm to the music. Turning to Bess, he swung her along with him.

In a few moments, her slim body responded to the age-old sob of the music, turning and twisting like a flame.

The mood caught her, and she became a part of the ritual, her skirts flying, her hair breaking loose from its tight restraints and flowing about her as though it had a life of its own.

She was the most exquisite thing Griffith had ever seen—a silver-gold radiance contrasting against the night. Not only the gypsies, but the villagers, as well, stopped to watch in awe.

The grace, the rhythm, the passion, with which they danced touched every person. As the music changed from brisk to sensuous, so changed the reactions of their bodies. They moved around each other warily, as though unsure of one another, yet drawn by mutual longing. The music soared, bursting into a throbbing beat of passion that sent them twirling faster and faster, until it ended and Bess fell back breathlessly in Griffith's arms, her hair trailing like a token of surrender across the ground.

Bess could feel the heat of Griffith's lips, only inches above hers. Slowly, slowly, he lifted her to her feet, relishing every moment he held the slim weight of her body against him. Her skin was covered with a thin sheen from her exertions, and her blouse clung to her youthful curves. He slipped his arm about her as they walked to the edge of the clearing, while the other dancers took the arena.

Shouts of pleasure and congratulations on their dance greeted them as they moved through the crowd. A mug of ale was pressed into Griffith's hands. He shared its contents with Bess as the villagers pounded his back and clasped his hand in good-natured camaraderie.

The hour grew late, and the jests became more ribald. Griffith took Bess's arm. "It is late," he said softly. "We must leave."

She nodded. It was, indeed, late. If they lingered, they would be missed at the castle. They had hardly started toward the trees at the edge of the campgrounds when a gypsy woman stepped in front of them, blocking their path.

"You have given us much pleasure this night," she told them, a smile on her craggy face. "We are most honored to have you share our humble festivities."

It was obvious that she knew Griffith's identity. He wondered how many others were also aware, but held his tongue, waiting to hear what the crone had to say.

"If you like," she continued, "I would tell your future."

Bess drew her breath in quickly. It was a sin, a terrible sin, to have one's fortune told, but Griffith had no such compunctions.

"And what see you in my future?" he asked, smiling.

"Give me your hand," the woman said.

Griffith held out his hand, and she took it in both of hers, turning toward the light from the fires as she gazed at it.

"Soon, far sooner than you know, you will accept your destiny. There is greatness here, and with it an equal measure of sadness and disappointment." The old woman turned toward Bess, and the girl instinctively hid her hand behind her back, but the old woman only suppressed a smile and continued. "This one—" she indicated Bess as she spoke "—when all others have failed you...this one will give you hope."

With that, she released Griffith's hand and disappeared into the darkness. Griffith stood for a moment looking after her until Bess tugged on his arm, reminding him that they must leave.

"She knew who I was," he said as they walked toward the looming shadow of Pembroke Castle.

"Perhaps she saw you in the hall," Bess suggested.

"That old woman couldn't have walked to the hall," Griffith answered. "She was so old and crippled, it would have been impossible for her to have gone so far."

"But your face is not unknown," Bess reminded him, "and you did nothing to hide yourself from them."

He placed his hand over hers, letting the subject drop. "Did you enjoy yourself?" he asked.

"I thought it wonderful," Bess admitted, "but I am embarrassed that I so forgot myself during the dancing."

"There is no need of that." Griffith squeezed her fingers lightly. "You were beautiful. No man could have asked for a lovelier partner. There wasn't a gypsy woman there that could have touched you.''

"Nor a man that danced as well as you, my lord."

"Bess and Giff, remember?" Griffith smiled at her.

Bess sighed as they neared the postern gate. "Yes, Bess and Giff, simple peasants, out for a night of revelry. But the night is over, and we are again Elizabeth, maid-in-waiting, and Griffith, lord of the realm."

"The night doesn't have to end," Griffith said, the memory of his passionate response to the haunting beauty of her lithe body blotting out all else.

Without letting her answer, he took her into his arms, covering her face with kisses—her eyes, her hair, the throbbing pulse in her throat, all knew his touch as she trembled beneath his onslaught. In a moment, it would be too late, the driving force that had burst between them would overpower even their most sacred vows, and he would take her here, outside the postern gate, like a peasant or an animal.

"Please, my lord," she gasped. "Please let me go."

Reluctantly he loosened his grip on her, drinking in the ethereal beauty of her face in the moonlight. "And if I say I cannot let you go?" he whispered.

He saw her answer in the tears sparkling against the deep pools of her eyes like tiny stars as once more he tasted the sweetness of her kiss before releasing her and opening the gate.

So great was their attention on one another that neither noticed the young prince watching from the battlements, his eyes bright blue slits in the blackness of the night.

Chapter Five

The trumpets began sounding with the dawn as errant knights arrived at Pembroke to participate in the jousting. The number of tents doubled as the morning light spread a rosy glow over the land.

"Do hurry, Bess," Mary scolded. "I don't want to miss a moment of this."

Bess smiled to herself as she fastened Mary's headdress with a flowing scarf. Mary wore a gown of blue, deep and rich, like the summer sky. Her scarf and headdress were of a lighter hue. The colors made her dark eyes sparkle.

Bess herself wore a gown of blue and gold—the Beaufort colors, as well she knew, though she feigned innocence in the matter. She continued with her mistress's toilette.

"There," she said as she tucked the last hair under Mary's headdress, "no finer lady could be asked for favor by any knight at the tourney."

Mary giggled prettily. "You look rather fine yourself," she said generously. "Now do hurry—my lady mother will be here at any moment."

As if on signal, the Lady Margaret came through the door, resplendent in a gown of brown and gold. "Ah, there you are, and all ready, too, I see." She nodded her approval as several of the other girls came hurrying up. Lady

Margaret and her daughter led their impromptu procession, the rest of the ladies followed neatly by twos.

The men who weren't participating in the jousts that morning smiled their approval at the bevy of beauties who passed by on their way to the field.

"I simply cannot tell you how excited I am," Ann was saying as they took their places on the pavilion. "I was unable to sleep the entire night."

"Then you snore while you're awake," Lucy chided, and Ann swatted playfully at her with a pomander.

"Girls," Lady Margaret admonished them gently, smiling at their teasing banter, "behave yourselves. The entry parade is about to begin."

The herald took his place in front of the stands, and the trumpets sounded again.

Knights burst onto the field in a brilliant array of colors, and the very air shook with the thundering of hooves as the great war-horses galloped past the stands. The sun reflected off the shining armor, sending shafts of light into the eyes of the spectators.

Bess held back the urge to cover her eyes and ears as the horses flew past. Each horse wore trappings in its rider's colors, and many sported plumes bobbing on their heads. The knights themselves were no less colorful than their animals. Some were preceded by standard-bearers, while others wore cloaks thrown recklessly over one shoulder as they held high their ornate ceremonial swords in a salute to the earl, who stood to receive their tribute.

"Aren't they just magnificent?" Mary gasped.

Bess, seated to Mary's right, nodded in agreement, adding, "But I cannot see how they can hope to fight with cloaks and trappings hampering them."

Mary smiled in a superior way. "Much of what they wear now is for exhibition only," she said knowingly. "They will not wear the cloaks or carry the jeweled swords when the joust begins in earnest, of that you can be sure."

All the time Mary was speaking, Bess's eyes searched through the maze of colors for Griffith. Long before she recognized his colors, she saw the red-gold lights of his hair as he galloped onto the field.

He towered head and shoulders above the other knights, although his horse was no larger than the others'. The size, the power, the skill, the knowledge . . . these things were all Griffith. Even the most chaste lady drew in her breath as he thundered toward the stands.

He drew his horse to a halt, bowing to the earl and then to the ladies. His eyes met Bess's, and he looked meaningfully into hers. She caught her breath, imagining his lips, hot and possessive, against her own.

Then he was gone, joining the others at the far end of the field, where they dispersed to their tents to await their events.

It was Lucy who first saw the dark, rather shabby knight standing at the edge of the field, staring boldly at the ladies in the stands.

"Who is that knave?" Lucy asked, turning toward Ann, "and why does he persist in watching us so strangely?"

Bess turned her attention in the direction Lucy had indicated, drawing her breath in sharply as she recognized Sir Morris. In her happiness, she had completely forgotten the man was at Pembroke, and that he had expressed the desire to take her back to her mother.

Her thoughts of Sir Morris faded when the trumpets sounded and the first joust began. As Mary had said, the men had, indeed, left their finery behind. Only the horses continued to wear the protective coverings that somewhat padded the blows should a lance miss its mark during the explosion of contact.

And explosion it was! Two knights rode toward one another, meeting with an ear-piercing screech of metal. A lance shattered, and Bess covered her face with her hands. To her surprise, when she again looked up, the men were still mounted and riding back to choose another weapon. They were allowed three passes, unless one of them fell. Bess felt her heart in her throat as she realized that Griffith would face such a match himself in a short time.

On the second pass, one knight was unseated, falling to the earth with a resounding crash. He lay immobile while the squires rushed forth and hurriedly removed his helmet. Within a few minutes, they had raised him to his feet and he was able to walk from the field with their assistance.

Meanwhile, his opponent was accepting his due applause as he cantered past the stands.

The herald had announced the fifth match of the day when Mary gave a little start. Bess looked at her in some surprise. Mary's eyes were bright with anticipation. Nervously she plucked at the scarf she carried, never allowing her eyes to stray from the far end of the field.

The knights rode out to present their salute at the center of the arena. Bess watched curiously as one of them—Sir Thomas of Essex—now rode forward, stopping before the pavilion and lowering his lance.

"I beg a token from Mary of Pembroke," he said as he bowed to her.

Mary was so flustered, she almost dropped the scarf brought for just this purpose. Finally, amid giggles from the other girls, she managed to secure the scarf to the lance. The knight retrieved it, waving it gaily as he rode back to his place.

Essex won easily and rode back past the pavilion to give a final salute to Mary. This time, he had removed his helmet, and Bess could see his face.

"He is handsome, is he not?" Mary asked as he rode from sight.

"That he is," Lucy agreed with a smile. "How lucky you are, Mary, to have such a man as your betrothed."

"Aye," Mary agreed, "you speak truly. I am lucky. The man is neither homely nor old. His family owns great estates, and he practices the ways of a true knight. There is no one luckier than myself."

"Nor lighter in the purse than your father," the Lady Margaret added cynically. "Your dowry must be honored now that the betrothal has become fact and the wedding plans have begun."

Bess sat in stunned silence. Mary's wedding plans... Bess had heard nothing of this, and from the looks of surprise on the faces of the other girls, they, too, had been kept in the dark.

She couldn't help but wonder if Mary would choose to take all her ladies to her new domain. It seemed more likely she would choose ladies from her new husband's estates. Bess wondered what would become of her should Mary decide to leave her at Pembroke. Lady Margaret's women were older, and it was doubtful they would take kindly to having a girl thrust into their circle.

The thought crossed her mind that perhaps she would be forced to return to her mother and Sir Morris. It was with real trepidation that she sought to ease her mind by watching the next match. To her dismay, Sir Morris himself was one of the participants.

He won the match, although there was some question of a foul, as he had dropped his lance below the accepted line. However, nothing could be proven, as the marshal had not been in a position to see, and Sir Morris declared staunchly that it was a fair blow.

The sun was high when Griffith took the field. He cantered toward the stands, carrying his helmet in his arm. After saluting his host, he spoke.

"I beg a favor, my lord." His voice rang loud and clear on the warm breeze. "I wish a token from Mistress Elizabeth."

The earl nodded his permission as Griffith dipped his lance toward Bess to receive her token. Somehow, the Lady Margaret managed to thrust a delicate scarf into Bess's empty hands. "Put it on the lance, child," she whispered.

Bess's hands were shaking, and she could barely hold the cloth, let alone secure it to the lance. Griffith smiled at her reassuringly. "Thank you, mistress," he said, "and be assured I shall endeavor to do you honor this day."

So overwhelming was the realization of the honor done her, Bess almost fainted as he galloped away. The most magnificent knight in Christendom had actually asked for her token. It was like a dream come true, and even as she saw him unhorse his opponent with one quick thrust, she could hardly believe it was happening. And, even more, that it was happening to her. And in that sweet moment Bess was very glad that she had left the convent. Very glad indeed.

It wasn't until late afternoon that the personal challenges began.

"But I thought they had finished with the jousting," Bess confided to Mary as they waited for the knights to appear.

"Those jousts were selected by lot," Mary explained, "but these men have some specific reason to challenge their opponent. Whether it is to prove their superiority, or for a personal grudge, or even because they feel they were not allowed a fair chance in the morning's matches. 'Tis the time for them to right their true and imagined wrongs."

Bess nodded and sat back to watch the matches. But only after several bouts had taken place was her full attention taken once more.

"Morris of Bladacglen challenges Griffith Beaufort!" The herald read out the words in stentorian tones.

A shocked silence fell over the crowd. It was unheard-of for any man to challenge Griffith—and a man of less than royal blood, at that. Griffith seldom honored any man by taking him on in individual combat, save certain friends whose prowess in the field of battle was tantamount to his.

The earl was on his feet in an instant.

"Sir knight, I fear that His Lordship cannot accept your challenge. Perhaps another of the knights would do as well?"

"No other knight," Sir Morris bellowed from one end of the field. "Griffith Beaufort has interfered in my personal affairs and caused me great distress. I choose to right this wrong on the field of honor."

"Your challenge is taken," Griffith's squire called out from the other side of the field. "My master will meet you for three passes or an unhorsing."

Sir Morris smiled. "Done!" He slammed down the face-piece on his helmet and wheeled his horse to the lists, where he would wait for Griffith to appear.

Within minutes, the trumpets sounded, as Griffith's squire had given the signal that his lord was ready.

Griffith spurred his horse on so violently the animal sat back on its haunches before plunging forward to meet the foe.

At the first pass, Sir Morris had aimed high, and his lance splintered against Griffith's shoulder. The men returned to their squires for new lances.

"Watch him, my lord," a squire shouted, slipping up beside Griffith's stirrup. "He drops his lance and hits along the edge of the saddle. My master is in sad shape from such a blow. He will ride no more this day, I fear, due to Sir Morris's tactics.''

Griffith nodded his thanks before he again thundered toward his opponent. He watched for the lance to dip as he rode forward. It wasn't until the last possible moment that Sir Morris, seeing that Griffith had covered himself well in anticipation of the blow, took Griffith's strike on his shield and ran his lance almost horizontally into Griffith's side as he passed by.

The crowd was on its feet as Griffith swayed for a moment before righting himself. Then he rode firmly to his squire and took another lance.

"It was a foul, my lord!" the young man cried. "Call it, and the marshal will stop the match and send the man away in disgrace!"

"Sending him away is not enough," Griffith said between clenched teeth. "I will send him to the devil."

With that, he rode back to his mark to await the third and final pass.

The crowd waited in silence, sensing that there was something more here than met the eye. Many of the men surmised that a foul blow had been dealt and that, by rights, Griffith would have been allowed to call an end to the match. He had not, however, and that in itself was ominous.

The trumpets sounded as the crowd came to life. The horses pounded forward, their great strides shaking the ground. As if one, the people in the crowd found their voices and rose to their feet, and the knights came together. There was a shattering crash, and Sir Morris was lifted from his saddle like a toy and tossed to the ground.

At the other end of the arena, Griffith circled his destrier and turned to his fallen opponent.

Griffith raised his visor, making a salute to the crowd before he cantered from view. It was only when he was well out of sight of the cheering multitude that he allowed himself to slump in the saddle, the pain from the tearing blow Sir Morris had dealt him finally becoming unbearable.

Bess sat in the stands, unable to cheer, or even to speak. It seemed as though she had been frozen the moment Griffith had sustained the foul blow. Her heart had ceased to beat. How could a man take such punishment without collapsing?

The day's heat had given way to an afternoon chill as clouds blotted out the sun and the mists began to form. Vapors rose from the heated ground as the knights again took the field.

The two factions paraded around once to the applause and cheers of the crowd before lining up on either side of the arena.

Prince Henry himself would ride at the head of one group of knights while his friend Charles Brandon led the other. The knights for the mock battle were chosen by luck of the draw. Excitement filled the air as the people looked forward to the grand finale of the games.

No one was surprised that Sir Morris did not appear. Nor would they have doubted had they been told that he lay unmoving in his tent while the castle leech made every effort to revive him.

Bess's eyes darted from one knight to the next. She found Sir Charles Brandon and Sir Robert Dymnock—she was even able to identify Sir Thomas of Essex—but she could not find the blue-and-gold colors of Beaufort.

The pennants waved bravely, adding their color to the trappings of the horses and the plumes and favors displayed by the knights. Each knight wore a short vest bearing the colors of the side for which he rode.

In honor of Prince Henry's presence, the knights had chosen white and green, while the other side had taken silver and black. Bess gave up all hope of finding Griffith simply by identifying him from his trappings, she would have to locate him by his size. But there was no man in the Tudor side who was large enough to be Griffith. While Dymnock was as tall, his body was slim and wiry. Brandon had the same broad shoulders, but he was shorter. The only man near Griffith's size was the young prince himself.

A flicker of fear crept through Bess's heart and lodged itself like a gnawing pain. Griffith was not there. He would not fight in the melee. Yet nothing would stop him from doing so, short of physical disability. He must be wounded. Bess sprang to her feet as the trumpets called out their challenge.

All eyes were on the field as horses and riders thundered toward one another. As the riders met, Bess slipped unnoticed from the stands. As she wended her way through the maze of tents, the sounds of the melee rose behind her. The crowd shouted wildly, urging their champions on to victory. Soon the knights would be returning, and it would not be good for her to be found here alone.

Her heart pounded painfully against her ribs as she hurried toward the edge of the camp. It was there that she found the tent she sought. Uttering a prayer of thanks, Bess hastened her steps.

"You can't go in there!" Prigge shouted, and grasped her arm as she would have entered. Then, recognizing her, he released his hold. "Mistress Bess, you should not be here," he protested. "You should be in the stands with the other women. It is unseemly...."

"He has been injured, has he not?"

The man nodded, almost imperceptibly, glancing about to see if anyone watched.

"Then I must go to him," Bess insisted, and again made to enter the tent.

"Mistress, I assure you—" Prigge got no further, for Bess slipped under his arm and with one swift movement was inside.

It took a moment before her eyes became accustomed to the dimness and she was able to make out Griffith's form, lying motionless on a pallet.

In her haste to reach him, she had not realized that his armor and tunic lay on the floor nearby and he was in a state of undress. His massive chest and powerful shoulders were bare, and the glimmer of red-gold hair on his chest gleamed in the flickering light. She had never seen a man unclothed before, and while she wanted to run away, she also wanted to stay.

She stared in wonder at the biceps developed through long hours of training with heavy swords. It was well-known that Griffith could wield the massive broadsword with only one hand, a feat equaled only by Prince Henry himself.

Bess had not realized the immensity of his body, but now, standing close, she knew he could have crushed her at will, had he so desired. Yet his touch had always been gentle.

Her eyes moved down over the outline of his body beneath the thin covering of linen. A pang of guilt washed over her, and she quickly returned her gaze to his face.

His eyes were closed, and he looked boyish, almost vulnerable. She wanted to hold him and protect him. As she sank to her knees, Bess became aware that Prigge had followed her into the tent.

"How long has he been so?" she asked in a hushed voice.

"Almost since he returned from the joust," Prigge fretted. "The castle leech came, but I have little faith in the man's ability. He bled him, but it did no good. I have sent for Master Aylesworth, the physician."

Bess laid her hand on Griffith's forehead. It burned beneath her touch, yet he moved slightly, as though he recognized her presence.

Her eyes took in the cruel bruises that marred his body—the swollen place on his neck where he had been struck during barriers, plus a myriad of lesser marks.

"Is this the only wound?" Bess asked.

Prigge came to stand beside her. "No, mistress," he said. "there is also this."

As he spoke, he lifted the covering, exposing the raw, bloodied gash in Griffith's side inflicted by Sir Morris's foul blow.

A gasp escaped Bess's lips. The pain she knew he must have felt seemed to surge through her own body.

Realizing there was no time to waste, she looked quickly around the tent. Spying a basin, she picked it up and handed it to Prigge. "Bring hot, clean water," she ordered.

Prigge returned a few minutes later. Bess bade him place the basin on a stool, and she knelt at Griffith's side. Gently she cleansed the area where the links of his mail had cut through his skin. She tried not to think of his pain as she worked. And she tried to ignore the new and tumultuous feelings that coursed through her body when she touched him.

She had learned a knowledge of herbs at the convent. Quickly she gave Prigge instructions to secure some common herbs. Soon he set to work brewing a mixture that they somehow managed to get Griffith to drink. Then, after making a poultice for his side, she sat back to wait.

"It will force him to sweat the poisons from his system," she told Prigge. "It is up to us now to keep him warm and comfortable. When he awakens, he should be all right."

Prigge nodded in agreement, unable to conceal his admiration for this girl who had done so much more than the resident leech.

The sounds from without indicated that the melee had ended and the knights were on their way to the castle for the feast that traditionally followed. Soon, undoubtedly, someone would come searching for her.

"Prigge," Bess said quietly, "they will be seeking me soon. I cannot leave him until I am assured of his well-being. Would you take a message to Mary of Pembroke apprising her of my whereabouts? I would stay with Griffith until he regains consciousness."

"I will do as you wish, mistress." he assured her.

Prigge had but stepped from the tent when Bess heard voices. Henry himself had come to see to his cousin's health. Prigge reassured the prince that Griffith was well cared for and Henry went on his way.

All through the day and into the following night, Griffith's body was racked with fever, while Bess stayed by his side, giving unstintingly of herself.

Then, when the night was full upon them and the torches flared, Griffith slipped into a deep and restful sleep. As his skin became cool to her touch, Bess sighed in relief knowing the fever had broken.

Where before she had pressed cool cloths against his brow, now she took dry ones, wiping away the moisture. It was late, and her body cried out for rest and nourishment, but still she would not leave him. She dropped her head against the coverlet. It was damp to the touch, and she knew she must change it. For a moment she thought of calling Prigge, but he had told her only a short time before that he was going to rest.

Taking fresh linen from the chest, Bess lifted the damp cloth. For a moment, her mouth went dry and her heart ceased to beat. He lay there before her and she drank in the masculine beauty of his body. His huge shoulders and full chest tapered to slim flanks and muscled legs, tightly corded and covered with fine hair the color of sunlight.

She likened him to the statues she had seen on a visit to London when she was but a child. It was as though life had been breathed into one of them. Her hands ached to touch him, to feel the warmth of his flesh against her fingers. She reached out, unable to restrain herself, memorizing his body with her eyes and hands. Realizing the enormity of what she was doing, she quickly stepped back and shook out the coverlet, laying it over his body as her guilt caused blood to sweep into her face.

Ashamed of giving in to her carnal desires, which must surely be the blackest of sins, Bess fell to her knees to beg God for Griffith's health and for her own forgiveness.

It was while she was so engaged that Griffith opened his eyes.

Bess's hair had fallen from its restraints and lay softly about her shoulders, like a shimmering veil. Her face was raised to heaven as her petal-soft lips moved in a silent prayer.

"Is it Bess?" Griffith asked weakly, raising himself on one elbow, "or is it that I have, indeed, died, and an angel has come to take me to my reward."

"No angel, I fear," Bess said, and she colored, remembering the sinful way she had drunk in the sight of his body. "When you did not appear for the melee, I realized something had happened, so I came."

Hearing voices, Prigge burst in. "My lord, I could not keep her out."

"I see," Griffith said, a smile playing about the corners of his mouth. "She overpowered you and made her way in."

"No, my lord, she..." Prigge faltered.

"Never mind, Walter," Griffith cut in. "It is well she came."

Prigge hurried from the tent, breathing an audible sigh of relief. Griffith reached beneath his cot and drew forth a scrap of cloth, which Bess recognized as the scarf she had given him as her token.

"I did not dishonor your favor, sweetheart," Griffith said as Bess seated herself on the stool near his pallet, "but I fear I have damaged it beyond repair."

She took it from his fingers and pressed it to her lips. It was torn and bloodied. "I shall treasure it all the more now that it carries the mark of your valor."

Griffith smiled at her words before he warned, "But keep its identity to yourself, as it is best if the people aren't aware that I have been injured."

Bess was aware of the constant power struggle between the king and Prince Henry. Since Beaufort was Prince Henry's man, it would do them no good if it was known he had been wounded while playing in knightly games that King Henry had specifically forbidden both the prince and his friends.

"We have tried to prevent that from becoming public knowledge, Prigge and I," Bess assured him. "But surely when you did not fight in the melee, they suspected, as did I, that you were injured."

"Those who think of it at all will believe there was too little time between the joust with Sir Morris and the melee for me to prepare myself. Then, too, many will swear that they actually saw me fight."

"I fear you are mistaken," Bess said, shaking her head, "for I knew immediately when you weren't among the knights on the field."

"Ah, but you looked for me through the eyes of love, sweet Bess, and so you saw what others would never see."

With those words, he took her hand in his and pressed her palm against his lips. His movement caused the covering to fall away, and Bess saw that his wound had opened as he stirred. The bandages were again bloodied.

"It should be tended, my lord," she whispered through dry lips, remembering the sight and the feel of his naked flesh. She turned away in confusion to seek clean linen.

Gently she removed the bandages. She tried to ignore the feeling of his eyes upon her. The heat of his gaze burned through her clothing. Her breasts rose and fell more quickly as her fingers lingered over their task, for she was unsure as to what would happen when she had finished. Injured or not, Griffith was still a virile, passionate man, and Bess realized she had placed herself at a disadvantage in coming to him. Yet she could not have stayed away.

Finally, the wound bandaged, Bess looked into Griffith's face. His skin was covered with fine sheen of perspiration.

"Forgive me," she said as she reached for another cloth, touching it to his forehead, "I did not mean to cause you pain."

"The pain you cause is not from your gentle ministrations—" Griffith caught her hands, holding them against his face "—but from my agonizing desire for you. A desire that becomes unbearable when you but touch me."

She would have pulled away, but he held her firmly.

"Feeling your touch, and wanting to return it," he continued. "To run my fingers across the cool satin of your skin. To feel you, to taste you." His voice was hoarse with desire as he lifted his hand and traced the line of her throat down across the neckline of her bodice. "To see, Bess, just that, sweetheart. Nothing more."

His eyes held her as in a trance, as the sound of his words wove a spell about her.

"Only let me look at thee." His voice vibrated with emotion as his fingers loosened her gown. "Would you have me beg?"

Beg? Ah, no, she could not make him beg. Surely there could be nothing so wrong in giving him the same right she had taken so surreptitiously only short time ago. She had gazed upon his naked body and rejoiced in its beauty. What harm could there be in granting him the same favor?

His hands slipped the bodice from her creamy shoulders. Her nipples grew taut as her breasts were freed to thrust themselves toward him. His hands cupped them tenderly. When she offered no protest, his fingers grew bolder, moving in circles about the firm, pink tips.

"A sip, Bess," he whispered, the heat of his breath burning against the sensitive skin. "Grant me a sip of your nectar. Restore my strength with it."

She stared at him, unable to answer. Her body had become a mass of tingling fire that shot down to the pit of her stomach and below, where it melted into desire.

His hands pulled her to him. She could feel the heat of his body, the burning heat of his breath as it seared across her breasts. With each labored breath, they drew closer, until his tongue reached out and traced her nipple before he took it into the moist cavern of his mouth.

Bess gasped for air as wild sensations shot through her body. Elation pounded through her blood as he suckled her. She felt as though she were dying, and she clung to him, her arms pressing him even closer.

He released her breast, covering it with his hand as his mouth sought its twin. The wild, maddening sensations sent her body arching against his, unmindful of the danger that throbbed against her body.

Sated with her sweetness, Griffith crushed her to him, relishing her moist nipples against the bare expanse of his chest. The touch of her flesh made him wild with desire. He had to have her now, regardless of the consequences, regardless of his vows to himself and to God that he would protect her virginity. Somehow he would take care of her, always, forever. She was his! He would never let harm come to her. She would be his pampered darling, his only love.

He drew her down beside him and pushed aside the remainder of her garments. His hand moved down her belly, and beyond, until it found the treasure that had heretofore known no man's touch.

With a groan, he buried his face in her softness, drawing her essence into himself. His hands stroked and teased. His tongue searched and tantalized until he was satisfied that she could wait no longer. Her breasts rose and fell as his caresses rendered her mindless with desire. Her body twisted and arched, moving with age-old rhythms for which she needed no instruction.

Each breath, each movement, told him of her unspoken need. She was ready and, God forgive him, he would have her!

But, slowly...slowly... He could not bear to see her trusting gaze cloud with pain. She must be taken with tenderness...while he gently taught her the delights of love. The moment was too precious, *she* was too precious, to be wasted in the haste of passion. They must reach the heights together, and together soar above the stars.

He bent, kissing the pink-and-white body that glistened in the torchlight. For a moment, his resolve weakened. His lips lingered as he fought a silent battle within himself. Then, suddenly, without warning, her body convulsed, and he tasted the sweetness that was hers alone. . . .

Griffith lay back on the narrow cot, holding Bess close against his body.

She trembled in wonder at his actions. Was this all there was to the mating of a man and woman? Surely the intimacies they had known had surpassed mere loveplay. She could feel her pulse pounding in each place his lips had lingered. It was as though he had drawn forth a new dimension of herself.... His mouth had invoked a magic spell, awakening her in ways she had never dreamed of. And while her body throbbed at the proximity of his, somewhere in her most secret being she felt a lack. She was satiated, but not yet complete... as though there were more wonders as yet unrevealed to her.

It was then that they heard Prigge's voice outside the tent, "Master Aylesworth, you came swiftly."

"When I was told Lord Beaufort had been injured, I came in all haste," the man answered.

With one swift movement, Griffith drew Bess's dress about her. By the time the physician entered the tent, she was standing silently beside the pallet as she tried to contain her throbbing heart.

"It seems my services were not so desperately needed as I had been led to believe." Master Aylesworth commented, inspecting Griffith's wound carefully. "Granted the wound looks a bit gory, but no vital organs were injured. It looks to be a flesh wound. It surprises me that you are still abed." He glanced at Bess, who stared in stunned silence at his words. "Then again, perhaps your prolonged recovery is understandable. I take it that it was not Prigge's gentle ministrations that have saved me such grief?" He glanced at Bess.

"This is Mistress Bess," Griffith told him, "and it is to her care that I owe my well-being."

The man lifted the cup of herbs Bess had brewed and smelled the contents. "Prigge has already apprised me of your concoction," he told Bess. "It did him no harm, but now the patient needs rest to regain his strength." He took fresh herbs from his packet and mixed it in a goblet of wine as he questioned Griffith on the tournament.

As Griffith responded to the physician's questions, Bess mulled the physician's words over in her mind. He did not seem to think the wound was serious, yet she had ministered to Griffith for the better part of a day and night. Surely he would not have allowed her to agonize over his hurts if he was not really ill. Yet he seemed to recover quite rapidly, once caught up in the throes of desire.

Bess waited for Griffith to speak to her, to explain his illness and make Master Aylesworth understand the seriousness of his condition. Instead, he continued his conversation with the doctor and ignored her presence. Perhaps this had all been a jest. A jest most damaging, for surely Bess had ruined her reputation by coming alone to his tent and staying throughout the night.

She could hear the physician's laughter, and Griffith's low chuckle. Was it her they were laughing at? Was it her gullibility where Griffith was concerned? Had he willingly forced her into a position wherein she had no choice but to be his mistress?

Oh, God! No! Please, let it not be true!

Bess slipped from the tent, glancing back to see Griffith resting comfortably as he related the particulars of his joust to the man. The fever was gone—if indeed it had ever been—and he no longer needed her.

Thinking Bess waited outside, Griffith joked with the physician until the herbs began to take effect. "Send Prigge and the girl to me," he said.

"Very well, but remember, you are to sleep now—and alone," the doctor muttered under his breath as he slipped into the starless night. "Prigge," he called, "your master requires your services."

Prigge, who had been talking to one of the squires, quickly bade farewell to the doctor and returned to the tent.

Griffith's eyes were heavy. "Where is Bess?" he managed to say as sleep threatened to overtake him.

"I thought she was here with you." Prigge looked about, as though expecting the girl to materialize.

"She went outside. Go and find her! It's unsafe for her to be alone in camp at this time of night!"

Prigge rushed from the tent. "I'll find her, my lord," he promised. "She will not have gone far."

Griffith sank back onto the pallet. The herbs had caused the aches to go from his body, and he floated on a sea of complacency and well-being. As he drifted between sleep and consciousness, his mind reviewed the tournament. The thundering of the war-horses, the pageantry, the banners streaming in the wind as horses and riders flew at one another in a panoply of color. Once again he was riding toward his opponent, bracing himself for the moment of contact. He looked toward the stands for one glimpse of Bess's sweet face, and as he floated on the edge of consciousness, he seemed to hear her voice screaming... screaming... screaming his name....

Chapter Six

Bess could not keep the tears from coursing down her cheeks as she made her way through the silent camp. To her shame, she had given in to her desires and let Griffith have his way with her. The hot blood rushed to her cheeks as she remembered the heat of his body against hers, the fire of his kisses, and her own uninhibited response.

Skirting the campfires and the men who were surrounding them, Bess had almost reached the edge of the camp when she adjusted her shawl about her head and shoulders. For one brief moment only, the moon reflected the luster of her hair, but that moment was enough to reveal her presence.

From a distance, Sir Morris of Bladacglen noticed the glimmer against the night.

"Jasper," he said, and touched the man next to him as they sat drinking with a group of mercenary soldiers about the campfire, "someone moves across the way."

"So?" Jasper took another swallow from the wineskin before passing it to the next man. "There are many who do not sleep this night, I vow."

"But this is not a knight." Sir Morris got to his feet. "This someone is a wench!"

Ignoring his aching head, he started across the camp, the other men following drunkenly.

They were not silent in their quest, and Bess could hear them laughing and jesting as they made their way through the brush at the edge of the camp. She quickened her pace, instinctively knowing that their presence boded her no good. Her heart pounded so loudly, she did not realize how near they were until a man reached out and grabbed her.

She screamed once before his hand closed over her mouth. Despite her wild struggles, he dragged her into the copse of trees that bordered the camp.

"Bring a torch," he commanded. "We'll see what prize we've found."

Within a few seconds, the light flickered through the darkness. Bess's eyes widened with horror as she recognized Sir Morris.

"Just as I thought." He laughed. "The Beaufort's doxy."

With a quick gesture, he jerked the shawl from about her head and threw it on the ground. Her hair cascaded about her shoulders, causing the men to grunt their approval.

Jasper, even in his drunken state, was aware of the danger they faced tampering with a woman who held the favor of the Beaufort. "Let her go, Morris," he urged. "She will bring trouble upon us. Beaufort has shown her favor."

"And she has obviously given all she has, as well." Sir Morris held the girl firmly, watching fear spread across her face. "Aye, look at her. She has shown him favors, and he is through with her! Why else would she be alone in the camp at this time of night? She has been cast out! He has tired of her, sending her away without so much as an escort. Why, he hasn't even given her a coin, so little was her worth."

His hand fumbled between her breasts as she struggled to be free of his hated touch.

"Perhaps she does have a coin," Jasper suggested, still unconvinced and worried about offending a great lord who was a guest in his master's house.

Taking Jasper's words as encouragement, Sir Morris moved his hands down the girl's body, lingering over the firmness of her budding breasts as the men called out ribald jests.

"There is no coin here," he affirmed, thrusting her toward the other men. "Hold her, and we shall see what delights the Beaufort has so recently rejected."

Jasper stepped forward, laying a hand on Morris's arm. "Think, man!" he cautioned. "If Griffith is not done with her, it could mean your life, and the lives of all of us." He glanced around the group as he spoke, and some of the others nodded drunkenly at the wisdom of his words.

But Sir Morris was not to be denied. "Had Griffith wanted her, he would have kept her with him," Morris insisted, the throbbing pressure of his lust overpowering all reason.

Jasper tried again. "Perhaps she ran from him, and he is still hot for her." Something about the girl told him that no man would send her off to fend for herself, regardless of how greatly she displeased him.

For a moment, Sir Morris hesitated. If the girl was as good in bed as her mother, she would be a toothsome morsel. Perhaps he should be less anxious to share her with the others.

He held up his hands. "Jasper has a point," he said. "Perhaps she did run from Lord Griffith, and he has not tired of her after all."

The men growled at his words. They wanted her, and she was theirs for the taking. One of them stepped forward, reaching out as though to touch her, but Sir Morris stepped between them. "Of course, it would be no crime to but look upon what the Beaufort has discarded. Perhaps she is diseased or deformed, and hence was rejected.''

The men shouted gleefully as Sir Morris drew his dagger and slashed away her kirtle. Her dress fell open, leaving only a diaphanous undergown to shield her white body from their lustful gazes. She was far more childish than Sir Morris had thought, her breasts not yet developed to their full promise.

''So this is the body that has charmed a lord,'' Sir Morris said as his hands moved down the gentle curves.

Bess struggled against her captor, writhing madly in her effort to get away, as she prayed that God would see fit to send the angel of death rather than let her be forced to submit to the will of these lustful animals. Desperately she begged for deliverance, swearing that she would never again think upon Griffith as she had in the tent. She knew that what she had done was a grievous mortal sin of the flesh and that she truly deserved to be punished for her indiscretions, but surely not to this degree.

A bolt of lightning cut across the sky, followed by a rumble of thunder, as though the elements themselves were angered by Sir Morris's use of this maiden. The men rolled their eyes in fear, but did not retreat. The shimmering body surrounded by silver-white hair had inflamed them to a point that fear of punishment was banished.

''Take her, and to hell with the circumstances!'' one of them cried. ''But for God's sake, hurry, for I cannot wait!''

Glancing quickly around the group, Sir Morris realized that keeping her to himself now would not easily be accomplished. These men wanted her badly. The wine had dulled their brains, even as it had inflamed their senses. Either he took her now, or he would have to wait and take what remained after the others had their fill. Ignoring the desperate fear in the girl's eyes, he stepped back to loosen his clothing. The men laughed at her struggles, which only served to inflame them more.

Bess managed to twist free of the hand that covered her mouth and scream again, the sound merging with the stormy night. Sir Morris moved toward her, and she was thrown to the ground, her arms held tightly above her head as she thrashed her legs wildly about, her actions only whetting the desires of the men.

"Griffith, Griffith!" Bess's piteous cries caught the wind and soared above the storm, and, as though in answer, a figure appeared at the edge of the clearing.

The men fell back in shock and fear, for, indeed, it was Griffith Beaufort who stood before them. Griffith, or an ancient god of war invoked by the plight of this hapless maiden. In his haste to answer her screams, Griffith had snatched up his sword and shield and, clad only in his linens, his cloak whipping out behind him, now stood like a god of vengeance. The wildly whipping firelight and the screams of the wind joined with his battle cry as he unleashed the fury of his mighty sword, casting men about as though they were leaves, defenseless against the storm of his anger.

They looked wildly about for leadership, but Sir Morris had disappeared into the darkness, while Jasper had been felled by the first blow.

Griffith dispatched the others quickly. They were routed by the time Prigge came running toward him.

Griffith ignored the man as he dropped to his knees beside the trembling girl. "It's all right, sweetheart," he murmured, cradling her in his arms. "I am here now. You are safe." Only his shortness of breath gave evidence of the effort the skirmish had cost him. He lifted her, wrapping his cloak about them both.

Only after she knew the safety of his arms did Bess begin to sob. He held her close, feeling her tears, hot with shame, running down his body.

The storm worsened, crashing about them so that even his words of comfort were lost in its sound. He did not need to ask the identity of the men who had assaulted her. He had recognized the weasel Sir Morris before the man took to the woods. But Griffith would not seek him out this night. His body ached from the rigors of the fight and the fever that had gripped him such a short time ago. But his main concern was for the girl.

Bess quieted under his gentle touch. He held her for a moment, and then turning to Prigge, said, "I am taking her back to the castle . . . now."

"But the storm . . ." Prigge protested.

"The devil with the storm," Griffith shouted over the wind, "I am taking her to the castle, where she will be safe."

"They will see you carry her in, my lord," the man told him. "She will be ruined!"

"I shall wrap her in my cloak. They will never be certain of her identity." Griffith enveloped her completely in his great cloak. Then without further ado, he carried his precious burden into the night.

The ladies-in-waiting were still feasting in the great hall when Griffith carried Bess to her chambers. She clung to him as he placed her on one of the beds.

Griffith looked down into the ethereal beauty of her face as his lips dropped tiny kisses on her skin. "I love thee, and I will never leave thee," he murmured against the fragrance of her body.

But instead of joy, he was faced with despair, for his words brought Bess back to reality. Tears formed in her eyes. She was yet unable to speak.

"What is it, my love?" Griffith asked, and kissed her tears away. "This is no time for tears, except those of happiness."

"Happiness for you, my lord," Bess managed, "but for me there is only disgrace. In the eyes of all I shall be a fallen woman."

"You are mine, and none shall treat you with anything less than honor and respect," he declared staunchly.

But Bess's tears had given way to sobs. "You don't understand!" she gasped. "I have forsworn my right to love you. To do so now would be the greatest of sins."

"Our love is no sin." He took her face in his hands, forcing her to look into his eyes.

"But I swore before God that if I were delivered from Sir Morris I would never allow myself to again desire you, in thought or in deed."

"Bess, Bess," Griffith told her comfortingly, "God does not punish those who love as we do. Our love is good and pure."

"How can you say this?" Bess questioned. "You know as well as I there can be no more than what we have now."

Griffith moved her body more closely against his. Her pliant form molded perfectly to him, her breasts against his chest, her belly soft and flat against his muscled firmness.

"But, sweetheart, we have so much. You and I, together. We have the world."

She would have protested the validity of his words, but his lips closed over hers, and his tongue found its way into her mouth as his passion found its response in her lovely body.

His questing lips found the little magic places that sent blood racing through her veins.

"Bess," he whispered against her shining hair, "listen to me."

She looked at him, her eyes deep with passion, yet touched with sorrow.

"I shall not leave you, Bess, nor shall you leave me. Do you understand what I am saying?"

"You are saying you want me to be your mistress," she said brokenly, "are you not?"

For a moment, he hesitated over the words that rose to his lips, weighing them before speaking them aloud. Then his love for her overpowered all else. "I am saying I wish you to be my wife, sweet Bess, my wife."

Bess's eyes opened wide, "I do not see the humor in your jest, my lord." She swung herself from the bed and snatched up a robe that lay nearby.

"It is no jest, sweetheart. No power on heaven or earth will keep me from marrying the woman of my choice," he declared as he came to stand behind her. "Even Henry says a man has a right to choose."

"Oh, Griffith," she whispered, then twined her soft arms about his neck, drawing his lips down to meet hers. "I think your mind is full of dreams."

"Just as my arms are full of dreams," he answered, "and the dreams are all of you, with your hair flowing across the pillows and your body warm and waiting for me to make love to you, again and again and again...." His words trailed off into the void of desire. But even as he would have said more, Bess slipped from his grasp.

"You know as well as I that Prince Henry means only that *he* has the right to choose the woman he will marry," Bess reminded him. "If you love me, you must let me go!"

Her eyes brimmed with unshed tears, and he felt desire surge and die as he released his hold upon her.

"I swear, on my chance of eternity, I will find some way to make you mine," he said as he went out the door.

The determination on his face frightened Bess, but she only whispered, "And so do I pray, my love, with all my heart."

Mary's ladies returned to find her sleeping and, seeing the dark rings beneath her eyes, assumed she had been waiting on their mistress and did not disturb her slumber.

Before long, Griffith and Bess were faced with the harshness of reality. Griffith's impending departure loomed before them like a harbinger of doom.

"I cannot take thee with me," he confessed. "Not now. But the time will come, and soon, when we shall be together, my darling."

They walked to their special place in the kitchen gardens, away from curious stares. Griffith's eyes rested on the little statue of the Virgin looking down on them from her lofty perch.

He sensed the doubt in Bess's mind when he spoke of their future together. Although she loved him beyond all else, she knew that the chances of his dreams for the two of them becoming reality were slim.

"Kneel with me, Bess." Griffith dropped to his knees before the grotto and removed the heavy signet ring from his finger.

At first his actions were lost on Bess. Surely he wasn't planning on making such an offering to an insignificant little statue in a kitchen garden. Then her mind focused on his words.

"With this ring, I plight my troth."

She lifted her eyes to his face, the confusion showing clearly in her expression as Griffith took her hand and placed the ring on her finger.

"Repeat the words, Bess," he urged. "As you love me, repeat the words of our betrothal."

Without moving her eyes from his, Bess repeated the traditional vow, and was bound to Griffith irrevocably and forever. It was only after his lips had claimed hers in a kiss binding their pledge that she dared look down at the signet ring that hung loosely on her finger.

"Griffith, you should not have given me this to bind our troth."

"And of all the things I treasure, I have said I treasure this ring most—but you, my love, I treasure even more. Therefore, from this day hence, my two most priceless treasures will be together, waiting for me to come and claim them for my treasure house of love."

Bess could not help but smile at his poetic words. Now, despite herself, she felt the stirrings of hope deep in her soul. Surely he would not have made so solemn and binding a vow unless he felt he would be able to honor it. A betrothal was the most sacred pledge that could be given, equal even to that of marriage.

Her other hand closed over the ring, still warm from his body, and she lifted it against her lips.

"Am I to be made to envy a ring when it receives the kiss for which my own lips hunger?" He bent down, claiming that which he craved, and she surrendered gladly, her lips an offering on the altar of love.

It was much later in the afternoon, and the courtiers had returned to the great hall, by the time Griffith and Bess returned to the castle. Their absence had not gone unremarked, but even the earl and his lady had not the heart to chastise them. With Mary, it was entirely another matter. Her mind was full of her own betrothal to a son of the house of Essex, and she hardly took the time to notice whether Bess was in attendance or not.

"Bess," Mary called from across the hall, "come and see the book Sir Thomas has given me."

Bess smiled brightly at Mary's happiness, glancing at Griffith for permission. He nodded, ''Run along, sweetheart. I have much to say to the earl before I depart.''

His words caused a shadow to pass over Bess's happiness, but she was soon caught up in the excited conversation with the other girls.

''Truly a book is a gift to be envied,'' Bess said, in awe of the little leather-bound volume with its gold-edged pages.

''I wonder if Sir Thomas realizes that our Mary has woefully neglected her studies, and knows hardly how to read this great and wonderful book.'' Ann teased, and laughed at the look of consternation on Mary's face.

''But I must know what it says, else what shall I say when he asks me of its contents?'' Mary cried in despair.

''You might tell him the truth,'' Lucy suggested, but her words only added to Mary's misery.

Bess took the little book from Mary's hand, turning the pages carefully as she looked at the beautifully written script.

''Why, this is a book of love sonnets,'' Bess said in wonder. ''I would assume your betrothed does not expect you to read them, Mary. It will be his task to read them to you, instead.''

The girls gushed with ecstasy.

''How lovely,'' Mary sighed. ''Who else but Thomas would think of such a beautiful thing.'' She retrieved the little book from Bess and held it against her heart.

Her action was not lost on her parents, who noted it as they spoke to Griffith.

''As you can see, our daughter Mary will soon be wed. At that time, there will be some changes in our household,'' the earl said officiously. ''What is your pleasure regarding Bess?''

"Bess may stay with Mary until she weds, then she will come to me." Griffith's words left no room for argument. Still, Lady Margaret could not hold her peace.

"Would it not be best for all concerned if she were to remain here at Pembroke, away from court gossip and cruelty?" she asked boldly, her feeling of responsibility for the girl outweighing even her fear of incurring Griffith's wrath.

"There will be no gossip or cruelty where Bess is concerned," Griffith told them. "I am making plans for her that will put her above all that. By the time Mary weds, next spring, those plans should be put into operation, and I will be ready to receive Bess into my household."

The earl drew in his breath, as though to speak again, but the flash of anger in Griffith's eyes silenced him for a moment. "Very well," he finally agreed reluctantly, "but should things not go as you have planned, the girl is welcome to stay at Pembroke."

"There will be no need," Griffith told them with the confidence of youth, "but I thank you for your offer, nonetheless."

He bowed over Lady Margaret's hand and went to retrieve Bess from the giggling mass of girls, unable to be parted from her by even the length of the room without feeling emptiness and longing. In a few days, he would be gone, and Bess would be forced to stay here, for he could not take her with him as he joined the prince in his progress across England.

And though his heart ached at the thought of being parted from her, Griffith would not allow her reputation to be tarnished by having her travel with him, as though she were nothing more than an occasional fancy. His love for her was too great for that. So great that it could only be assuaged by marriage. And somehow, during this progress, Griffith must approach his cousin and ask Henry to lend his royal support to Griffith's petition to wed.

For all his brave words, Griffith was not certain Henry would be inclined to do so, for although Henry declared for all to hear that a man should be allowed to wed the bride of his choice, the bride to whom Henry referred was of royal blood and a princess of Spain, while Griffith's choice of bride was the daughter of a lowly knight and brought naught, save her beauty, to the wedding bed.

There was no guarantee his plea would be heard, much less accepted. And for a lord of the realm to marry against the wishes of his monarch was political suicide, if not grounds for a charge of treason, depending on the mood of the king.

He could but hope, and he pushed his worries aside as he drew Bess's hand through his arm and walked with her toward the huge, blazing fireplace, savoring their time together.

Chapter Seven

Griffith found his time with Bess had been far too short and far too precious. He was again on a tour of royal progression with the prince, while she was left behind at Pembroke. Griffith had made certain Sir Morris was well gone. There had been nothing more he could do to the man without adding to the gossip concerning Bess and himself.

He went on about his business, but his heart, and, for the most part, his mind remained at Pembroke Castle with Bess.

Meanwhile, Bess was living in a dream world where even her friends were not admitted. Their teasing words did no more than slip past her, and their queries went unanswered.

In contrast, Mary of Pembroke was more than happy to tell about her amours with her betrothed. Although he, too, had gone back to his own estates, Mary talked of him as though he were still in the castle. Her plans went on at a brisk pace, and within a matter of weeks it seemed every woman in the castle was stitching on her wedding gown and working on linens for her household.

"And as soon as I am settled in my new home, dear Bess, I shall find a suitable husband for you." She smiled graciously, completely ignoring the look on Bess's face. "It's too bad my lord Griffith didn't leave you a portion for your

dowry, but being a man, I don't suppose he thought of it. Of
course, you could petition him for something after he returns to London, but then he might think you presumptu-
ous, and that wouldn't do, either.''

"I want nothing of Griffith that he does not give freely,"
Bess said, touching the ring that hung suspended between
her breasts.

A look of distress crossed Mary's pretty face. "To be
sure," she agreed. "Still, a little remembrance for your care
when he was wounded could have been put to good use."

Bess looked away. She was aware that Griffith had spoken to the earl, warning him that should harm befall her
there would be dire circumstances for all involved, regardless of rank or status. Bess was also aware she was being
guarded and the only times when she was not closely
watched were when she was in the solar with Mary and her
mother, the Lady Margaret.

Although Bess realized Griffith had done this for her
protection, she longed for the days when she had been able
to go where she wished without worrying about whether or
not she was free to do so, or in danger if she did.

The days of winter were rapidly approaching and Bess
waited breathlessly for some word that Griffith would return. Although she had not expected him to write to her, she
was disappointed when no message arrived and could hardly
hold her feelings in check as Mary glowed with happiness
over the missives she received from Thomas of Essex.

"You needn't look so miserable, Bess," Mary said as she
patted the girl comfortingly. "The time will come, and soon,
I'll warrant, when you will have a man of your own to read
you pretty words of love, just as I do."

Bess did not speak as she stood in the icy courtyard where
the girls had gone to receive the rapidly approaching messenger.

Through the open gates of the castle, Bess was able to see far into the distance as the clear, cold air enhanced her vision. There, a great way down the road leading to the castle came a lone horseman. Even at first glance, Bess knew the man was far too small in stature to be Griffith, but it was as though every nerve in her body were suddenly throbbing to the beat of the horse's hooves. Griffith...Griffith... Griffith...

As the figure grew larger and took on color and proportion, Bess could see that the man was from the house of Tudor.

Mary's face lit with excitement when she realized they were receiving a message from the royal family.

"Run, Bess," she urged. "Tell my father the king has sent a messenger."

Bess did as she was bidden, but her heart told her the message was not from the king, nor was it for the Earl of Pembroke.

Bess arrived back at the huge double doors of the castle just in time to see the earl take a packet from the breathless messenger. The young man looked past the earl and smiled into Bess's eyes, as though telling her he knew there was news for her, also. Bess dropped her gaze immediately, as was seemly for a girl of her age and station. It would do no good for any man to think her bold. God knew, she had displayed her boldness enough locked in Griffith's wild embrace. She felt the blood rise to her face, but she could not know how fetching she looked to the young man who had raced to Pembroke from Greenwich to deliver his tidings.

It was a delighted gasp from Mary that brought Bess back to herself. "Oh, Bess, isn't it wonderful? Have you ever heard of anything so exciting?"

Bess stared at her blankly, and Mary laughingly continued. "Didn't you hear what my father just said?" At Bess's imperceptible shake of the head, Mary gave her an impulsive squeeze. "The prince, you goose—the prince has requested we come to Greenwich for Christmas. And, of course, a request from the prince is tantamount to an order. We must begin packing at once."

Grabbing Bess's hand, Mary raced up the stairs to the solar.

Brightly colored gowns, robes and cloaks were flung indiscriminately about the room, which looked like a displaced summer flower garden when the Lady Margaret entered.

"I see you girls wasted no time." She smiled at their excitement.

"Oh, Mother," Mary said as she ran to the older woman and took hold of her arm. "Do you think Tom will be there?"

"I wouldn't be a bit surprised if he were. The court at Greenwich is a gay place at Christmas, and all those who seek enjoyment will surely make it a point to be present. Where Prince Henry is, there will be music and laughter."

In contrast to her words, Bess's face crumbled as she fought to contain the tears that threatened to undo her.

"And, pray, what ails you, child?" Lady Margaret asked, placing her finger under Bess's chin and lifting her face to be scrutinized.

"I will not have to go to my mother in Kew while you and Mary are gone, will I?"

"Had you planned to go to visit your mother over Christmastide?" The Lady Margaret looked from Bess to Mary for verification before continuing. "Because if you have, I'm afraid you'll have to change your plans. The prince has specifically requested you come as Mary's companion and share the festivities."

The air went out of Bess's body in a sigh of relief. She hadn't been mistaken. There had been a message for her from Griffith. Her heart lurched madly beneath her demure bodice. She would see him again, be near him, touch him, and feel him touching her. She hugged herself in delight as she started across the room to help Mary with her packing. It was important to finish quickly so that she could do some packing of her own.

Mary had sent Bess on an errand to the kitchens when Bess again saw the messenger. He sat at a table near the fires, warming himself in the glow.

"And you must be Mistress Bess," he said as she walked past him.

"I am indeed, but how did you know?" she asked. "I'm certain we've never met."

"Lord Beaufort told me to seek out the fairest flower of winter, a pale rose kissed with the golden light of a frosted morn, and she would be the one. From the moment you stepped through the doors, I knew it could be no other than yourself."

Bess smiled in pretty confusion. "Lord Beaufort spoke of me?" she asked softly.

"He spoke of you when he asked me to deliver this message into your hand alone. I confess I was a bit taken aback, wondering how I would accomplish such a feat without having the whole castle down on me, but luck was with me once again, and here you are, and here is the message."

The young man drew a rolled parchment from his doublet and offered it to her. Bess took it hesitantly, turning it in her hands until she found the Beaufort seal. She held it against her breast, her face shining with happiness.

"I thank you, master..." She hesitated, not knowing the man's name.

"Talbois," he told her, "Will Talbois, at your service."

She held out one hand, still clutching the scroll with the other. "Then you have my heartfelt thanks, Master Will."

He bent over hand, kissing it lightly and releasing it before she could begin to pull it away. "It was my pleasure entirely, mistress."

Bess smiled at him, then hurriedly turned and all but ran from the room. She could hardly wait to find some privacy in which to read her communication from Griffith. It wasn't until she was well on her way to her room that she remembered her errand for Mary.

The morning of their departure was sparkling-bright, with air so fresh one could taste it. Wrapped snugly in their fur-lined cloaks, Bess and the other maids-in-waiting rode down the frost-edged road, their faces reflecting their excitement.

It was doubtful any of the company except Bess actually realized to whom they owed their good fortune. In his missive to Bess, Griffith had admitted he could no longer live without seeing her sweet face and would have her company at Greenwich if it meant moving the whole of Pembroke Castle, brick by brick, and housing every man and beast in its confines.

Bess had smiled at his impetuous implications, for she knew it was well within his power to send for her alone, and that she would have gone to him despite cost or consequences.

As they rode along, they saw woodmen choosing the tree trunks that would be used as Yule logs during the holiday celebrations. Little groups of young people were out picking holly branches to decorate their hearths, and many of them waved at the procession of nobles that passed them in laughing abandon.

When they arrived at the castle, it was alive with guests, and huge fires blazed in the many hearths. As time neared for the Christmas revels, Will Talbois was made the lord of misrule and conducted the ceremonies, glowing with happiness at his good fortune in having been chosen for the role.

The ladies' party from Pembroke were taken to the suite of rooms set aside for them. The maids-in-waiting would share a common room but Bess was appointed personal maid to Mistress Mary and given a tiny room of her own, that could be reached from Mary's room, or from the hall itself, should she need to run errands.

Bess was rather glad to have a place to herself. It was an unprecedented luxury, and although some of the other ladies looked askance upon it, they kept their counsel, for none of them wanted to go to the kitchens in the dead of night to get the hot water with which Lady Margaret insisted on starting the day.

For the first days of their visit, Bess waited breathlessly for a summons from Griffith, and although he made every effort to be near her, their meetings were always public and handled with the greatest of decorum. It was Elizabeth Blount, come to visit her sister for the revels, who, in her love for meaningless gossip and her enthusiasm for introducing her new friends to everything and everyone at Greenwich, inadvertently explained the situation to Bess.

"And the woman there, by the prince, the one who always looks as though she's about to cry, that is the Princess Catherine of Aragon, the widow of Henry's brother, Arthur. It is rumored Henry wishes to wed with her, and he demands propriety be upheld to the utmost when she is present."

Now Bess looked at the young woman with interest. If this was true, it would explain why Griffith had never sought Bess out. Although Catherine was some years older than Henry, she was short, coming barely to his shoulder even with the high headdress she wore. Now and again she smiled up at him, quietly, as though giving him the counsel of her superior age and knowledge.

Griffith stood with them, deeply engaged in conversation, obviously not taking much note of her suggestions yet listening to them politely. Time and again his eyes would wander across the room to where Bess stood talking to Elizabeth Blount and the lord of misrule. Finally, unable to leave the princess and unwilling to forgo Bess's company any longer, Griffith came toward them, with Catherine in tow.

"We could not resist," Griffith said as he approached them. "You looked as though you were enjoying yourselves so immensely, I came to join you."

"Will Talbois has shed his role of lord of misrule for the evening, and is playing the jester instead, my lord," Bess exclaimed, laughter ringing in her voice.

"Then I assume you are enjoying yourself."

"'Tis truly wonderful, my lord," Bess told him. "There is beauty everywhere about me. From the myriad of candle-laden chandeliers, to the forest of holly and ivy that decorates the halls. I have never tasted such food in my life. I fear I shall leave here as plump as one of the little birds on which we dined."

"Then perhaps we should tell the musicians to strike up their instruments, and we will counteract dinner with the dance." With a wave of his hand, he summoned the minstrels and within minutes he had excused himself and Bess from the company of the others and was leading her onto the floor.

"Should you not have danced first with Princess Catherine?" Bess asked demurely.

"The princess does not care much for dancing. She is far more content to watch," Griffith explained. "It will do her good to hear lighthearted banter for a while, and take her mind from her worries."

Bess could see that Griffith pitied the poor princess, whose gown was in sad repair, albeit clean and neatly patched.

"Has she so little, then, my lord?" Bess asked, acutely aware of the newness of her own gown, and even more aware that her good fortune had come only after she received favor in Griffith's eyes. Her station in the household at Pembroke had improved. She even received a tiny allowance for her services, the first money she had been able to do with as she chose. Discreetly but determinedly, her wardrobe had been replaced with newer, more fashionable things. She smiled up at Griffith. He seemed surrounded by the golden aura that had attracted her to him from the first.

His robes were of red and gold velvet that complemented the rich tones of his hair, and which absolutely shone in the candlelight as they moved around the room, executing the intricate steps to perfection.

"Do not fret over the princess, Bess, Henry will see to her welfare. Instead, think of the wild music, and the gypsies when we danced around their campfire, fair Bess. Each time you move, I remember how you danced with me that night."

She laughed up into his eyes, seeing her memories reflected there. "I cannot tell you how often I have thought of that night...and others...." Her voice caught in her throat, and Griffith's hand tightened on her.

"And I," he whispered, "I have longed to relive those moments, or to find them anew in your arms."

They continued the dance in silence until the music ended and Griffith led her from the hall.

They entered a small wood-paneled room where embers glowed in a fireplace. He walked over to the fireplace and stirred the embers to life, thinking as he did that it was in this same way that Bess stirred him to life, for his life was bleak and cold without her, despite all the people who surrounded him.

He turned to her, thinking to speak the words that filled his heart, but her face, the way her lips parted in expectation, made him forget all else but his need to feel her mouth beneath his. He enfolded her in his embrace, touching her gently at first, as though he were afraid she might disappear. Then his kiss deepened and was fed by hers until it burst into flames of long-restrained passion that could not be quenched by anything less than the fiery liquid of love, flowing from one to the other until even their souls were seared with desire.

"I shall come to thee, beloved," he whispered as the sounds of voices outside the door came closer. With that, he released her, and she sank onto a low chair, her face lost in the shadows as the door opened and the Princess Catherine peered into the room.

"I thought I heard someone in here," she said.

Griffith suppressed a smile as his eyes met Bess's, both of them knowing full well no voices had been heard.

"I was giving Mistress Bess news of her mother, as I had promised when we last met at Pembroke," he lied gracefully.

"How thoughtful of you," Catherine said, with true admiration in her voice, "But the ballet is about to begin, and since Henry has an important role, I'm sure you will want to see it."

Griffith held out his hand to Bess. He was pleased to see how well she had managed to compose herself after their impassioned embrace. The Princess Catherine preceded them from the room and was well down the hall before they entered it.

"Come," Griffith offered, "I will find a place where you will be able to see clearly."

Bess gratefully accepted his offer, but her heart was still pounding wildly in the aftermath of his kisses and his promises.

As she lay nestled in her sumptuous feather bed that night, her mind flew over the events, the words and the deeds of the evening.

Bess had been weak with longing as they sat together watching the ballet. It did no good to try to shut him out of her mind. He was always in her thoughts, placed before all else in her prayers, her vows of chastity, even her fear of damnation and her love of God.

She sighed. No, there would be no opportunity for him to come to her without compromising them both, and she knew he would not risk the prince's wrath, especially with the princess in residence.

Bess had settled herself to sleep when she heard a scratching on the door. She sat up just as it opened and a monk, robed and cowled, entered the room.

"Forgive me, good brother," she said, peering through the dim light given out by the dying fire, "but I fear you have come to the wrong place."

"Nay, my child, I think not," a muffled voice intoned from deep within the dark cowl.

"But I have no need for a man of God." She cowered behind the questionable protection of the covers as he came nearer.

"I've come to hear your confession, my child," he persisted. "Confess to me that you love me and have lived for this moment as have I." He threw back his cowl, and his hair gleamed golden in the firelight. "Confess to me that you want me, that your body aches for the touch of mine, heart against heart, flesh against flesh, as mine aches for yours."

He threw down the robe and stood before her, his naked body shimmering like a white-hot flame. He took the final step that separated him from the bed and drew the quilts from her hands before he slipped beneath the covers and took her into his arms.

"Confess," he whispered as he rained tiny kisses on her hair, her eyes, her lips. "Confess..." His mouth found the secret spot on her neck that sent her writhing so delightfully against him. "Confess..." His words were slurred now, as he became more demanding, more knowledgeable of the secrets of her body. His hands memorized and remembered, stroking her soft curves, caressing her firm breasts, before losing themselves in her silken heat as she cried out her love in mindless rapture.

For long moments they shared new experiences in one another's arms as he guided her hands, allowing her the adventure of discovery and himself the ultimate in pleasure, until it became as though the pores of their bodies had fused, making them one being, floating in a pocket in time.

Bess's eyes shone with love as he found the very core of her body, intimate, evocative, erotic, invoking tremors that shot through to her soul. She trembled against him, demanding that he give all that his caresses promised.

"Patience, my love," he said soothingly, as his caress took her to where she was all but mad with desire. "Patience, and we shall have all the delights of which we dream and more...much, much more." She waited, her body poised and ready, willing to accept Griffith as her lover, despite the circumstances, now or in the hereafter.

He moved over her, a white-hot sword burning the length and breadth of her body. It must be like unto dying, she thought, for it was as though all her life were rushing through her mind. Her heart pounded so loudly it blocked out all else as blood rushed madly through her veins. She waited for the one fatal, irrevocable step to be taken. The swift, silent pain that would make her his forever. She forgot to breathe, steeling herself against what she knew must come. Her head grew light, still she felt nothing and time hung suspended.

Trumpets sounded in her brain, and the pounding of a hundred running feet echoed through her breast. The world became a vacuum of sound, louder and louder. She opened her eyes, suddenly aware that the sounds reverberating through her body were not those caused by the culmination of love.

The castle was alive with frantic activity.

"What is it?" Bess managed to gasp.

Before Griffith could speak, there was a hammering on the door. "Mistress Bess, Mistress Bess, come quickly! Word has arrived the king has taken to his bed. Prince Henry is preparing to go to Richmond immediately. Lady Margaret is in a desperate state. You must come at once!"

"Of course!" Bess managed to say with a mixture of disappointment and relief. "Tell her I will be there right away!"

There was the sound of feet scurrying down the hall before Bess again faced Griffith. "You must go, my lord. Your presence will be required far more than mine."

Griffith nodded in agreement. "Bess, I would not leave you this way." He reached out and pulled her into his arms for one more bittersweet moment. She let the sheets drop from her fingers as flesh sought flesh. "I love thee," he whispered as his lips moved across her hair and down to her shoulders. "Regardless of the outcome of this night, I love thee." With one last, desperate kiss, he gathered his robes about him and hurried out the door.

Rumors abounded during this time of unrest. Bess paid little heed, as she knew most were idle gossip and would come to naught.

Even when the rumors concerned Griffith, Bess managed to push them aside. It was true that they had not been alone together since the ill-fated night when he had come to her room disguised as a monk. But Griffith was obliged to spend his days and nights with Henry, and the young prince's life was in a state of flux as the reins of power slipped from the hands of the dying king into those of his son.

"I swear each word Prince Henry utters is repeated as though it were the word of God," Mary of Pembroke watched Bess put the finishing touches on her hair. "All he need do is suggest something, and gossip has it down as fact."

Bess nodded. "It is difficult to cull truth from fiction."

"They say that he is adamant about marrying Princess Catherine," Lucy offered from across the room. "And well he may be, for who dares gainsay a king?"

"Prince Hal can deem himself lucky that his father was not able to secure the alliance on which his ministers have been working," Lady Margaret said officiously, "else there would be no question as to whom he would marry." She looked at her daughter, making certain she had the girl's attention. "I can tell you that the earl and I were quite concerned over some of the rumors. It seems the prince cares little for the desires of his liege men. His full purpose is to secure his kingdom, if he must join every eligible nobleman to the daughter of a foreign power to do so.''

Bess felt a tingle of apprehension at Lady Margaret's words. ''It is difficult to understand the change in him,'' she said slowly. ''Henry has stated many times that a man should be allowed to marry the woman of his choice, rather than being bound by political alliances.''

Lady Margaret chuckled. ''That was before the political alliances were to Prince Henry's advantage.'' She sensed the girl's concern and decided to change the subject. ''Be that as it may, we will be forced to put up with the gossip and the intrigue for a while longer, since the earl has decided to remain here until...'' She let her words fade into silence and crossed herself, unwilling to mention the inevitable death of the king.

The rumors escalated, and Griffith's name was prominently mentioned. Bess could no longer ignore the gossip, and she decided to tell Griffith of the rumors when they next met.

He entered the room to find her standing in the candlelight near the fireplace.

''Bess, love! What a welcome surprise. I did not think to find you here at so late an hour.''

''I have no wish to sleep, my lord,'' she replied.

''Nor do I, my love!'' He came toward her, intent on taking her in his arms.

Deftly she moved away.

''Forgive me, my lord, but there is something I must ask.''

He paused, letting his arms drop to his sides. ''Very well, sweetheart. Ask what you will.''

''I've heard the prince has arranged a betrothal for you. I've heard he insists you wed according to his wishes, to help secure his hold on the crown.''

Griffith sighed. Henry had only broached the subject to him that morning and already the palace was abuzz with the news. He had not been able to talk privately with Henry at any great length to express his own wishes, and had hoped Bess would not hear of it until later.

"Henry mentioned something about a foreign alliance requiring my... services, but nothing was settled. Henry is not yet king. There are many possibilities that must be explored. The betrothal was one of them. It is speculation, nothing more."

"But an order from the king cannot be ignored," she reminded him.

Griffith did not answer. There was no need. Bess was well aware of the truth in her words. There was little Griffith could say to deny them or to ease the pain both felt so acutely.

His heart wrenched within him as Bess turned away.

"It was all a sham, was it not? Our betrothal, the ring, even your love for me... All a sham..."

"Nay, sweetheart, I swear it. My love for you has not lessened. It is still as strong as it was the first time I saw you. I will speak to Henry. He will understand. What he is proposing is a political alliance, Bess. It has naught to do with love."

"It has much to do with *our* love, my lord," Bess responded softly. "I love you, and I believed in the love you professed to have for me. I believed we would someday ferret out a life together, in spite of the odds against us. But I will not be your mistress, and now it seems I cannot be your wife."

He placed his hands on her shoulders and turned her toward him. Looking into the depths of her eyes, he whispered, "Bess, believe me, I love you. None other, only you!"

"I do believe you, my lord, and well you know the extent to which I return that love, but I will not live as my mother lives with Sir Morris. Not even for you! Rather I would return to the convent than face a lifetime of shame!"

"Bess," he pleaded, but she turned away and made her way toward the window. He wanted to follow her, to take her in his arms and kiss away the lines of pain that had formed about her mouth, but the solid defiance of her straight back kept him at bay. He knew she was suffering, even as he suffered. Once Henry was king of England, his word would be law. If he wanted Griffith to marry for a political alliance, it would be done.

With a heavy heart, Griffith went to his apartments, leaving Bess to fight her phantoms alone.

At the end of April, in the first bloom of the English spring, King Henry VII gave up the ghost, and his son, Henry VIII, was proclaimed king of England.

Within hours, the scepter was passed and young Henry seized the reins of power.

Any unhappiness that Bess might have felt was lost in the excitement and pageantry of the court. If anyone noticed that she was more quiet than usual, or that she spent less time with Lord Beaufort, nothing was said.

Time and again Bess felt Griffith's eyes following her. She carefully ignored him, making certain she was busily engaged at all times.

Griffith, miserable, followed her to her room. He tapped lightly, but no sound came from within. After waiting several minutes, Griffith realized he would have to either break down the door or leave. Reluctantly he decided on the latter course, resolving to speak to Bess on the morrow, whether it be her wish or not.

Bess leaned against the inside of the door. The wood felt cool against the heat of her brow. Her hands still rested against the heavy bolt. It was only with the greatest of willpower that Bess had managed to keep from tearing open the door. She longed to feel Griffith's arms about her. To hear his voice, whispering against her hair, reassuring her, wiping away her fears. Still, she knew her wishes would lead, ultimately, to a night of impassioned lovemaking, and that could not be.

For Bess had decided to return to the convent rather than jeopardize her immortal soul, and that of her lord and love, Griffith. It was only a matter of time before his nearness and her weakness would render them unable to resist the inevitable culmination of their love.

Only by absenting herself could Bess resist the temptation that burned so insistently between herself and Griffith. Burned, like the eternal fire of hell.

It was late in the afternoon before Griffith sought her out. She knew he was there without looking up. Her heart pounded wildly, and she strengthened her resolve. She must be firm. It was not only her life and her immortal soul that were at stake, but his, as well.

"Come, Bess." He held out his hand and helped her to her feet. "I would talk to you."

Bess placed her sewing on the low stool. The time had come to face the issue.

"I have spoken to Henry," Griffith began. He waited for Bess to respond but she held her silence, unable to utter a sound over the wild pounding of her heart. His next words would shape the remainder of her life.

She looked straight into his eyes, making it difficult for him to continue, to say the hurtful words that must be spoken.

"This alliance must be made. It is mandatory for the good of the country to secure the goodwill of the people as quickly as possible."

Bess swallowed. Her voice caught in her throat and held there choking back any sound. The pain she saw in his eyes was reflected in the depths of her soul.

"No, no..." Her lips formed the words, but gave forth no sound, for her grief was overwhelming, her sorrow too deep for words. She had believed, somewhere in her most secret heart, that their love would prevail and Griffith would find a way to bring the young king around to their favor. But such was not the case.

In the end, she could but bow her head in submission as tears of despair spilled from her eyes and trickled down her cheeks.

Griffith longed to take her in his arms, but knew he dared not touch her until this dilemma was resolved. She could not know of the heated argument between himself and his cousin Henry. An argument that had ended with the young king issuing the ultimatum that if the proposed political marriage did not take place, Griffith would be taken to the Tower of London and charged with treason, and Bess would be sent back to her mother in disgrace as having interfered with the wishes of the king.

"We carry the same blood in our veins," Henry had said. "And while you are my friend, that very blood also makes you my enemy. For through the Beaufort blood you can lay claim to my throne. Therefore, you must either be with me, or against me. There is no gray area here."

"But you know I love Bess," Griffith protested. "I have told you many times that I wished to wed with her." It was as though some evil spirit had overtaken the body and mind of his lifelong friend.

Henry sighed, sensing the other man's thoughts. "My father's kingdom was secure. He no longer needed to strengthen his stronghold. My situation is somewhat different. I must use every possible ploy to make certain that I will not be overthrown while my kingship is being established. I am truly sorry, Griffith. If it were possible, I would gladly give permission for you to marry the daughter of a petty knight. However, such is not the case. I need loyal men to secure the lands and alliances that may look to test my strength. If you are, indeed, my loyal subject, you will do as I command. If you thwart me, you will suffer the consequences."

No, Bess did not understand, nor would she. But the situation into which they had been thrust forced the words from Griffith's lips. "You may understand my words, but you cannot fully understand the urgency of this situation."

"Nor do I wish to," Bess returned. "It is enough you have been chosen by your sovereign to play a major part in his plans. You will do what you must, as will I."

"Bess, you can become a lady-in-waiting to Catherine. Henry plans to marry the princess, and has graciously offered to place you in her service. We would see one another often. I will spend a great deal more time in Henry's court than at any of my own establishments. My betrothed is but a babe. She will not be of an age to marry for over a decade. It is but a political alliance, not an affair of the heart. She will remain with her parents in a foreign land. You would never even see her."

"But I would know she was there, my lord, and that someday she would be your true and lawful wife." Bess shook her head, fighting down the tears that threatened to undo her. "I will return to Saint Lawrence of Blackmore Priory. If they will have me, I will take my vows."

"Think what you do! You will shut yourself away from the world." His body shuddered as he fought his emotion. "I will never see you again."

Bess longed to reach out. She could not bear to see him suffer so, to see the pain in his eyes. Yet she knew his slightest touch would be her undoing. She stared straight ahead, holding herself away from him.

"Very well." He took her silent stiffness for rejection of his plea. "I will give you sufficient dower to ensure your acceptance into the order."

She opened her mouth to object, but he held up his hand for silence.

"The dower is for the care you gave me during the hours after the tournament. I would do the same for my squire." He brushed the matter aside. "I leave with Henry on the morrow. I'll see that you have an escort to your destination."

"I will pray for you, my lord," she managed to answer. "I will pray for you, forever."

But Griffith was gone, and her promise fell on deaf ears.

Chapter Eight

To say the days passed quickly in the convent would be a lie. To say they passed slowly would be equally misleading. Bess had been placed in charge of the wicket gate, a job that kept her relatively busy, for there were many pilgrims and travelers, and the convent had proven to be a convenient stop.

The days merged into weeks and the weeks into a painful blur that prolonged into months. News came to them regularly. Thus, all the prayers in the world could not keep Bess from hearing of the coronation of Henry VIII and his marriage to the Spanish princess who was now queen of England.

And, try as she might, Bess had been unable to escape the news of the betrothal of Lord Griffith of Beaufort to the infant daughter of the Earl-Marshal of Calais. The betrothal might be hailed as a stroke of genius by the court and touted for its popularity with the commoners, but, somewhat to Bess's satisfaction, it seemed it was not made in heaven, for it would be years before it could be consummated, due to the age of the bride.

It was partially the feeling of smugness that came over her whenever she heard of the Beaufort's betrothed that kept Bess from taking her vows. Although her dower had been

paid long ago and in an amount large enough to have ensure her the position of mother superior sometime in the
future, Bess found it impossible to pledge her life to God
when her dreams were still haunted by a man. She would
never be able to count the nights she had awakened, her
body burning with remembered passion, longing for the
fulfillment it would never know. Nights she had spent
kneeling before her prie-dieu, until the bells at dawn called
her to another day of labor in the service of others.

In a combination of penitence and pique, Bess returned
Griffith's letters unopened and thus retained her sanity. For
there were times when, if she saw it written, she could not
have resisted his request that she come and share his life.

Her beauty turned from the first flush of innocent youth
to a haunting maturity. Her features became finer, more
sculptured. There was a look of poignant longing that never
left her as she resolutely kept her head bowed and bent to
her many tasks around the convent.

Saint Lawrence of Blackmore was not a large community, and many of the nuns were old. They were more than
happy to have younger shoulders on which to lay the heavi-
er tasks. Therefore, Bess worked until her mind and body
were exhausted. As she lay on her pallet each night, she
prayed only for a deep and dreamless sleep, but that was always denied her. Despite her weariness, she let Griffith creep
into her dream state and make love to her memory as surely
as if he were with her in fact.

She prayed, she confessed, she did penance, but to no
avail. Her whole being dwelt on the love she held for Griffith. She could not drive him from her thoughts or from her
heart, and although she loved her Lord God, she loved
Griffith, as well, and it was her never-dying love for him that
sealed her lips and forced her to remain a postulant rather

than take the vows, which would quickly have put her in a position of authority and honor.

If she could only go but one night without Griffith slipping into her dreams. Just one night without waking to the bitter loneliness of spending her life without him.

And although the mother superior counseled that once she took her vows her heart would be filled with the love of the Lord, Bess wanted a lord who would fill her arms, as well. A certain mortal lord to whom she had given her heart and soul and from whom they could not be reclaimed.

As the travelers came more and more frequently, it became Bess's habit to make the rounds of the stables before retiring, as she did now. She walked silently. Only the swishing of her skirts and the shuffling and munching of the livestock broke the hush of the night.

Satisfied that all was well, Bess started up the back stairs of the convent. It was a covered area, sheltered from the wind and rain as much as possible for the convenience of the good sisters, who must perform their tasks regardless of the elements.

Bess was halfway up the worn stairs when she heard men's voices. Apparently they were standing just beneath her vantage point, and their voices floated up unhampered.

"We foresee no problem, sire." The voice boasted surety. "The king rides out often, with only one or two of his closest friends as a token honor guard. They will be taken unawares and before they know what has happened to them, they will be ours."

There was a moment of silence as Bess wondered whether she should take the chance and try to move on into the safety of the convent. What was it to her whether they took the king or not? Had it not been for Henry, she might, even at this moment, be safe in the arms of the man she loved.

As a nun, Bess had no place in secular plots. She could relay her information to the mother superior and be done with it, or she could disregard what she heard and let Henry fend for himself. Before she could make a prayerful decision, the man's next words caught her attention.

"Our agents tell us he often rides with only one or two of his gentlemen. They are not heavily armed, as they go merely for the sport of small game. The king is very depressed at the queen's inability to bear him a living son, and wants to be as much alone as possible."

"There will be ten of us," another voice added. "We should be able to handle four lightly armed men with ease, even if two of them are renowned as the fiercest fighters in the land."

"The stakes are too high to take any chances!" the first voice reminded them. "France will pay a huge amount to have Henry under her power, even if it is only until they can force him to grant concessions they would otherwise never attain."

"What of the others? The French said nothing of their disposal."

"Our orders are to secure the person of the king. We can take no chances. The other members of the party must die. Only Henry will be taken alive."

"Then it is settled! We will meet on this day a week hence at the Northumberland Road. Henry and his party will be hunting there. The woods are thick. We should take them with relative ease."

Bess was unable to move for some minutes after she heard the men move away. It was as though her soul had frozen within her. When feeling returned, it was in the form of such palsied trembling she was obliged to lower herself to the stairs because her legs would not hold her. These men planned to capture the king and kill his companions—and, merciful heaven, Griffith was a constant companion of the king.

She rested her head upon the cool stones, as though their age and strength could give her the answers for which she now prayed.

Memories assailed her. Memories she had blocked out these many months, memories that flooded through her with such force that she clung to the stones as though the earth itself trembled.

Griffith...burning with the passion of life, as she had first seen him. Griffith...towering above all as he achieved his victories on the field at the tournament. Griffith... dancing with wild abandon in the light of the gypsies' fire. Griffith...of the gentle hands and magic lips that turned her body into an instrument of desire that throbbed to the rhythm of his passion. Griffith...who had allowed her to go from him when he could not offer her marriage, as well as love.

Would that brilliant light be snuffed out by these men who thought only of profit? Somewhere deep in the recesses of her mind, Bess realized that the reason she had never dared take her vows was due to the faint glimmer of hope that someday Griffith would come for her and, through a direct miracle of God, they would be reunited.

Devastated by the truth, Bess lay limp and exhausted, her mind remembering hazily more recent days. Had it only been earlier that week that the mother superior had called Bess into her cell and asked her intentions regarding her final vows?

"I am an old woman, Elizabeth," she had said, "and I am not long for this world. I would like to think the priory will be placed under your able hand when I am gone. It cannot do this if you are not a member of our order. The other nuns are old, like myself, and, like myself, wish to see you take the responsibility when the time comes.''

''Please, Reverend Mother, do not speak of such things,'' Bess had pleaded, but the woman had held up her hand for silence.

''Death is only another part of life, Elizabeth. It must be faced, but more than that, it must be planned when possible. Our Lord has given me that option, in answer to my prayer. Now it is time for you to make your prayer. If you do not know which path to take, ask the Lord to show you the way. If you are sincere, as I believe you to be, he will hear your prayer and grant you an answer.''

''I will do as you ask, Reverend Mother,'' Bess had promised, but it was with true fear in her heart that she had knelt in prayer, a fear that reached its culmination with the conversation of the men in the courtyard, for Bess knew her prayer had, indeed, been heard and answered.

There was no question in her mind as to what she must do. There was no one else she could trust. She must go and warn the king . . . and Griffith.

Reasoning it would be better if no one but the reverend mother knew where she was going, Bess hurried to her cell and wrapped a few things into a bundle. She had no clothes other than her habit, as her lovely gowns had been given to the poor.

Now, hurrying through the dark, drafty halls of the priory, Bess was reminded of the first time she had seen Griffith in the chapel at Pembroke. She tried to keep her nervousness from showing in her voice as she scratched at the door of the reverend mother's cell.

''Who is there?'' the soft voice called.

''It is Elizabeth, Reverend Mother. I must speak to you.''

The door opened, and Bess slipped into the sparsely furnished room. Even in the dimness of candlelight, the reverend mother's eyes missed nothing.

"You are carrying a bundle," she observed. "Where do you plan to go?"

"Reverend Mother, I fear a grave problem has come to my attention. This evening, as I returned from my chores, I overheard some men speak of attacking the king. I must go and warn him."

The old nun's head jerked up. "Are you certain?"

"Yes, I am!" Bess's voice left no room for further question.

"We could send for one of the men in the village. Undoubtedly one would be willing to go in your stead."

"No, Reverend Mother! If the men notice any undue movement in the village, there is no way of telling what they might do. No one must know but the two of us. None will suspect a nun on a mission of mercy."

"It is too dangerous! I cannot allow you to do it."

"You cannot stop me! I have not yet taken my holy vows, and am free to go out into the world as I please."

The older woman nodded her head at the girl's words. Her heart was heavy, for she felt she would never again see this young woman upon whom she had placed so many hopes. But it was the king's life that hung in the balance and, truly, a nun would be far better able to gain access to him than any villager.

"Will you not at least take Dan, the stable boy? He would offer some protection."

"If he is gone, the men would surely notice," Bess told her. "It is better I go alone, and swiftly. They will not guess the absence of one nun, and should they, you could say I have gone for medicines and supplies."

"Where do you go?" The mother superior took a bag of coins from her small coffer.

Bess paused. "I will not tell you. That way they will not force information from you, should they suspect the reason for my leaving."

"You are wise as well as good." The older woman smiled her blessing and pressed coins into Bess's hands. Above all, the girl was beautiful, the woman thought, looking into Bess's face. Surely it was a desperate measure to send this lovely, innocent creature out into the world again. She bent her head, uttering a silent prayer for forgiveness of the infirmities that did not allow her to take the girl's place. But she knew it could not be.

For some reason unknown to mortals, the Lord had deigned to send Bess as his messenger to save the king of England, and far be it from a lowly prioress to question his motives.

"Take these coins, and the better of the nags in the stable. And Godspeed!"

Bess gave the woman a quick embrace and slipped silently into the night. The horses knew her, and were quiet as she entered the stables. She saddled her horse with little problem and led it out through the back entrance, toward the fields. The gate was some distance away, but the path was not paved with stones as was the one in the courtyard. Bess made good her escape, pausing for one last moment to glance back at the walls of the convent. It was completely dark, save for one little light, in the mother superior's cell, where Bess knew the old woman must be praying.

Bess had no map, and was obliged to stop and ask for directions. For the most part, people were more than happy to help the dusty little nun who rode on so diligently. She fabricated a story, uttering a little prayer for forgiveness each time she told it.

"And we have heard of a marvelous herb growing only in the forest in Northumberland that cures the painful crippling of the bones that comes with age," she deftly told a group of noblemen and merchants who had paused to give her directions. "I have been commissioned by my mother superior to bring some of it back to the convent, to see if it will ease the pain in the older nuns."

One of the men hesitated, then reached into his pocket and drew out a piece of parchment.

"This is a map that includes the area into which you are going. As you are a nun and a messenger of the Lord, I will trust it to you for the remainder of your journey. My name is on it. I am the Baron of Oatlands, and you may send it to me after you return to your convent."

"I will, and with thanks!"

The smile that lit Bess's face startled the man. He had not before realized the woman to whom he spoke was a beautiful human being. It worried him that she traveled alone.

"Of course, should it be your wish, perhaps you would let an old man accompany you...."

She saw the concern in his eyes and knew he wished her no harm. Truly, she would have welcomed his protection, but who would protect him if she was set upon by the men whose plan she hoped to thwart? No, she could not allow him to take that chance.

"There is no need," she told him. "You have already done more than enough, and I will remember you in my prayers." Bess urged her horse forward and was soon out of sight.

The map proved to be a great help to Bess, but because of the age and disposition of her horse and the many times she had become lost in the early part of her journey, time was running out. Now, instead of asking directions, Bess asked what day it might be. Surely the men, with their faster steeds, were already in the area. Bess became more and more cautious as she neared her destination. It would not do to lose all now that the time was at hand.

She did not reach the forest of Northumberland until the morning of the planned fatal day. The mists were still on the ground as she plodded onward, leading her horse, who had gone lame during the long night's ride.

The forest was large and vast. Its very size intimidated Bess. How would she find a small party of men in this maze of trees and brush? And then, what if the men she came upon were the wrong ones?

Resting against the trunk of a tree, Bess finished the last of her bread and cheese and allowed the horse to take his fill of the rich green grass that abounded there. She must form some plan. She couldn't spend the day wandering about the forest in the hope she would come upon the king and Griffith. At the thought of Griffith, her heart turned over within her breast. She caught her breath. She realized she was nearer to him than she had been in years. Nearer than she had been since she had seen him last, that fateful day at Greenwich. Would he have changed? Would he recognize her? And, if he did, would he treat her coldly, or would the spark of love shine in his eyes, as it did in her memory?

She got to her feet. She would follow the path to the hunting lodge. It was still early. Possibly the men had not yet taken to their horses. If she could reach them before they left, there would be no danger.

Bess took the reins. If her nag was discovered alone in the woods, the outlaws would be alerted to trouble. It was better she take the horse with her, she reasoned, and she dragged him along behind her.

As it happened, it was the horse who alerted Bess to the presence of others in the vicinity. He whinnied a greeting, and Bess dropped the reins and scurried into the brush.

Two men appeared on the path before her. Huge men, clad in hunter's green. They rode with majesty, although, to be sure, there was an aura of dejection surrounding them. They spoke quietly as they moved toward her.

Bess stared, hardly able to believe her luck. One of the men was Henry, the king. He had waxed plump, and his massive body was well padded with the fruits of good food and drink. It was an older Henry, not the carefree prince with whom Bess had been briefly acquainted. The man next to him . . . dare she look? Having once let her eyes feast on the long-remembered features, could she look away? Her need to know of his safety prevailed, and she looked hard. It was, indeed, Griffith. A magnificent Griffith, whose body had filled out, most probably from long hours in the saddle and long campaigns fighting for his king.

They did not see her at first, and she was free to look her fill at the face of the man she loved. Then, remembering her mission, she stepped into the path, only to be stopped by a burly guard.

"Go and beg elsewhere!" the man commanded.

"I have a message for Lord Beaufort," she gasped as the man tried to push her from the path. But Griffith had ridden on, paying her little mind. "I must speak with him!" she cried out in desperation as Griffith and the king moved farther away.

Somehow the desperation in her voice reached Griffith and caused him to hesitate.

Reaching inside her robes, she clutched the precious ring he had given her so long ago. A ring that had never left her body in all that time. Breaking the chain on which it hung, she thrust it at the guard. "Take it to Lord Beau—hurry, there is no time to waste!"

The moment the ring touched Griffith's hand, it was as though lightning had struck him. Surely this woman was here to tell him that Bess was dead, or in dire need, or had taken her vows and could no longer keep the ring in her possession.

"How came you by this?" he demanded, riding back toward her.

The little nun dropped to her knees.

"My lord, beware! There is a plot against the king! The men are coming. They will attempt to capture him this day...."

The conspirators, realizing their plan had been thwarted, burst from the thick foliage. "Silence the woman!" one of them shouted.

Bess's head exploded with pain as the force of the blow knocked the wimple from her head and she fell, unconscious, to the ground.

Henry and Griffith dared not take a telling blow, as they wore no armor, and did not carry shields. For a few minutes, Henry fought a fully armed knight with nothing more than a hunting knife, a feat he knew he would relish relating, should he live to do so.

After dispatching one of the knights, Griffith took the man's battle-ax and tossed his sword to Henry.

Without further ado, Henry sliced into another knight. By now, there were only three outlaws still astride their horses, and Henry and Griffith were beginning to enjoy themselves, knowing the remaining men were no match for their superior skill.

Without speaking, the two men deftly led the others away from the still form that lay across the grass. While Henry only knew he would do all in his power to protect the little nun who had warned them, possibly at the cost of her own life, Griffith was strangely perturbed.

His eyes kept returning to the unconscious figure, the worry on his brow not for himself or his king but concern for the woman, a concern enhanced by a spark of recognition he dared not acknowledge.

Chapter Nine

"Well done, cousin!" Henry clapped Griffith on the back as the men assessed the damage around them. "We have them all! None escaped!"

But Griffith's eyes were on the woman who still lay at the edge of the clearing. Henry noticed his cousin's preoccupation.

"Go on, then. The little nun saved our lives. See if she has survived the ordeal. She was struck a mighty blow, for one so small."

Griffith started across the clearing, aware that Henry was giving orders that the prisoners be kept alive as long as possible for questioning. Ordinarily, he would have pitied the poor devils, for their lives were forfeit whether they talked or no, but, looking at the unconscious woman, all thought of pity was erased from his mind. As he neared her, he noticed the thick mane of white-gold hair flowing across the grass. Surely there was no other hair like that in Christendom. It had burst loose from its bonds and lay about her like a veil, tinged now with the red blood of sacrifice.

Griffith swallowed with difficulty, afraid to move, afraid of what he might discover when he touched the unmoving body. Gently he turned her over and looked into the face of his beloved.

"Bess," he whispered. "Merciful God, let her be yet alive. I cannot bear to be parted from her again."

He prayed that the words, strained from his soul, had not fallen on deaf ears as he lifted her into his arms and searched for a pulse beat with his lips. It was there! It fluttered tremulously against his mouth. She lived!

He looked down at her. Her eyes were ringed with dark shadows of fatigue. How she must have struggled, to reach them in time, he thought as he traced the lines of her face. The harsh effect of the elements were written on the skin of her face, skin that should have been protected. He would see to it that she was protected, now and forever, he vowed as he lifted her into his arms.

"Does she live?" Henry called as his cousin approached.

"She does, but barely." Griffith's eyes never left her face.

It wasn't until Beaufort mounted his horse that Henry had a clear look at the girl. Something about her touched his memory. Something about her white-gold hair—and the preoccupation of his cousin.

Then it came to him. "Was this not the little wench you were so taken with at Pembroke some years back?"

Griffith knew it would do no good to lie. Henry had a mind like a steel trap. "It is she!"

"I heard the girl had gone to a nunnery," Henry mused, his unusual powers of memory doing him proud once again.

"She must have come here from Saint Lawrence of Blackmore Priory," Griffith told him.

"I would flatter myself that the girl had come to save her king, but now I cannot help but wonder if it might not have been you she felt she must save, rather than myself." Henry's laughter echoed through the forest. "'Tis no matter! She has been of great service to us, and we are grateful. I will send for my chief surgeon to tend her wounds, but I leave it up to you, cousin, to see she is rewarded properly for her service to the crown.''

Henry's words were tantamount to an order. Griffith realized there were unspoken meanings stemming from Henry's flawless memory, and could only hope that it was in the king's heart to grant Griffith his request of long ago.

''She may have already taken her holy vows and be lost to me forever.'' Griffith nearly choked on his words. ''Even if she lives, it may be too late.''

The steady hoofbeats against the moist ground echoed the words again and again as Griffith carried Bess toward the hunting lodge.

Too late ... too late ... too late ... Was it indeed too late for the love that flamed so brightly in his heart?

Prigge met them at the gate. ''My lord, we heard rumors of trouble! What has—?'' His words stopped short as he became aware of the still figure in Griffith's arms. ''My God! It's Mistress Bess!''

''I will take her to my apartment,'' Griffith announced. ''Send the physician there when he arrives.''

Henry nodded in agreement. ''Do you want to come down when the prisoners are questioned?''

''Prigge can keep me informed. I will come if you have need of me, but I do not wish to leave Bess until I know how she fares.''

Griffith did not bow to his king, nor did Henry expect it. They had just been through a harrowing time together, and the closeness of their relationship made them more than sovereign and subject. The bond of blood and battle had, for a few moments, made rank unimportant.

The bedchambers Griffith used while at Northumberland were sumptuous, with hangings of black velvet and cloth of gold. Prigge had turned back the fine linens on the

bed, and Griffith laid Bess down carefully. His arms ached,
not from the weight they had borne, but from the loss of it.
He wanted to hold her again and never let her go.

Prigge tried to move Griffith aside. "I will see how serious her wound is, then attend to you."

"There is nothing wrong with me," Griffith said
staunchly.

"It is difficult to believe all the blood on your clothing
belongs to Mistress Bess," Prigge muttered as he bent over
Bess, carefully dabbing at the blood in her hair.

But Griffith took the cloths from Prigge's hands, unable
to bear the thought of anyone touching Bess save himself.

"My lord, you must rest. Even His Grace has gone to his
chambers. Only the prisoners are not given the courtesy of
a few moments of peace." Prigge tried to pry his master
from the side of the unconscious woman, but his arguments were in vain.

"By your own words, I am undeserving of rest," Griffith said as he looked into the sympathetic eyes of his man-
servant and companion, "for am I not a prisoner, forever
tied to vows that cannot be broken save by God himself?"

Prigge looked somewhat confused. "You are no prisoner, my lord. Indeed, you are the very soul of freedom."

"But it is Bess who is tied by vows. Holy vows that must
not be broken, on pain of everlasting damnation."

"You do not know this," Prigge pointed out.

"She was in the convent for a considerable length of time.
There was ample time to complete her training. Her dower
was paid. She wanted never to see me again, and would have
stayed true to her vow had the king's life not been in danger. No, I fear it is too late. If I were wise, I would leave her
now and not rekindle the flame or open the wound of love
that festers within me, never healing, never giving me a
moment's peace." He sighed and looked at her still, pale

face. "But I am not a wise man, I am a fool, and more than that, a fool in love. Go, fetch news of the prisoners. I wish to be alone with her."

Prigge looked anxiously at his master. He feared for the souls of both these people whom he cared for. He had never forgotten Bess, and he admired the strong stand she had made against the powerful man who was his liege. Surely no man would have stood more staunchly against so great a lord of the realm. Yet she, rather than surrender her virtue to a man who could never marry her, had chosen to take the holy vows. Would her resolve be as great when she opened her eyes and was confronted by the man she had loved so much? Would her faith in God be strong enough to sustain her? Prigge had no answers, and there was nothing he could do but hope for the best for all of them.

The surgeon had come. At Griffith's insistence, the man had only bound the wound in Bess's scalp, although he had wanted to bleed her. One look at the scowl on Lord Beaufort's face and the notion was put aside. The surgeon made no attempt to disguise his desire to leave as quickly as possible. Each time he laid hands on the young woman, Beaufort looked as though he might attack him. Did the fool think that he, a physician, would molest a nun? Let the overzealous nobleman do the menial tasks, then, he thought as he packed up his instruments and made for the door.

"The nun would be more comfortable if she was not bound so closely in those bloodstained robes. I could send—"

"There is no need to send anyone," Griffith snapped. "She will be well cared for." He tossed the man several gold pieces to pay for his services, as well as his silence.

Griffith sat silently at the bedside. A hundred times his hands reached out to loose the voluminous robes that covered Bess's body. He had no way of knowing what a nun wore beneath her robes of office, and fear and anticipation stopped him before he could begin his task.

Unbidden memories swept through his mind as he recalled how he had gone to Bess wearing nothing but the robes of a monk. Had his mocking of a man of God cursed their relationship?

It seemed as though from that night on they had been doomed to be torn apart. Why, it had been that very night that the castle was sent into a state of flux when word came that the king had taken to his sickbed, whence he would never rise.

The great hope Griffith had known over the crowning of his friend and ally, Henry VIII, had been quickly squelched when the young king flatly refused Griffith's request to marry Bess.

Bess moved restlessly as the medicine the surgeon had given her began to wear off. It sounded as though she whispered his name. He bent more closely to catch the words.

Her head pounded as if a hundred horses galloped across her skull. She knew not where she was. Her body was ensconced in feathery softness, quite unlike the pallet on which she slept at the convent.

But she wasn't at the convent. She had been forced to leave. To go out into the world, alone, with only fear and desperation as her companions. She had to deliver a message... No, not a message...

If only her head did not ache so terribly, perhaps she could remember. It was not a message, but a warning! A warning to save the king, and... Griffith!

Marshaling all her strength, Bess managed to open her eyes.

"Was I... in time?" she whispered brokenly.

"Yes, my love, you saved both the king and myself. All the outlaws were killed or captured."

She tried to move her hand toward him. She needed to be reassured that he was, indeed, whole and unhurt, but the effort was too much for her. Her hand dropped back onto the counterpane. "Thank God, you live," she murmured as she slipped back into the world of semidarkness, where she floated just above her exhausted body.

At first she felt nothing, but then the tight bonds that held her were loosened. She breathed deeply as the stiff, sticky robes fell away. Hands lifted her tenderly. Griffith's touch, so well remembered as intimate, was now impersonal. They did not linger or caress. Was she no more to him than any man-at-arms who had fallen wounded and must be tended on the field of battle?

Desperately she tried to force her way through the thick, muddy darkness. She tried to tell him there was no need for him to minister to her thus. She would be as well tended in the servant's quarters, where the women would see to her needs until she was well enough to return to the convent. She would not humiliate him, or herself, in this way. It was unseemly for a man to nurse a woman. But, God forgive her, her body had sprung to life at his touch. Each pore yearned to experience more of the maddening electricity that shot through her veins. Surely it could not be so great a sin to only stay silent a moment more, relishing the anticipation of his touch as he sponged her body.

She felt him dry her with thick, thirsty toweling, lingering a moment before removing the rough texture. Cool now from the tepid water, her body was once more exposed to the air. Then a burning droplet touched her skin and trailed down the side of her breast into nothingness. It was followed by another, and another. Unable to understand what was happening, Bess forced her eyes to open.

What she saw through her lashes made her gasp in disbelief. For it was tears that burned a sensuous path down her body. Tears that fell from Griffith's eyes. Her mind, numbed by pain and medicine, was unable to comprehend what she beheld, but the spark of undying hope awakened in her heart, and, clinging to that hope, she allowed herself to drift into the neverland of sleep.

Griffith forced himself to cover the alabaster body that gleamed in the candlelight. Never had he seen anything more lovely. The promise of womanhood had been more than fulfilled by the lush curves and deep valleys, the moonlight and shadows spread before him. He trembled at such beauty, for it was the beauty of the woman he loved.

The awakening she had experienced so long ago had only made her more desirable. There was nothing about her that was not perfection in his eyes. It was as though he had molded her himself. He longed to touch, to kiss, to explore, the way he'd done in the past. She was his. So much a part of him, he could not differentiate the warmth of his body from her warmth.

He wondered if he could stand the torment of holding her again without renewing the love that called out for fulfillment. He would not take her while she was unconscious, but he knew he would do all in his power to make her his own, as soon as she was able to comprehend his desire.

If it cost him his eternal soul, so be it! Gladly he would trade it for a night lost in her love, in her arms, in her soft, sensuous body. If there be sin, it was that a body such as hers was hidden beneath a nun's shapeless habit. For hers was a body that cried out for a man. Not any man, but one willing to love to his greatest capacity. To show tenderness and restraint in awakening her, and then to lift her, and himself, to the heights that were reserved for lovers who are willing to sacrifice all to achieve ecstasy. To hold back, though the blood pounded through his veins like a million horses riding into battle. To wait, until neither of them could stop the wild culmination of their union. To feel the surge of power as the explosion rent bodies joined for eternity. To die, and be born again in her arms, in her heart, in her love . . .

When her breathing assured him the worst was over and Bess slept peacefully, Griffith was finally able to rest.

True to his vow, he did no more than lie next to her, savoring the warmth of her naked beauty. He marveled at the smoothness of her skin as she moved toward him, unconsciously seeking the comfort of his arms. It was like satin drawn across mail, he thought as she curled her body to fit against his. He was almost afraid to move, to touch her, for fear that his hands, callused from many battles, might injure her petal-smooth skin. She was so different in texture from himself, he could hardly believe they were of the same species. His body, scarred and covered with thick red-gold hair, and hers, white as ivory. A skin so fair, so translucent, the blue veins shone through against the column of her throat and down across her shoulders—like the markings on a map setting the course through the valley and up the gentle rise of her breasts.

A shock shot through his body, causing him to stiffen in sheer desire as he remembered her sweetness. Like honeymead, like the nectar of the gods, she had spoiled him for all others.

Somewhere in her dream world, Bess was aware of Griffith's presence. Her hand moved across his belly and up to tangle in the mat of hair on his chest. She awakened and began twisting the hair about her fingers, rubbing it as a child rubs a silken coverlet or a favorite toy. She felt tension in the muscled arm beneath her, but she was used to only the most rudimentary sleeping accommodations, and the hardness did nothing to add to her discomfort. Indeed, it was Griffith who suffered, as each gentle touch caused his body to be racked with the pain of unfulfilled passion.

Not realizing the tumult she caused him, Bess slipped back into the healing darkness of sleep, assured of her well-being by the strength and warmth of the tortured man beside her.

The soft breath teasing against his skin told him that Bess slept, but it was many hours before Griffith could join her. He spent hours unmoving, relishing her presence, even as he was tortured by it. His whole being cried out for her, even as his mind told him he must not take her in a manner less than beautiful for both of them.

No, their love could not be, unless Bess was both willing and free to join him in the ultimate fulfillment. He had waited for such a long time—what were a few hours more? But for Griffith, they were hours of agony.

There was but a memory of pain in her head when Bess finally awakened. The deep and secure peace she had known in her slumber had served her well, and much of her physical strength had been restored. Her mind was another matter.

She was unsure how much of what she remembered was only the dreams with which she had been plagued for so many nights, and how much truth. There was a hollow in the bed where a body had lain beside her. Surely some of her dreams were, in fact, real.

She sat up, realizing for the first time that she was naked, only her hair covering her. Before she could rectify her condition, Griffith entered the room, stopping short as he took in her pink-tipped breasts that peered from the thick veil of hair like rosebuds in the snow, her wide azure eyes, and her dew-kissed lips, parted, as though waiting for a lover's kiss.

Her whole pose was the ultimate in seduction, but innocently so, and therefore much more enticing.

He steeled himself against the unbearable temptation that all but overwhelmed him, and jerked the quilt up around her shoulders. "Cover yourself, woman, you'll catch a chill."

His voice was more gruff than he had meant it to be. It took all his strength to keep from trembling as his fingers touched the cool skin of her shoulder. "How do you feel?" He found himself unwilling to remove his hand from even the most minute contact with her body. "I have ordered broth and bread, if you are hungry."

Bess's eyes locked on his face. He had aged, but it had given him even more character. His skin was scarred from battle. She could see lines of suffering, lines of sorrow, that had replaced the laughter she remembered so well. If she had thought the younger Griffith was desirable, she found this man irresistible. Her eyes traveled down to where his hand still rested against her shoulder. The hand was scarred now, and heavily callused. Still, she remembered the magic it had invoked in her body. Then it had been the newly callused hand of a young man, untried in the battles of life. Much more exciting was the touch of his hand now. Much more exciting was the husky depth of his voice, which sent shivers coursing through her body. How she longed to hear that rough voice murmuring words of endearment against her skin, awakening her desire as only he knew how to do.

She understood why she had never been able to accept the commitment of the convent and take the final vows. Surely she could not be shut away before she was allowed to be fully alive?

Her love, her longing, was clearly reflected in Bess's eyes, yet Griffith did not move. It was more than he had dared hope, if what he saw was true. Still, she might only be grateful he had cared for her. With her next words, she might demand he return her to the convent, and how could he bear it?

He stepped back, closing his eyes against her pleading gaze.

"I am authorized by the king to grant you anything you wish for saving our lives," he managed. He didn't want to look at her, to see the gentle curves outlined beneath the bed linens, to see her face as she told him she would take a little bag of gold and return to the convent whence she came. He didn't want to hear her tell him she had taken the irrevocable vows and was now a bride of Christ and lost to him forever. He didn't want to hear her reprimand him for lying next to her and coveting her lovely body.

But she did none of those things.

"You," Bess whispered. "You are all I want, in heaven or on earth."

The longing to touch him was too great. Bess knew Griffith suffered as greatly as she, just as she knew there was only one way to assuage that suffering. Overwhelmed by his presence, and unable to weigh the consequences of what she was about to do, Bess reached out and took Griffith's hand, pressing the callused palm against her lips.

"You are all I want," she whispered, and released his hand. It dropped against the softness of her breast as she lifted her arms to welcome him. Her fingers explored the craggy planes of his face and down his cheeks and neck, finding each new scar, each line that had not been there before.

Remembering the many nights she had relived each place his lips had touched, she sought out those places on his body, and nibbled at the little pulse that throbbed in his neck.

Griffith could not move, could not believe this was happening to him. Not in his wildest dreams had he dared hope she might take the initiative. It was as though he were paralyzed as he let her explore his face and neck. Then, dizzy with desire, he felt her hands slip beneath his robe as she drew him to the bed. The robe fell open as she rose to her knees beside him. Slowly, slowly, her hands and lips explored the hard planes, the tense muscles, of his burning body, her fingers outlining the scars.

He watched her as she moved above him, pressing tiny kisses down the length of his body. Her body was a torch of delight as she swayed in a dance of desire.

Griffith's breath caught in his throat, such was the response she elicited as she caressed him. Although he had yet to touch her, she could not help but know of his desire, for his body throbbed, though he willed himself to be still as she continued her exploration.

He could feel her hands moving down across the hard muscles of his belly. Her face was close behind. So close, he could feel her breath rippling his hair. He tensed, willing himself to be still, but it was too much. If she so much as breathed upon him, he would explode, unable to control himself.

It must not be so! He had dreamed of this too long to have it less than perfect. She must be with him in this act of love.

Sinking his fingers into her hair, he drew her face toward his. Her eyes were heavy with desire and her lips soft and pliable with the abandonment of love. His hands found her breasts, drawing out each note of passion to the ultimate. He explored her wonders, running kisses down the sweet curve of her hip and across her thigh.

Bess began moving rhythmically as his lips forced all conscious thought from her mind. There was only desire, as old and as primitive as time. Desire, begging for fulfillment in the silent voice that cried out above all the sounds of the world, until it was lost in the voice of eternity as he entered her body, stroking her to fruition as the rhythm of need intensified.

Together they rose to meet the voice, to become one with it, as they were one with each other. Their eyes locked as each perceived the wonder, the love, and finally the fulfillment, on the other's face. Then the world exploded in a panoply of light, and they were catapulted above it and lost in time and space, where there was nothing but sensation and love.

Griffith lay against her, his face buried in the gossamer softness of her hair. Somehow he felt he must have her promise now, while they still shared the glow of love.

"Promise me . . . promise me you'll never leave me!" He whispered the words against her beautiful face.

"Never, never, as long as you love me!" Bess cried.

"I could never stop loving you," he told her, "or wanting you. As I have wanted you these long, lonely days, these weary, hopeless nights."

"And I you, my love, wanted you so desperately I felt I could not take my holy vows and dedicate my life to God. All the while realizing I had no place in your life, save one of shame."

"There is no shame in our love, sweetheart." He breathed a sigh of relief as he drew her more closely against him.

She held her breath, waiting for him to repeat the magic words telling her he wanted her to be his wife, but he continued kissing her until she realized he had said all he intended. She could not suppress a sigh of disappointment.

Griffith interpreted her sigh as one of contentment, a contentment he felt he understood and shared. To him there was no need for further words. He loved her, as he always had, and his love was returned. She had not repeated her vows, and would not return to the convent. He would have no other as his wife. When the proper time came, he would quietly ask the king for permission to marry Bess, and they would continue as they were, their love supplanting all else. In his mind, the path was clearly marked. He never gave thought to the possibility Bess did not know or understand his intent.

Chapter Ten

For Griffith, it was a time of interminable bliss, for Bess a time of anxious waiting. Surely Griffith's feelings toward her had not changed so greatly that he would take all she had to offer without giving thought to the holy vows of marriage. She could not understand his attitude, and although it was obvious he loved her, he had never offered to return the betrothal ring he had given her so long ago. Instead, he wore it on his finger, as he had when first she met him.

To Griffith, the ring held special meaning. He had taken it, still warm from her body, and placed it on his hand. To him, it was a symbol of her love for him, and the sacrifice she had made to save him. He looked down at it, remembering her loveliness, and her love. Even when he was apart from her, he felt joined to her through the ring. Soon, he would give her a ring of great splendor. The ceremonial ring his grandmother had worn. Somehow he had realized he could present it to no one but his beloved Bess. He smiled at her as she sat with the other ladies of the court. They looked like a wreath of bright flowers surrounding the queen in her drab clothing.

The queen was again in mourning, for the loss of her last child. Another son... another hope of England laid to rest.

The king was beside himself in an agony of doubt. Henry lay awake nights trying to discover where the blame might lie in his inability to beget a living male heir to the throne of England.

The men stood at the long windows overlooking the castle gardens. "There are other women, Griffith," the king said sagely.

"Not for me, Your Grace. I have waited for Bess these many years, and she for me. I intend to make her my wife."

Henry was silent. He would much rather have heard Griffith say he was only having a light affair with the woman, but Henry, for all his faults, was a romantic, and Griffith's love for Bess was romance at its most classic.

"With or without the approval of your king," Henry finished for him. "I well remember feeling much the same way about Catherine. I would consider marriage with no one else. No other woman would do, and look what my devotion has gained me. A barren wife who spends her days praying and crying, and her nights crying and praying. I wish you better luck in affairs of the heart, cousin. The only thing that keeps me from taking a woman like your Bess is the threat that she would plead her belly each time she wanted something. Women are prone to do so, I am told."

"Not Bess, Your Grace," Griffith assured his liege. "She would never use a child to make me marry her. Nor would there be a need, for marriage to her is all I desire in this world."

"I think the wine has gone to your head," Henry told him as they turned back into the room and walked toward the queen and her ladies, who had congregated near the fire. Henry's voice carried to Bess's eager ears. "I will take your request under consideration and see what can be done to nullify your betrothal. You will have my decision before Michaelmas."

Griffith glanced at Bess, his happiness at the concession he had just gleaned from his king shining in his eyes. But Bess did not see. Michaelmas would be too late. For Bess carried Griffith's child and, according to her best calculations, would come to term in the early fall. By the end of September, it would be impossible to keep her condition a secret. It would be the talk of the court.

So far, their love trysts had gone unremarked, for Griffith made his frequent nocturnal visits with the greatest discretion. But it would not be long before she would be forced to let out the seams of her gowns and her condition would be obvious.

She would be disgraced. And Griffith would think her scheming and venal.

Making her curtsy to the queen, Bess left the room. She had almost reached her apartments when she heard footsteps behind her. Before she could secure herself within, Griffith was beside her, his arms enfolding her against the encrusted velvet of his tunic.

"I saw you leave the others and begged the king to excuse me so I could be with you for a little moment," he said.

In his happiness Griffith could not but think she teased as she resisted him, and while a teasing Bess was something new to him, he found her even more enchanting. His ardor knew no bounds as she struggled against him, and his powers of persuasion became more and more inventive as she persisted in denying him.

As his passion mounted, Bess's own desire flamed. Try as she might to deny him, her body responded to his caresses. His lips covered every inch of exposed skin, from her smooth forehead to the gentle curve of her breast, before his hands deftly exposed even more. Her breasts grew taut with anticipation as he worked his magic, tantalizing her, until his mouth found hers.

Like a flower opening its dew-kissed sweetness to the warmth of the sun, so she opened to him, unable to resist the urgent persuasion of his lips as they drew the nectar from each honey-filled treasure. Now it was his turn to tease, to torment, in the game of love. She lived only to feel his hands, his mouth, his throbbing body, covering her, entering her, fulfilling the promise he made with each new caress.

Desperately her body moved against him in anticipation of being joined with him. Her mind was whirling. Surely he must love her... No man could make love with such tender abandon if he did not love the vessel into which his efforts poured.

She felt his lips drawing her out of herself, drawing her into the dark, swirling void where passion was all. And then they were one, riding through the darkness and bursting together into the light. He would have pulled away, but her legs locked about him and he was sealed tightly against her slender beauty on the rumpled bed.

"I love you." Her words were hardly more than a whimper. "I cannot help myself."

"Nor can I keep from loving you," he admitted. "Neither would I try, for loving you is all to me. Just holding you, feeling the smoothness of your body against mine, I cannot think how I could have lived so long without you. I could never do so again."

She knew she could deny him nothing.

When his arms were about her, she found it impossible to think, to believe in anything but his love.

Desperately she racked her brain for a solution. But clear thought would not come with Griffith's face floating before her. Would it always be so? Would he always come to haunt her, his magnificent body driving her to the pinnacle of desire?

Oh, pray God he would, and that her confession would not turn him away from herself and her love.

He held her close. Their bodies still touched at each intimate point. He kissed her face lightly, feather kisses, given with a smile.

"I have wonderful news, sweetheart," he confided. "The king has promised to consider our plea. I feel certain he will give in to our wishes and nullify the sham betrothal I have been forced to endure. It is only a matter of time before we can be wed."

"A matter of time..." Bess repeated.

Griffith was beside himself with happiness. "Henry has promised a decision by Michaelmas." He stopped kissing her and drew back enough to look into her eyes. "It is nothing, after the many months we have waited."

Oh, how was she to tell him and destroy the happiness he knew at achieving his goal against Henry, the king. She could feel his questioning gaze.

"It is too great a time to wait for an answer, when one has less than nine months to make ready." She felt the color rise to her cheeks as she completed her statement and wondered if Griffith was wise enough in the ways of women to know of what she spoke.

He took her shoulders and held her away from himself as his eyes scanned her body.

"Bess! What are you saying?"

"Only, my lord, that before the end of summer my condition will surely be obvious to everyone."

"A child?" he gasped. "Our child?" His face shone with awe. "You are saying you will give me a son?"

Bess lowered her eyes. "I do not know that it is a son, my lord. But surely there will be a child. A child born of our love."

He crushed her to him. "You are right, my love. I will present my petition—nay, my demand—to Henry, and he shall not deny me. I swear it."

And again she was engulfed by his kisses, and time stopped until they awoke in the light of a new day. But the day was not to be as bright as the morning light had promised. For Henry had left during the night. And, being unable to find Griffith, he had taken Sir Charles Brandon with him.

Griffith went to Bess's apartments later in the day, desolation written all over his handsome countenance.

"No one knows when the king will return. He became morose and depressed during the night. It is said he and the queen had words. He called his men together, and those who answered the summons went with him. No doubt to gain his ear and his favor."

"But surely he could have guessed where you would be. You said yourself that it is no secret to Henry that we love one another."

"I doubt Henry has yet discovered I am not among his entourage. When he realizes I am absent, it is most likely he will be piqued with jealousy and believe I hid in your arms to avoid being with him."

Bess gasped aloud, seeing their chance of happiness slip away. "Surely not! His Majesty must know that you have put him before all."

"Before all but you, my love. All but you, and Henry knows it too well."

"Then you think he will deny our petition and refuse to grant our request, even though he pledged that he would grant my every wish after I saved his life?'' Tears fill Bess's eyes. ''Is his life suddenly worth so little to him, then?''

''I know not what my king will do. I only know that we must do everything we can to protect your reputation and the life of our unborn child.''

''What do you mean?'' Bess asked, hardly able to believe her ears, much less her eyes. Griffith's face was filled with concern, rather than the joy she had hoped to bring him with her news.

''There are many who would begrudge you your child and try to destroy our chance of happiness. You must leave the court before your condition becomes obvious.''

''What do you mean? How can you say such a thing? I have never harmed a soul here, and have no enemies. I will go to the queen. She has said many times how grateful she is that I saved her husband's life. She will help us.''

''It is from the queen that you have the most to fear,'' Griffith warned. ''You think to go to a barren woman and tell her that you are pregnant with the illegitimate child of a lord of the realm? How do you think she will take that news, when she still wears mourning from the death of her last child?''

Bess put her hand over her mouth. Indeed, she had not thought of the situation in that light.

''Have you seen any lady of the court carrying a child?'' Griffith persisted.

Bess searched her memory. ''No married women, and surely none that are not married. I cannot recall anyone among the queen's ladies-in-waiting that might be pregnant.''

''Do you not recall those pleasant days of Christmastide, before Henry became king?'' Griffith reminded her. ''It was then he first made it known that Catherine would not tolerate anything but the highest morals among her ladies. That has not changed. What has changed is that since Catherine is unable to bear a living child, she will not have any woman who might be in a position, or a condition, to do so in her midst. Once with child, a woman is banished from the court."

He took Bess's soft shoulders in his hands, relishing the wonder of their silkiness. "If the queen was to learn that you were pregnant with my child, like as not she would dismiss you from the court and send you back to your mother.

"With Henry gone there would be no one to gainsay her."

Griffith paced back and forth across the floor, his brow furrowed with worry. "There is only one thing to do. You must ask the queen for permission to leave, before she suspects you are with child. Tell her you wish to visit ... someone ... anyone...."

Bess bit her knuckle. The only person she wished to be with was Griffith. How could she hope to lie to the queen and be believed? If only Mary were here. Mary of Pembroke, now of Essex, would know how to handle the situation.

Bess jumped to her feet.

"That's it! I'll go to visit Lady Mary of Essex. I have not seen her since her marriage. No one would doubt my sincerity of purpose in visiting my girlhood friend."

Griffith swept her into his arms. "Ah, what an intelligent, devious little vixen I have given my heart. Most surely the queen will allow you to go without a thought. And I shall go with you. Together we will spend halcyon days and impassioned nights, until Henry releases me from my enforced betrothal and frees us to marry."

He swung her around the room, lost in the euphoria of love, until they collapsed, overcome with giddiness and longing.

* * *

It wasn't until some time later that they realized their plans were not destined to proceed exactly as they had hoped, for Henry sent word that he had need of his cousin and grieved for his presence.

"If you are with me, dear cousin," the king wrote, "I know we can work out an arrangement suitable to all regarding the circumstance in which you find yourself through your efforts on my behalf.

"As you are no doubt aware, these situations must be handled with the utmost care, and I feel it will behoove us all if you are at my side when the final arrangements are put down.

"I go now to Calais, and expect to meet you en route prior to my arrival if you truly desire my help in freeing you from this unwanted betrothal."

"He makes it sound as though the betrothal was originally of your doing!" Bess could hardly hide her outrage at the king's choice of words.

But Griffith only patted her warmly. "It is the way of kings, my love. Nothing is ever their fault. That would not be 'kingly.' Now do not give it a thought. Henry can see that I am released with the least possible diplomatic difficulty. I will meet you at Essex when I return. In the meantime, have a happy visit with your friend Mary."

He wrapped her in his embrace. "Oh, my love," he whispered against her hair, "when we are next together, we shall indeed be as one. Not only in our hearts and our bodies, but in our souls through marriage, and for all eternity. Now kiss me again, for I must go and arrange with my king to finalize my marriage to the woman I love above all else."

Bess melted in his arms, quashing down the fears she knew in approaching the queen to ask for a favor, and wishing, somehow, Griffith could be at her side.

Bess went to the queen early the next morning. She found her in the chapel. It was strange, Bess thought as she approached the woman, that her love for Griffith should continuously center around a chapel.

She felt as though she were being torn apart. How could she bear to be apart from him now? How could she bear not seeing him for days and weeks on end? How could she live without feeling his lips, hard and demanding, against her own? Her resolve weakened. She would follow him. They would face Henry together.

Just then the queen rose to her feet, and Bess knew she must stay with Griffith's plan.

She dropped to her knees before the queen and timidly asked that she be allowed to leave her service to visit her friend, Mary of Essex.

"But I thought you enjoyed our company!" The queen was plainly surprised by Bess's request.

"Oh, I do, Your Grace, but ... but I cannot remain here any longer. You see, Lord Beaufort..." Her words faded to nothingness. Admittedly inept at lying, Bess had talked herself into a corner. Only silence could save her now.

So, it was an affair of the heart. The queen smiled to herself. It would do Griffith no harm to worry a bit about this young woman, whose love he obviously took so for granted. The queen nodded her head. Permission was granted, and Bess's secret was safe. And Catherine felt sure that Bess would soon return to court, for if her memory had not failed her, Mary of Essex would come to join the queen's ladies for her period of service in midsummer.

Bess arrived at the Essex estates in a modicum of style; the queen had provided generously for the one who had saved her husband's life.

Mary was delighted at Bess's arrival, and the two women spent many hours reminiscing.

"I must say I was surprised when I learned that you had accepted a position among the queen's ladies. You always seemed more comfortable in a more quiet, circumspect situation," Mary observed as they walked in the gardens.

"It is still so with me. Only Lord Beaufort keeps me in the hustle and bustle of the court."

"And where is Griffith?" Mary wanted to know.

"With the king. Griffith hopes to convince Henry to nullify his betrothal so that we can be married."

Mary's eyes widened. "It is possible. The king was very grateful when you saved his life. It was then you should have asked your boon, rather than waiting until our good king has forgotten how close he came to being taken. Why, your bravery was the talk of the land. I do not see how Henry can possibly deny you anything within reason."

"It is only that he seems to think my request somewhat unreasonable," Bess admitted as she took the fallen petals of rose and crushed them in her hands.

"And Lord Beaufort? What are his feelings?"

"Much the same as my own," Bess assured her. "He urges Henry to give us permission to wed."

Mary reached the end of the path, and was about to start back toward the castle when she turned to her friend. "Court gossip does not quickly reach us here. If the king rescinds his command that Griffith wed the child from Calais, we will be the last to know. That is why I look forward to serving my time at court. Come back with me, Bess. We shall have such fun together."

Bess caught her breath. She could do nothing but tell Mary and swear her to silence. "I cannot go back now."

"But why?" Mary asked. "You were sent here with all honor and comfort. The queen cannot be angry with you."

"She would quickly make her anger known if I returned to serve her." Bess drew in a deep breath. "You see, Mary, I am with child, Griffith's child, and should the queen learn of my condition before we can be married, she would hold me in disgrace."

Mary gasped and put her hand over her mouth. "You sly minx! All this idle chatter about Griffith casually trying to get the king's permission to wed with you, when actually you are in desperate straits." She put her arms around the girl in a quick embrace. "Do not fear. We will think of something. And in the meantime, you will stay here at Essex, while I go to court and find out what is happening."

Bess's eyes went to the huge castle. "I have chosen a poor time to visit," she said.

"Not a bit of it," Mary assured her. "And before I leave, I will see you installed in the dower house, with your own servants. The house is not large, and it sits some distance from the castle along the east end of the estate. Some years ago, it was the main road into the estate. That is why I want you to stay there."

Bess looked at her friend askance.

"The midwife lives in the old gatehouse, only a short distance away. She will be there, should you need her." Again Mary gave her friend a little hug. "You see? We will have you all taken care of while you wait for your Griffith to come."

Bess smiled in relief at her friend's idea. So pleased was she with the idea of having a house of her own that she did not see the worry in Mary's eyes, for an unmarried, pregnant woman was easy prey to a man's whims.

But surely Bess knew Griffith far better than did Mary. Still, she remembered the concern her parents had known when the Beaufort showed interest in Bess when first they met at Pembroke. And Mary had no recollection of any marriage being mentioned between Griffith and Bess at that time. Indeed, it was another union, far less honorable that had set Mary's father and mother wondering as to Bess's probable fate.

But the die was cast, and Bess would be subject to her fate, with or without Griffith as her husband. Mary could do no more than try to keep her friend as safe and happy as possible.

Upon their return to the castle, Mary proceeded to give orders to open the dower house. She told the servants that Bess was married and had come to Essex to live while she awaited her husband's return.

"Well, most of it is true," Mary said with a giggle when Bess upbraided her for fibbing. "I never thought to be a nun, so a tiny lie, well placed, and for the good of another, will be of small consequence when my sins are totalled up before God. Besides, what harm can a little misinformation cause?"

Bess acquiesced to her friend's persuasion. "What harm, indeed?"

Chapter Eleven

While Bess's situation was not common knowledge, it did not take long for the servants to gossip a bit about the lovely young woman who awaited her husband while comfortably ensconced in her own private lodgings on the Essex estates. Bess's mother heard them quite by accident.

Edwina, who still held her position as a seamstress at Kew, was buying needles from a tinker who mentioned the apparent good fortune of the Lady Bess.

"The girl must have married wealthily," the tinker said, warming to his theme as he became aware of the woman's interest. "It is said she saved the king's life and was rewarded with a large sum of gold. She is living in the dower house at Essex, so there must be some truth to it."

Edwina's eyes narrowed. So her daughter had done well for herself. The last news she had had of the girl was when Bess returned to the convent, intent on taking the holy vows; still, tinkers were renowned for knowing all the gossip, and this man was particularly knowledgeable.

She planned to share the news with Sir Morris the moment he returned, but, to her surprise, he greeted her with more affection than he had shown since their first days together, and his words sent all thought of Bess fleeing from her mind.

"My love, I've decided it's time we should wed!" he announced.

Edwina had long since given up hope he would ask for her hand. In truth, Morris visited her at Kew only when he was in need of money, to take the paltry funds she managed to ferret away from her sewing. But now that he had asked for her hand, Edwina was determined to do everything in her power to see that he had no time to change his mind.

"When?" she asked, as quickly as she was able to find her voice.

"As soon as possible. I believe I can secure a new position, one of great importance. I want you by my side, as my wife." He carefully concealed the fact that he had heard Bess was installed at Essex, and was apparently well able to support both of them. It was to his advantage to marry Edwina now, for what doting husband could possibly turn out his bride's mother?

Edwina, overcome by the suddenness of his proposal, completely forgot the news about her daughter. It wasn't until the vows had been said and they had left Kew that Edwina began to understand something of her husband's motives.

"And now I have another surprise for you," he told her as they rode through the green countryside. "We are going to visit your daughter, Bess. I know how you have longed to see her again."

Edwina was confused. She had never expressed any desire to see Bess. Indeed, it was just the opposite. Edwina hoped never to see her lovely daughter again, for rumors of Sir Morris's interest in Bess had run rampant after his encounter with the girl at Pembroke some years before. Had he heard the rumors too? Quickly she strove to make up for her lapse. "I had completely forgot, in all the excitement. I heard Bess was married and living at Essex."

"Know you the name of the husband?"

"No... but he must be a close member of the family, for I was told she was installed in the dower house."

Sir Morris allowed himself a cunning smile. "All the more reason for us to visit her and wish her well in her new estate. With a house at her disposal, there should be no question of accommodations that befit her parents."

They grinned at one another as they continued their journey, certain all would work to their advantage.

Through the long days of summer, Bess awaited the all-important message from Griffith. Certainly it would come soon. She had already received several messages declaring his love and devotion, as well as those bright missives from Lady Mary, who had adapted to the bustle of the court and was gleaning every bit of gossip that came her way. Henry seemed to be doing nothing more than enjoying himself with hunting and jousting, both in England and across the channel in Calais.

As far as the king and his entourage were concerned, they seemed to be on nothing more exciting than a holiday, and, try as she might, even Lady Mary could learn nothing more.

The queen had let it be known that she was somewhat piqued when Bess did not return to court with Mary. Nonetheless, she eventually forgave Bess, who had spent a great deal of her life sequestered in a convent and undoubtedly found the turbulence of court life exhausting.

Meanwhile, Bess scanned the horizon for word from Griffith. Word that would free her from the doubts and fears that had become her constant companions.

How she longed to hear his voice and feel his strong arms around her. How she longed to place his hand against her belly as their child quickened within. Longed to let him know the strength of their son, and it must be a son. Griffith's heir. Their link to immortality.

Her every day was spent watching for the long-awaited arrival of her love, and her nights were spent dreaming of the moment when they would be together again.

The arrival of Edwina and Sir Morris was hardly met with fanfare. The castle was the hub of the area, and was bustling with activity. They were hustled from the courtyard and given scant directions to the dower house by the chief steward.

"Bess!" Edwina called as she spied her daughter.

For a moment, Bess could do nothing but stare in shock, but then she moved toward them. She managed to embrace her mother, noting her brassy hair and heavily powdered face, but Bess could not force herself to embrace Sir Morris. His scowl was her reward as she moved away from his outstretched hands.

"You must be polite to Sir Morris, Bess. He is your stepfather. We are married."

"You have my best wishes, Mother," Bess said, without enthusiasm. She winced as Sir Morris embraced her, managing to squeeze her tender breast without her mother's observing.

He smiled in satisfaction at the brief moment when her fullness filled his hand. This was surely not the red-eyed waif he had taken from the convent, nor even the slim white body that often haunted his memory. This was a woman, lush and ripe. He envied her husband, and hoped the man would not be in residence, for Sir Morris knew he would not be able to keep his hands or eyes off the girl, and there would be many chances to fondle her, with them living in such close proximity.

As soon as they were settled, Sir Morris announced he would take himself to the castle, where a large party of some import had arrived. It was during his absence that Edwina found time to talk to Bess.

"I am so happy for you, daughter," Edwina said as she ran her finger across the carved rosewood back of a little chair. "To see you here, with all that any woman could ask of life is the culmination of my dreams for you. Every mother hopes that her child will know such riches and such happiness, as you no doubt realize."

Bess looked at her mother in surprise. It was true that the women did not know each other, but Bess had hoped for one brief moment that her mother would have some hidden intuition that would bridge the gap of misunderstanding between them. But it was not to be.

Edwina had no idea of the path that had led Bess to her present circumstances. She knew only that Sir Morris had ordered her to establish a good rapport with Bess, and she hastened to do so.

"I cannot help but think that you have been wiser than myself. I could not free myself from Sir Morris. His hold over me has sent me to the heights of ecstasy, as well as the depths of hell. I have lost everything your father left me, but all the passion a woman could ever hope for I have found in Morris's arms."

Edwina saw the look on her daughter's face, and hastily tried to explain. "It is not as though your dear father did not love me. He did, Bess. Truly he did. It was just that he knew nothing of the art of love. He had no idea how to please a woman.

"He seemed to think the culmination of the act itself must hold some magical spell, and nothing more was necessary. I can tell you that even as a bride I was sorely disappointed, and thought there must surely be something more than I had been given. But it was only after your dear father's death that I learned the truth of what I had missed.

"Sir Morris introduced me to the arts of love while you were away in the convent. Truly, that was one of the reasons I decided you need not stay."

Edwina shook her head, dabbed her eyes with the tip of her sleeve and began to pace back and forth across the floor.

"I could not leave you there. Not my daughter, my very own child. Not after I had learned that there was more to life than caring for your home and bearing children without screaming the house down.

"You must believe me when I tell you that it was not only Morris's demands that we must have more money that led me to take you from the convent so many years ago. I felt that you had the right to know love, passion. And from the look of your face and the shape of your body, I believe it to be so."

The woman's words did not ring true, and Bess did not believe her for a minute. It was obvious Edwina wanted something, and would go to any lengths to get it.

"You have the king's ear, from what I have been told," Edwina gushed. "Henry himself has given you a gift of gold and seen that you are married wealthily, so to live in comfort, as a reward for saving his life. Is that not so?"

Something in her daughter's demeanor made Edwina lean forward, as though to pull forth the answer she so desperately wanted to hear. But Bess's words shattered her hopes.

"It is not so, Mother," Bess told her. "The king has yet to grant me a farthing for saving his life. This house in which I am living is given through the charity of my friend, Lady Mary, and the child I bear is at this time destined to be a bastard, for I am not wed to his father, or any other man."

"Surely not!" Edwina was on her feet. "You jest with me," she said. "You think your joke very funny, but I am not fooled. I know the fate of ladies-in-waiting who do not conform to the strict moral code of the queen of England."

"Nonetheless, what I tell you is the truth. I live here through the goodwill of Lady Mary, and have no way of knowing what the will of the king will be regarding my condition."

Edwina pressed her hand to her lips. "How could you?" she demanded. "I left a fine position as seamstress to the ladies of Kew to come here. I will never be able to go back and hope to assume the same prestige that I knew when I left. I will be lucky if I don't have to start all over again!" Edwina dropped onto the chair and buried her face in her hands.

"You were not asked to come here, Mother. Pray do not forget that there was never any time I sought to deceive you. Instead, it is you who have deceived yourself. About me, and about Sir Morris, as well."

Edwina drew herself to her feet. "I may have deceived myself about you, Bess, but Sir Morris would never deceive me. He loves me to distraction, and has these many years. I will not allow you to speak against him in my presence. After all, you must remember that he is my husband, and therefore your stepfather. As an unmarried woman, you are subject to his full control over you and your estates, as dictated by the laws of the land."

Edwina's dictum rendered Bess silent, for she knew without question that in her last declaration, at least, her mother was correct, and her soul was suddenly cold with fear.

Much to the exasperation of Sir Morris, the first person he saw when he reached the castle was the newly arrived Baron of Oatlands, a man to whom he owed a great deal of money.

Having been plagued by a tally of bad luck in his jousts and feats of arms, Sir Morris had taken to gambling, borrowing money and offering, instead, the promise of property he did not possess. The generous old baron had seemed an easy mark, until he investigated Sir Morris's claimed assets and found them to be nonexistent. Sir Morris had been forced to beat a hasty retreat several times to keep from facing the baron's wrath, not to mention the threat of debtor's prison should he not soon render the amount due.

"What brings you here, Sir Morris?" the baron asked bluntly as he barred the younger man's escape. "I know of no tournaments planned in this area."

Sir Morris laughed ingratiatingly. He would make Bess give him the money he owed this man, and the sooner the better. "My wife longed to see her daughter, who has her own establishment here on the estate."

Sir Morris did not add that the establishment had been a definite disappointment to both himself and Edwina. However, Bess had seemed happy enough with her lot. It was in his mind to ask some questions of the servants and find out more about his stepdaughter's position in the household, as well as her husband's prospects.

"How commendable," the baron was saying. "I, too, came searching for someone. I met a little nun on the road some months ago. She seemed quite lost, and uncertain as to how to reach her destination. I feared for her safety and lent her a map.

"The map was returned in good stead, and the messenger said it had come from the Essex estates. The short note carried apologies at having not been more prompt, but explained that she had met with an accident. I found myself concerned for the woman, and decided to stop on my way to Oatlands and inquire as to her health."

Sir Morris's eyes shifted from one group of servants to the next, trying to weed out a face that he recognized. He paid little mind to the old man's words, seeking only to leave his presence before the conversation turned to matters of money.

"I have only just arrived myself," Sir Morris admitted as he took in the size of the baron's traveling entourage with envy. "I know nothing of the household, but should I hear anything of an ailing nun, I will let you know."

Without further ado, Sir Morris made his bow and went on his way. Nun, indeed. Surely the old man was in his dotage, chasing across the countryside looking for nuns.

Unfortunately, Sir Morris was unable to learn anything about Bess's situation, other than that his stepdaughter was a close friend of Lady Mary and the two women had spent a great deal of time together prior to Mary's departure.

Somewhat piqued by his lack of success, he made his way back to the dower house. Surely Bess was not drawing on her friendship with Lady Mary in order to have a place to live. The girl would have been returned to the convent, had the king not planned to reward her with generosity, both monetary and through the marriage bed.

His mouth twisted into a sinister smile as he thought of the favors that would be his due as the husband of Bess's mother. Perhaps, through Bess's influence, Sir Morris and Edwina could hope to be appointed to service at court. Many other knights had been raised above their own estate by marriage.

But first things first, and the first thing he must do was to tell Bess that he needed money, before the baron became a bore with his demands.

He had no more than stepped into the entry hall when Edwina burst into the room.

"Bess is not married!" she cried. "And, even worse, she carries a child and refuses to name the father. I could die of humiliation!"

Sir Morris felt as though he might die, too, although humiliation had nothing to do with it.

He was filled with rage. "How could she do this to us?" he raved. "She has misled us and brought us here under false pretenses."

Edwina buried her face in her hands, overcome by tears. Sir Morris pushed her aside, his mind, his body, his whole being, suddenly possessed by the thought of Bess. Lovely, delectable, wanton Bess. No longer a virgin child, to be guarded by the lords of the nobility, but a fallen woman. Nay! More than that. A fallen nun who had gone back on her vows and forsaken her God.

Luck had, indeed, played into his hands. The girl, delectable as a ripe peach, had suddenly fallen into his grasp. Living in the same house with her, with only his wife to deceive, it would be but a short time before he found his way to Bess's bed, and who could say him nay? Was she not admittedly a fallen woman? He chuckled licentiously, rubbing his hands in anticipation.

"How can you look so pleased with this state of affairs?" Edwina demanded. "This is ruin! Bess is only here on Lady Mary's charity, and we are not welcome to stay."

Sir Morris grabbed his wife's bony shoulders, cruelly digging his fingers into her flesh. Truly, he had more reason to be upset than she. Had he not given up his freedom in the thought he would marry the mother of a great lady and be cared for the rest of his life? Now he was saddled with the burden of not only a wife, but her daughter and the daughter's bastard, as well.

Ah, but the daughter! To lie with her was worth any sacrifice. To bend the proud Bess to his will and watch her beg him to be kind to her and her bastard child would make him very happy. He would keep Bess so busy satisfying his sexual needs that she would be too exhausted to think of any other man. And when he had his fill of her, he could peddle her lush, young body to his cohorts, playing on the fact that she had enticed lords of the realm. Errant knights and soldiers were impressed by such recommendation, and would, no doubt, pay well for her favors.

Yes, all would be well. Sir Morris's only regret was that he had been so hasty in marrying Edwina. Had he waited, he might have had the lovely Bess to wife.

Over the next days, Bess kept to her rooms as much as possible. She could not help but see Sir Morris's covetous eyes roaming over her body. He watched her constantly, causing her great discomfort.

It seemed each time he passed, Sir Morris managed to brush intimately against her, or touch her in some familiar manner. It was with relief that Bess was called upon to dine at the castle and see to the needs of the guests.

Bess recognized the Baron of Oatlands as her benefactor of the map, but held her counsel. He had asked about the condition of the little nun, and Bess had assured him that she was well and had been nicely provided for. Having attained his purpose, he seemed eager to continue on his way.

"I shall be stopping at Greenwich," he told Bess as they consumed the evening meal together in the great hall of the castle. "Should you decide you need a change of scenery, I would be honored if you would accompany me."

It had taken him but a few minutes to assess the situation between Bess and her stepfather. The baron did not like the way Sir Morris looked at this fair daughter of England. It bothered him that he must go and leave her at the man's mercy, but he had no choice, for she was not of his blood, unlike his own daughter, who had met with tragedy years ago.

The baron's daughter had possessed the same fresh loveliness that attracted men with shadowed souls. Men such as Morris of Bladacglen. She had begged him not to force her to marry the powerful lord who asked, nay, demanded her hand. But the baron had been blinded by the man's charm and soothed by the riches that would ensure his daughter a comfortable and prosperous life.

Such had not been the case. The man had been cruel and unfaithful. He had beaten his wife when she did not immediately become pregnant, and when she failed to produce a male child, he had thrown her down the stairs.

By the time the baron reached his daughter, she had been a broken, dying woman. He had taken her to Oatlands and buried her with her babe. His grief and guilt had been unbearable: in his pride he had sacrificed her young life.

He had vowed before God that he would never allow any man to so abuse a woman again, but now, faced with a similar situation, he was powerless—the laws of the land were against him.

His only recourse was to offer to take Bess away. An offer that she quickly, albeit somewhat sadly, refused.

"Thank you, I shall stay here." Bess said hesitantly. She, too, dreaded the day when Sir Morris's lust would unleash itself in her direction.

"Would that I could stay," the Baron of Oatlands remarked from across the table. His smile was kind, and his manner gallant, in a rough way. Only his body—though still strong enough for him to don armor and participate in battle—showed the weight of his many years.

Bess smiled at him. He had been kind to her, and they had passed several pleasant hours in quiet conversation. He reminded Bess of the father she missed so sorely.

As the servants cleared the tables away, Bess sought a corner where she could observe the room without exposing her person to Sir Morris. Before she could gain her goal, he was upon her, running his fingers across the nape of her neck.

"Ah, my sweet Bess, did you enjoy your dinner?"

"Everything is more tasty when you are away from me," she responded, pulling away from his touch.

"You needn't play the innocent virgin with me. I know you carry some man's bastard, and I can imagine, oh, I can just imagine, the delights he knew in getting you that way." His eyes crept insidiously over her body. His voice became strained and hoarse as his gaze rested on her high, firm breasts. "I can remember the delights, dear Bess. Oh, yes, I can remember only too well."

"Apparently your memory does not serve you as well as you would have me believe," Bess returned. "The woman and the body you remember no longer exist. As you have so succinctly pointed out, I am large with child."

"The child is of no concern, and can be eliminated one way or another, if it interferes with my pleasures." Sir Morris smiled wickedly as he saw her reaction to his threat against the welfare of her babe.

There was true fear in Bess's eyes now. He saw it, and relished it. It excited him as greatly as the lush body he intended to possess, no matter the cost. And soon, it must be soon or he would go mad with desire.

He would have reached for her then—the urge to touch her was more than he could stand—but a voice behind him stopped his action.

"May I have the honor of walking with you in the garden, my dear?" the baron asked, having seen the alarm on Bess's face. "They tell me the roses are especially beautiful this time of year."

Bess nodded in agreement and took the older man's arm.

Sir Morris would not be put aside so easily. "And I shall go along, to keep you both company."

The baron drew Bess nearer himself. "I do not remember requesting your company, sir knight!" he said as he escorted Bess across the floor.

"The man is a clod and a lecher!" the baron growled as they made their way out the door. "Why do you let him near you?"

"He is my stepfather. My mother has only recently married him. They are staying in the dowerhouse with me." Bess drew a shuddering breath. "I live in constant fear!"

The older man patted her shoulder in a clumsy effort to comfort. "Have you no one who would protect you?" he asked, unable to believe a woman so young and beautiful would be without male protection.

The look on her face told him more than any words might have imparted. For a moment, she saw Griffith clearly, as though he were there in the garden. He would have protected her—aye, to the death—but he was not here.

She longed for his nearness. The touch of his hand. Even when she was in the convent, she had known she had only to send word and he would come to her aid. Instead, it was she who had gone to Griffith's aid. Her effort had cost her everything, including her good name, her self-respect and her heart, for Griffith held her heart for eternity.

She lifted her eyes, soft and tear-filled, to the baron. He caught his breath. Never had he seen anything more beautiful than this girl, who silently pleaded for his help and understanding. He took her hand and led her back toward the terrace. Without realizing it, Bess had acquired a champion.

The time at Calais stretched long through the days. Negotiations and diplomatic innuendos skimmed through the air at all hours of the day or night. Henry scowled and fumed. He was tired of the whole ploy and thought Griffith should see that nullifying the betrothal was ill-advised and should be forgotten.

But Griffith did not forget. Daily he reminded Henry of his promise, not only to himself, but to Bess, as well.

"She did only what any other loyal subject would gladly do for their king," Henry declared when negotiations had broken down once again.

"She did far more than any woman would have thought of doing, as well you know. And, as her sovereign, you promised to grant her wish. She took you at your word, and now you seek to find a way to make her change her mind. I tell you, it is too late. Her mind cannot be changed." Griffith's arguments became more forceful as the days passed and the time element came into full swing.

Henry did not answer his cousin. Instead, he looked out over the garden where the tiny child who was Griffith's betrothed played among the fountains.

"Look at that!" Henry crooned. "Have you ever seen a lovelier creature? She will grow to be a great beauty, mark my words. Why can you not wait for her? In the meantime, you are free to love your Bess without interference, and, for that matter, the royal approval. Even the queen dares not gainsay me in this."

"I want children of my own, not to raise one that I must later wed. The daughter of Calais is, indeed, beautiful. But she is a babe. I want a wife. I want sons and daughters, and I will wait no longer. With or without your permission, I shall marry Bess."

"You would defy me?"

"I have put your wishes and your throne above everything in my life, Your Grace. Now it is time for me to put someone before you."

Henry did not wish to lose the good graces of his cousin. The man was a powerful lord and a good ally. He was loyal and intelligent. There was also the fact that, as long as Griffith was a king's man and sworn to Henry's cause, there would be little chance of his conspiring against his king, as was the wont of those carrying even a drop of royal blood in their veins.

Henry heaved a deep sigh. "The marshal will demand a great deal of money to salve his wounded pride," he reminded Griffith. "It is not money the crown is prepared to pay. It must come from your coffers. Are you sure Bess is worth so much to you?"

But Griffith did not flinch over the loss of the child's dower, or the fine against his estate. "It shall be as you wish, Your Grace," he agreed. "As long as I can take Bess to wife as soon as we set foot in England."

"It may be somewhat longer than you hope. The marshal comes from a great and powerful family. To spurn his child is to impugn his honor. It must not seem as though you have cast the child aside because you cannot wait to wed with another woman. To do so would mean destruction of all that I have planned so carefully." Henry paused and stroked his chin, deep in thought.

"I want your word that you will not so much as see Mistress Bess until I specifically deem it safe to do so. Do you understand?"

Griffith opened his mouth to protest, but Henry cut off his words. "After you make my plan known to her, she must not expect word from you, and under no conditions will she be allowed to communicate with you. You will not see her. You will not speak of her. And you will not make love to her, for I will not allow my carefully laid plans to be destroyed by your insistent amours."

Henry saw that he had dealt his cousin a powerful blow, but he would not back away from his decision.

"If you agree to my terms, I will offer the marshal another prospective bridegroom for his child, pleading your age as the deciding factor."

Griffith swallowed his ire. There was no way but that of the king, and Henry was the king, and not likely to allow anyone to forget that fact.

"It shall be as you wish," Griffith agreed.

"Fine, fine," Henry said, clapping him on the back. "I will speak to the marshal after the tournament next week. He should be in a fine mood by then.

"Now, be off with you." He waved his hand toward the door. "And do not look so smug, for if all else fails in these negotiations, I shall decree that your firstborn son marry the little girl, though she be his elder."

Griffith was shocked to a sudden standstill, and he stared at his king, temporarily unable to speak. Did the all-knowing Henry guess Bess's condition? But the king's next words eased Griffith's mind.

"Granted, it will be a while before Bess has a child," Henry mused, "but wedding a woman somewhat older than the husband is not untried. Catherine is some years my senior, and look how happy we are."

Griffith dared not meet his cousin's eyes, lest the king read the truth therein. Henry was no longer happy with his Spanish princess, and it took very little to see that this was so.

Carefully keeping his eyes lowered, Griffith bowed out of his king's presence. Henry had said he would do nothing until after the tournament. That gave Griffith the better part of the week to let Bess know of the king's decree.

He would go to her. He would tell her and make her understand the political ramifications that faced both them and their monarch. And for one more time he would make love to her. Should Henry learn of his tryst and object, he would insist that he had thought he had permission to apprise Bess of her king's decision during the week of grace.

With a song of love in his heart, and no thought in his head save that of Bess, Griffith went to gather what he would need for his journey.

Chapter Twelve

There was only one way the baron could devise to protect Bess, and that was to rid her of the presence of Sir Morris. He decided to put off his departure until he was certain she was safe from her lecherous stepfather.

His first act was to seek out Sir Morris and demand payment of his debt.

"I have waited a goodly amount of time for you to pay me the monies you owe me," he reminded the knight. "If you will not honor your obligation, I will see you tortured until you pay."

Sir Morris paled visibly at the man's thinly veiled threat.

"I will see what I can do, my lord," Sir Morris told him, hedging, "but surely you can see that I have many responsibilities to attend to at this time, and..."

"I see that you are lusting after your stepdaughter rather than going out and trying to earn your keep as a mercenary knight." The baron's gaze never faltered, and Sir Morris flinched, realizing that the man would, indeed, carry out his threat. "If you refuse to pay what you owe, I must take matters into my own hands."

"I'm sure something can be worked out," Sir Morris said as he backed away from the baron. "I'll talk to you about it on the morrow." With that, he bolted and almost ran from the man's presence, all but tripping over a young squire, who fell back in nimble confusion.

"Are you hurt?" the baron asked as he approached the boy.

"No, my lord," the lad answered.

"Have you business at Essex?" the baron inquired.

"I come with a message for Mistress Bess. Know you where she might be found?"

The baron hesitated, appraising the boy before he decided to answer. "You will find her walking in the garden," he replied, having decided the boy had passed his inspection. The baron was about to ask whom the lad served, but he sped away with the agility of youth and the baron was left alone with his thoughts.

"We must leave immediately," Sir Morris announced as he approached Edwina. "With luck, we may be able to put you back into service at Kew, although I doubt not that you will be forced to start as an apprentice."

He pitilessly ignored her little sob as she thought of the endless nights she must again spend sewing in the candlelight as she had done when first she had taken the position. She wondered if she would be able to achieve the fine work that had held her in such good stead during the past years. She was older now, and her eyes did not function as clearly as they had in the past.

"Oh, Morris, must it be so? Can we not stay here a while longer? It is so pleasant here."

"You'll not find it pleasant in debtor's prison," he snarled, "and that is where we'll both find ourselves, if the Baron of Oatlands has his way."

"That nice old man?" Edwina asked in surprise. "Why ever would he want to harm us?"

"That nice old man loaned me several hundred pounds. Money that I have never been able to repay. Now he demands his payment, and at once."

"But why did we stay, after you knew he was here?" Edwina asked, well aware of the times they had been forced to leave rather abruptly due to her husband's many debts.

"I thought your daughter's windfall would hold us in good stead. I had planned on asking her husband for the money I needed, but alas, there is no husband and there is no money."

"Perhaps if Bess asked the baron he would give you a bit more time," Edwina suggested. "The man is quite attracted to her, as anyone can see."

In his heated pursuit of Bess, Sir Morris had given no thought to the baron's interest in his stepdaughter. A thought took seed in his devious mind. It was worth exploring, for it could be the answer to all his problems.

Already besotted with Bess's charms, the baron might be coaxed into accepting the girl without a dower, freeing Sir Morris from his debt at the same time.

It was worth a chance, Sir Morris calculated. Definitely worth a chance. If all else failed, he would take Edwina and go. Perhaps he would even take Bess. If the baron was not around to champion her, there would be no one to say him nay in his plans for his stepdaughter.

"Pack our things and be ready to leave on the morrow," he ordered Edwina. "If my plan does not come to fruition, we will be forced to leave in all haste."

"But where are we going?" Edwina questioned timidly, afraid that he would leave her behind.

"Be it to heaven or to hell, we shall not go alone." He laughed aloud at his private joke, and laughed even louder at the look of confusion on his wife's face. What might seem like heaven to Sir Morris would undoubtedly be a living hell to Bess—and to Edwina, for that matter. The thought of playing a reluctant daughter against a jealous mother made him laugh harder.

"One way or the other, I intend to win at this game, and I care little who is hurt in the play," he boasted as he started toward the room they shared, with Edwina scurrying behind him. "Tomorrow morning I will settle a debt for good and all," he said. "Just be ready to leave, and have your daughter ready to leave also, else she will travel with what she wears on her back."

Bess felt her heart lodge in her throat when she saw Griffith's squire hurrying toward her.

The boy dropped to one knee and held out a roll of parchment. Bess took it from him and broke the seal, her fingers shaking with anticipation.

"Where is he?" she asked. "Why hasn't he come to me direct?"

"He must keep his presence a secret," the lad answered. "It is worth his life, and yours most like, to be discovered together."

"But we have been together these many months," Bess protested, thinking the squire had lost his wits. "Why should we hide now?"

"By order of the king," the boy said softly. "Please, m'lady, come with me and ask no more questions, for Lord Beaufort can answer them far better than I."

With that, he took her hand and led her through the back of the garden, where they disappeared into the forest.

The squire took Bess along a little-used path that led to the ruins of a chapel. She stopped and looked about, expecting Griffith to appear. When he did not, she looked at the lad askance. He smiled at her unspoken question and gave a shrill whistle before disappearing along the path whence they had come.

Somewhat bewildered, Bess was about to follow him and demand an explanation when a figure emerged from the shadows. With a little gasp, she ran to Griffith's arms.

Lost in the wonder of his embrace, Bess all but forgot her questions. How could life hold anything other than love and beauty when they were together? Their minds, hearts and bodies joined in all-consuming love.

At first, there was no time for words. Their lips met and parted in hungry kisses that would not be denied. And once their arms had had their fill of holding tight the throbbing bodies, their hands began a search through layers of clothing, desperate to touch the burning flesh beneath.

Griffith lifted Bess in his arms and took her within the fallen walls, to a grotto where he laid her on a bed of sweet-scented grasses.

Her ripe beauty spilled into his eager hands as he removed her clothing, laying bare her pink-and-white loveliness beneath his adoring gaze. His hands cupped her cheeks as he kissed her eyes and her lips before burying his face in the lush splendor of her breasts.

She moaned in pleasure as he touched and teased with his lips and hands, tantalizing each budding nipple with his fingers and tongue before drawing it into the moist warmth of his mouth.

Her hands caught and held, lost in the thick golden mane of his hair, as her body arched in response to his stimulation. Then her nimble hands fought to remove the clothing from his body.

Laughing at her efforts, he freed himself of his remaining garments, and she reached out to grasp his manhood and draw him deep, deep into the silken folds of her body. The boldness of her action dispelled all ability to think from

Griffith's mind as he lost himself in the tunnel of passion that rendered him completely and irrevocably hers, for all eternity.

When the storm of passion had passed, he lay beside her, suddenly aware of the changes in her body. Gently, tentatively, his hand caressed the small mound that comprised her belly.

"I did not think," he said apologetically. "In my need, I forgot about the babe. Think you we did him harm?"

"There can be no harm for our child from our love," Bess assured him. "Like myself, he welcomes his father's touch."

With something akin to wonder, Griffith's lips touched every inch of flesh covering her stomach. "I thought you would be much larger than this," he murmured as his kisses moved across her breasts and to her waiting lips.

"I hold our babe tight against my heart," she told him with a smile.

"As I hold you in mine," he whispered against her breast. "But I would rather hold you in my arms, as I do now."

"And so shall it be," she assured him. "We could be married here at Essex. The priest is discreet, and asks few questions."

Griffith raised himself on his elbow and shook his head. "Bess, I'm sorry, but I did not come to wed with you today. I came in defiance of the king's order, and should he learn of our tryst, there will be the very devil to pay."

"But what has happened? I thought he had all but agreed to our proposal."

"'All but agreed,' indeed," Griffith said. "It seems the marshal of Calais feels his family honor is impugned by a broken betrothal, and hints that he will be forced to sever relations with the king's emissaries if his daughter is passed over for another woman. Therefore, Henry has decreed that there shall be no hint of my intent to marry you until the marshal is satisfied with the arrangement.''

"But, Griffith, although my body does not overflow with the abundance of our child, it is still only a matter of weeks before the babe will be born. Surely there is something you can do to facilitate this matter."

He looked into her tear-filled eyes, unwilling to hurt her more, and unable to keep the truth from her.

"The king has decreed that until the betrothal is officially nullified we must not, under any circumstances, have any contact with each other. To disobey is to lose the king's favor, and any hope we have of becoming man and wife."

Bess gave a little sob. "Oh, but my love, your messages held me firm against my loneliness. How will I survive these last weeks without them?"

He cradled her in his arms, rocking her as though *she* were the babe. "We have each other at this moment, and the memories of the love we share in these hours must suffice until we win the right to be together forever."

Her arms crept about his chest as his questing kisses followed the line of her face and moved down her neck, but Bess's mind was in turmoil. With the king's order threatening their very lives together, Bess dared not tell Griffith that Sir Morris was in residence at Essex. For Griffith would never leave her alone in the man's company, and should he confront the evil knight, there would most surely be a fight that would reach the ears of the king.

With a little sigh, Bess lay back in Griffith's arms, allowing his kisses to run the length of her body. She resolved to live this night of love to the fullest, and not reveal the depth of her fears. Somehow she would find a way to handle Sir Morris herself.

* * *

Assured in his own mind that Sir Morris would be forced to leave Essex, the baron was making ready to return to his own estates when the knight approached with his offer of a way to pay off his debt. It took the baron but little time to squelch Sir Morris's hopes.

"I have made it known that I do not want another wife. At my age, a wife would do me little good except to cuckold me." It was the truth, and the baron had no trouble admitting it.

But desperation put words in the mouth of Sir Morris as he realized his mistake and saw opportunity slipping away. "I said nothing of a wife," he contended, congratulating himself on his cunning. "It is a child I offer. A child conceived of handsome parents with good lineage. A child of which you could be proud. It is well-known that you long for an heir for your estates."

The baron gave Sir Morris a sharp look, but said nothing.

"If I could produce a child of good lineage to be raised as your heir, would you cancel my debt and give me a stipend in token of your gratitude?"

It was true, the baron had no heir to his estates. When he died, all his lands and holdings would revert to the crown. His eyes narrowed. "I want no child of your blood, Sir Morris."

"The child is not mine," Sir Morris assured him. Would that it were, he thought, for he would claim the little bastard, had he the memories of its conception. "The woman was at court for a time, and has been seduced by one of the nobles. The child promises to be handsome and intelligent, except perhaps in matters of the heart." He chuckled at his own joke, and was pleased to see the baron barely suppressed a smile.

"Very well, Sir Morris, if the child pleases me and his lineage meets with my approval, I will name him my ward and dismiss your debt. When may I see this little paragon?"

Sir Morris shifted nervously. "It will be several weeks, my lord," he admitted. "The babe has yet to be born."

The baron mounted his horse. It occurred to him that Sir Morris's stepdaughter looked to be with child, but it was beyond belief that the man would barter away his wife's grandchild. Besides, Bess would never agree to such a thing, of that he was certain. He was about to send the man packing, but something held him back. "Bring the mother to Oatlands. I would want the child to be born on my lands, in any case." He looked down on the face of the knight. He did not like the man, and definitely did not trust him. It was the distrust that caused him to add, "It would behoove you to make certain both woman and child are in good condition when they arrive. With that thought in mind, I will leave my coach at your disposal. And, Morris, transport the woman in it. Do not gamble it away."

Without a backward look, the Baron of Oatlands galloped through the castle gates, while Sir Morris mused that transporting Bess to Oatlands would be gamble enough.

Bess slipped into the house as the first glow of dawn touched the sky. Her body felt as rosy and glowing as sun's first light, and she hugged herself as she changed her clothing and made ready to face the day. Although she knew that the next few weeks would be difficult, her body was still caught up in the euphoria of remembered love.

It occured to her that the baron would have returned to his beloved Oatlands by now, and she was saddened that she had not been able to bid him farewell. How she wished Sir Morris had gone away, too.

As if in answer to her prayer, there was a timid knock at the door, and she opened it to see Edwina's anxious face.

"Good morrow, daughter," the woman said. "I came to tell you that Sir Morris and I have decided to return to Kew, and want you to join us in our journey."

Bess turned away quickly to hide the unseemly joy on her face when she heard her mother's words. With a lightened heart, she composed herself and swiftly but firmly refused her mother's offer.

Sir Morris returned to the dower house to find Edwina's bags stacked neatly in the hall and the woman beside them wringing her hands.

"She will not come, Morris," Edwina whined. "I have begged, pleaded, cajoled, and she will not pack so much as a tippet."

Sir Morris cast a disparaging glance toward his wife and started up the stairs. "She will come. Have the footmen load the baggage, then send them away."

He did not bother to knock on the door, and was disappointed to find Bess fully dressed and standing in the center of her room. "Your mother says you do not wish to join us on our travels."

"That is correct," Bess said shortly.

"Very well, then. The choice is yours. We simply wanted you to know that you were welcome." Morris did not move nearer. He stayed by the door, leaving it wide open. "The least you can do as a good and dutiful daughter is to come say farewell to your mother, and offer us a stirrup cup, as befits a good hostess."

A look of uncertainty passed over Bess's face. What the man said was true. It was common courtesy to offer a stirrup cup to guests. "Very well," she said, and swept past him and out into the hall.

Sir Morris did not try to touch her or impede her progress as she went to the sideboard and poured wine into the heavy cup. Bess handed the cup first to her mother, and watched with a feeling bordering disgust as the woman drank greedily before reluctantly passing the cup to her husband.

Sir Morris scarcely touched the wine and took a small scrap of cloth from his sleeve with which he made the motions of wiping the rim as he slipped a powder into the cup before passing it to Bess. "Surely you will join us in a toast of farewell and finish the last of the cup. There are but a few drops."

Bess saw that what he said was true. Relief at their departure took hold of her, and she lifted the vessel to her lips and finished the dregs. They tasted somewhat bitter, but that was to be expected, as far as Bess was concerned, since they had touched Sir Morris's lips.

Giddy with relief, Bess walked with them to their carriage. In a matter of minutes, Edwina and Sir Morris would be gone from her life. It couldn't be soon enough, although she made a silent prayer that she would be forgiven for feeling such euphoria at being rid of her mother.

Bess staggered dizzily as Edwina released her from a cloying embrace. "I hope all goes well with you, daughter," Edwina said in maternal tones. "If you need us, you have only to send a messenger." She squinted her eyes against the sun. "You should go back into the house. You look a bit pale."

As Edwina spoke, Bess reached out to steady herself. With one smooth movement, Sir Morris swept her into the coach and ordered the coachman to drive through the back gate of the estate. "Keep her quiet," he ordered Edwina.

Bess dropped into a nether world of darkness and drugged wine.

* * *

Bess was aware only of constant jolting, and liquids, all containing the same bitter taste, when she asked for food or drink.

It seemed like a lifetime before they came to a prolonged halt and Bess heard a voice that gave her hope. It was the voice of her friend, the Baron of Oatlands.

He would help her. The baron would save her from Sir Morris and his plot, whatever it might be. She tried to pull herself into an upright position as the door of the coach opened and she found herself looking at the baron with haunted eyes.

His face registered shock and dismay at her appearance, and her presence. "Is this the woman whose babe you have promised me?" he demanded. "Is this the woman whose child you want me to take?" Cold fury filled him as he realized Bess was hardly able to focus her eyes. But even in her half-conscious condition, his words registered, and she made to get out of the coach.

"Not my baby!" Bess cried. "I will not let you take my baby."

She tried to brush past the baron, but he caught her as she stumbled through the door and held her fast.

"There, there," he crooned. "No one will take your baby from you. Not while there is breath in my body." With that, he half carried her from the portico and into the entry hall.

From the start, the older man had been sorely troubled by Bess's plight, but due to his advanced age, he had given little thought to taking another wife. Now he must make a decision, and make it quickly, for he knew he had met an adversary in Sir Morris, who was as devious as he was ruthless. And while the Baron's body had slowed somewhat with the weight of years, his mind worked as quickly as ever. He immediately began adding demands to the settlement of the debt, to keep Sir Morris off balance. Demands that separated Bess from the clutches of her stepfather.

Sir Morris was hard put to hide his frustration. While it was true he had been unable to get away from Edwina long enough to seduce her daughter, he had made elaborate plans to do so. He cursed himself for not tossing his wife from the coach and taking the daughter while she was drugged and unable to oppose his carnal appetites. Now the baron's offer to take Bess, without a dower, as his wife, settling lands and monies on her and even giving a stipend to Sir Morris and Edwina, was more than his greedy soul could resist. He could not turn down such an offer, regardless of his base desires.

He would force the girl to agree to marry the old man and make her bastard child the baron's legitimate heir.

"Then we have a bargain!" the baron said as Sir Morris forced his mind back to the matter at hand.

Sir Morris signed the betrothal agreement, as did the prospective bridegroom. "Bring the girl here to me this afternoon, and I will present her with the betrothal ring and settle the lands upon her, as agreed."

Sir Morris licked his lips. "And the stipend you specified."

"It will be waiting," the baron assured him, hardly able to keep the smile from his lips. "Provided Bess remains untouched by yourself," he reiterated.

Sir Morris was so consumed with greed, he didn't even see the path down which he was being led. The baron was hard-pressed to hide his delight. The sooner Bess was taken from her stepfather's clutches, the better for them all. It would be interesting to see how Sir Morris reacted when he found he was not to be allowed access to any of the properties settled on Bess. The man and his wife would have the small stipend, as agreed, but would receive nothing more.

It was all the crafty old soldier could do to keep from laughing aloud as he watched Sir Morris strut pompously from the room to relay the news to his stepdaughter.

Chapter Thirteen

If Sir Morris thought Bess would take her sudden betrothal in good stead, he was very wrong.

"I will not marry him!" she declared bluntly.

"Ah, but you will, lovely Bess. I have here the betrothal agreement, signed and sealed. You have only to go to him and receive the ring. Think how lucky you are, my dear. Your child will be born legitimate. The heir to the lands and titles of a baron. Your poor mother will not have to face the disgrace of having a bastard for a grandchild."

"My 'poor mother' should have no trouble with that," Bess fired back. "She seems to have an affinity for bastards. After all, she married you!"

He snatched her up and shook her until the coils of her hair fell down about her body in a silken veil.

Her head was still reeling when he pushed her back and crushed her against the wall. "Believe me, Bess, what I suggest is for your own good. The child you carry will be born the legitimate heir of the Baron of Oatlands, or it will not be born at all. For if you will not have the baron, I will force you to accommodate my carnal demands until your body expels the little bastard from sheer exhaustion. Then you will belong completely and absolutely to me, and I will use you as often and as wantonly as I please. I know sexual diversions that your highborn court dandies have never imagined."

His hand dropped into her hair, twisting into its softness. She tried to hide her fear, but he forced her to look at him.

"Eyes like yours drive a man mad. They drive all reason from his mind, and leave him a victim of raw desire," he whispered hoarsely. "You were always meant to be mine. The delights of your body, known to the fullest extent by myself. Oh, do not fear, my sweeting. At first you may cry for me to stop, as I teach you the rudiments of love, but in a short time you will forget the pain and beg me to take you, again, and again..." His voice became hoarse with building desire as he visualized how he would use her.

"You are mad!" she gasped.

"It is your beautiful, wanton body that makes me so," he countered, and he rubbed suggestively against her. "Shall I show you, sweet Bess? Shall I prove to you that you can hate and fear me and still be unable to stop me from bringing forth the response that I desire?"

She tried to pull from his grasp, but he held her fast.

"Your struggles only serve to excite me the more." He practically choked on his passion, not to mention his words, as lust vied with greed.

Bess knew nothing of the ultimatum given by the baron, and was unaware of the battle that waged in Sir Morris's avaricious soul. He wanted Bess, but he also wanted the money the baron offered, as well as to be released from the debt he owed the man. To take her now might mean his life.

"Either you wed the baron, or you bed me, as my mistress."

"My mother..."

"Your mother is a drunken sot, who even now lies snoring with her wine bottle. You can scream the house down, and she will never hear you! Once you are mine, she will cease to exist. She is old, and has outlived her usefulness.''

The black, staring eyes, the slurred words and the spittle frothing on his lips warned Bess that the man was, indeed, mad. He would rid himself of Edwina and force Bess to take her mother's place without compunction. She could barely tolerate the touch of his hands; anything more would be worse than death itself. She must free herself from his close proximity. She must have time to think, to plan, to decide which course to take before the only course left was pain and death at the hands of this cruel, merciless man.

''Which will it be, Bess?'' His hand slid down her body. ''Do not make me wait too long for your answer, or my good sense may be overridden by my desire. What matter if you know one more man before becoming the baron's wife? He will never know of our little ruse, anyway. One man, more or less, should be of no consequence to my pure little would-be nun.''

Bess jerked away and ran toward the door, but he was too fast for her. His hand grasped her shoulder, while the other delved into the front of her bodice, and they tumbled to the floor. He sighed in sheer ecstasy as his hand kneaded her tender breasts.

''I've never forgotten the feel of your skin, the scent, the taste....''

His breath came in great gasps as he nipped at her breasts, unmindful of the hurt he caused.

Realizing that she must stop him or risk the life of her unborn child, Bess agreed to his proposal. ''I will do as you ask, but only if you let me go, now! Continue, and I will tell the baron everything! He will not want a wife who has been so recently used by another man.''

She could feel Sir Morris shaking with indecision.

He wanted her! He had never wanted a woman more, and he was on the verge of taking her then and there, and the baron be damned! But he would be damned, also, for the baron would hound him to the ends of the earth for the money he owed if he did not fulfill his promise. Morris released her and stood for an agonizing minute, gazing hungrily at the rise and fall of her breasts. "I am a fool to let you go so easily. But I cannot take the chance, even for so sweet a morsel." He turned away, fighting the urgings of his frantically aroused body.

"There will be another time, sweet Bess. The baron is old, and cannot live forever, and when he dies, I will be there to give you . . . succor."

Bess sank to the bed as soon as he had left the room. Her body trembled so uncontrollably, she was hardly able to properly cover herself. Her trembling turned to sobs as she clutched at the silken coverlet.

"Griffith, Griffith . . ." she moaned to the empty room. As she had in years past, she reached unconsciously for the hollow area between her breasts where Griffith's ring had lain for so long. The emptiness there was only another reminder that he was gone and her life was empty without him. She knew the obstacles he faced, and she dared not petition him for help, or all would be lost.

Somehow, she must find a way to rid herself of Sir Morris. The baron was her best hope, but she could not marry him or lead him to believe she would do so.

She would tell him the truth. All of it, and pray that he would understand and be willing to help her, regardless of the circumstances.

Drawing herself to her feet, she went to the basin and splashed cool water on her face before sending a message with the little maid that she must speak to the baron before the betrothal.

The baron agreed to see her and sent his man to bring her to his private gardens. He watched her come toward him, shining with youth and beauty, and prayed that she would allow him to help her through her dilemma and thus free him from the guilt he felt over the suffering and death of his own daughter many years before.

"You wished to speak to me?" he asked.

The baron's voice was soft, but Bess felt threatened nonetheless. She squared her shoulders and held out her hand. "There is something I must tell you," she admitted. "And I thank you for seeing me, although I know it is against convention.

"That little worm, Sir Morris, has been beside himself trying to keep us apart until after the betrothal," the baron said, his eyes sparkling with admiration for the young woman.

Bess barely suppressed a giggle when the baron called her stepfather a worm, and looked with some semblance of hope at the situation. "It is about the betrothal I wish to speak. I cannot marry you, my lord, and a betrothal would be sinful in the eyes of the Lord."

He drew her down beside him on a bench near the sundial. "I want no misunderstanding between us, Bess. I no more desire a wife than you desire an old man for a husband. It is obvious that you have been loved, and loved well! But where is the father of your child?"

Bess gasped aloud, but did not answer his question.

"Is it that the father of your child will not, or cannot, give you his name in marriage?" he asked gently.

Bess bowed her head. "He is betrothed to another—a child—by order of the king, and has gone to petition for release from his vows. But the procedure takes longer than we had hoped. I waited each day at Essex for word that we were free to wed, and although he wrote to me often, our plan was never mentioned. Now he will not know where to find me. I must get back to Essex, else he will think I have deserted him.''

"You are in no condition to travel, my child. This trip has taken its toll on both you and your babe. We will send him a message. He will realize you have come to me in order to protect his child. You have but to give me his name, and I will see that he is apprised of the situation.''

"But why should you do this for me?" Bess asked.

The old man stared at the sundial. "Once, many years ago, I forced my daughter to marry a man she did not love. It was a political marriage, with all the trappings of wealth and social prominence. The coup of the decade, some said.''

He shook his head and wiped a tear from his eye. "He was a cruel, ambitious man. When she did not immediately become pregnant with his child, he flaunted his mistresses and brought his bastards to be raised in the castle. He came to her only to assuage his anger at her barrenness. And when, by the grace of God, she did finally carry a child to term, it was a girl.

"Some said she fell down the stairs trying to escape her husband's wrath. Others swore that he dragged her from her bed and threw her down them. Either way, she was broken and dying when I reached her and brought her home.

"I destroyed the man and his house, but it did not remedy my own sin. I cannot see another woman destroyed by a cruel, avaricious man. I will protect you from Sir Morris if you will let me, in the hope that somehow my daughter will forgive me and that God will have mercy on my soul.''

Bess bowed her head and closed her eyes as the horror of his story and the similarity of her own situation struck her.

Her hesitancy caused the old man some concern. "Bess—" his voice rang with earnestness "—I would give you my protection. Can you not give me your trust in return?"

Bess lifted her head proudly, meeting the baron's eyes. "The man is Griffith Beaufort."

The baron caught his breath. "Cousin to the king. So that's the way the wind blows. Does Sir Morris know the identity of the child's father?"

"I think not," Bess said. "I have told no one but yourself and my friend Mary. But I dare not write to him, for we are under order from the king to have no contact with each other until Griffith's betrothal is nullified."

"Thank the Lord," he said, releasing his breath. There was no telling what a man like Morris of Bladacglen would do with that information, he thought. "There will be no true betrothal, but Sir Morris must never know."

He held out his hand and helped her to her feet. "I will send your Griffith a note informing him discreetly of your whereabouts. He can come for you here as easily as at Essex, and I will know you are safe."

Bess smiled up at him. "You are more than generous, my lord."

"And you are more than beautiful. Now come, we have much to do."

The ceremony took place in the Lady Chapel. Sir Morris insisted that both he and Edwina had the right to be present, and was angered to find the ceremony had started before they arrived. They had but entered the door when the priest intoned, "Present the ring."

The baron took a ring from the small finger of his right hand and slipped it on Bess's finger. He deliberately mumbled his response for her ears alone.

"I pledge my protection to you and your child, and as token I give you the ring that belonged to my daughter, and pray that she can forgive me for my transgressions against her."

Bess touched the ring to her lips and then placed her hand in those of the baron. "I'm sure she has already given you her forgiveness and her blessing."

"Speak louder," Sir Morris called as he pushed Edwina toward the nave. "What did you say about a blessing?"

"The pledge has been made and heard by God," the priest declared. He made the sign of the cross over Bess and the baron, and closed the huge Bible somewhat abruptly before genuflecting on his way out of the chapel, not speaking to anyone, as he had been instructed to do. Although to save his soul the priest could not understand why a ceremony to pledge protection of a woman had been necessary. But such were the ways of the nobility, and who was he to argue?

Besides, after any ceremony, a goodly feast most usually followed, and he had never been one to argue with an evening of food and entertainment. He had hardly reached the castle when he realized that the baron's guests, Sir Morris and his lady, had mounted their horses and were trotting through the castle gates.

It seemed a shame that the knight and his lady would miss the feast. The priest had just started back across the courtyard to suggest to the baron that their departure might be postponed when Sir Morris looked back over his shoulder with such malevolence in his face that the little priest abandoned his endeavor. Perhaps a banquet without guests would be preferable to the presence of the surly man and his sniffling wife, who now dabbed her eyes and blew her nose as she followed in her husband's wake.

And so, my lord, I invite you to partake in the excellent hunting that abounds this season at Oatlands. Be assured you are always welcome in my home. Mistress Bess Blummer has agreed to act as hostess after surviving an unfortunate misunderstanding with her stepfather, Sir Morris of Bladacglen. She will be staying in my home until suitable arrangements can be made for her future.

Bess leaned over the baron's shoulder and giggled at his evasive wording.

"That should suffice," the baron told her. "He will know that you are well, and waiting for his return." He turned to the young messenger, who stood proudly in his new livery. "You must deliver this to Lord Griffith Beaufort, who is said to be with the king in Calais. I want no dallying along the way. The sooner the note reaches Lord Beaufort, the better it will be for all involved."

Ian, the young footman, bowed his head and pulled his forelock. The journey to Calais was long and tedious and smacked of danger. He was pleased that he had been chosen to go, and wondered at his luck, for this was his first assignment of such magnitude. He was anxious to leave as quickly as possible. Despite his master's warning, he planned to stop at the Boar's Head Inn, where the maid was exceptionally well endowed, and while she had thus far given him but little notice, with his new livery and the coin in his pocket she could not help but be impressed.

If all went well, Ian would most likely be able to spend even more time with the girl on the way back. The thought brought a smile to his face, and it was with real anticipation that he mounted his horse.

Ian reached the Boar's Head on the second day. To his delight, the maid had few duties to perform. Indeed, the only guests were a knight and his lady.

"Oh, la, dear Ian," Gert said, grinning flirtatiously as she took in his newly acquired accoutrements, "but I can always make time for you. I only wish you could stay a bit longer. We could have a bit of fun together, given time to get to know one another."

"What of your duties?" He wondered how much time he dared spend with her if he rode day and night after he left.

"There is but the one couple, and, although they do nothing but complain about the food and service, they have been here for several days. I look for them to try to get out of paying their bill with one complaint or another." She giggled and glanced over her shoulder to the table where Sir Morris of Bladacglen was dourly drinking his ale. "I think the man would have liked to have taken me for a tumble, but his wife watches him like a cat at a mousehole."

As though sensing that they were talking about him, Sir Morris banged his cup against the table. "Service! Let's have service here!"

Gert went to get the man another drink, and Ian sat across from him at the table.

"Rather quiet here," Ian said nonchalantly. "But it makes for a nice place to relax."

The man gave what was obviously meant to pass as a smile. "I would have enjoyed myself a lot more, had the maid been more willing and my wife less vigilant."

Ian nodded. "A wife can be a great burden sometimes."

"My wife is a burden all the time," Sir Morris complained. He watched as the younger man removed his cloak, instantly recognizing the badge of the Baron of Oatlands.

Sir Morris felt the blood rush to his face. His abrupt dismissal still rankled, and he knew again the anger at being so poorly treated by the baron.

"But what brings you so far from your master's estates?" Sir Morris asked, as casually as possible. Perhaps the baron had had a change of heart and wanted him to return.

"I go to Calais to deliver a message." He sighed as he looked toward Gert.

"Calais? You go to see the king?" Sir Morris asked, hiding the concern in his voice. Surely the baron would not go back on his word and take his claim for the money owed him by Sir Morris to the king?

"I have had the pleasure of seeing the king—" Ian guffawed "—but I have yet to see enough of Gert's charms."

Sir Morris knew he must see what was in the message. "From the looks of the wench, I'm sure she is as grieved over the situation as yourself." He nodded toward the girl, who grinned at them as she filled the mugs with ale. "The trip to Calais is a long one, too. By the time you return, she will undoubtedly be serving many guests, and have no time for your amorous pursuits."

Ian nodded morosely. "My exact thought," he agreed.

Sir Morris drained the last dregs from his cup and craftily assessed the young man. "It happens that my wife and I are traveling to Calais to join the king. Perhaps, if you requested my assistance..."

Gert undulated toward the table, a mug overflowing with ale in each hand.

"I could not ask such a favor of you, sir knight," Ian said as Gert rubbed against him. His words did not ring true. He could ask. He wanted to ask. Regardless of the consequences. The only thing he could think of at that moment was the time he would spend with Gert.

Sir Morris furrowed his brow, as though in deep thought. "I might be willing to take your message to the king, while you stay here with Gert."

"Oooh, lovey, that would be so nice," Gert said as she kissed Ian warmly.

"But my master..." Ian began, rather halfheartedly.

"Your master need never know. What better messenger could he have than a knight of the realm? I will have access to the king that you could not hope to achieve."

"But I-I have no way to repay you...." Ian was stammering beneath Gert's renewed affection.

"I like a man who does not want to be indebted," Sir Morris said garrulously. "If it suits you, you can pay for my board here at the inn. Then we are even."

Gert frowned and tugged on Ian's sleeve in an effort to warn him that the knight owed a great deal of money, but the young man was too far gone with desire. "Agreed!" he said as he swept Gert into his arms.

"Very well, then," Sir Morris said, and smiled. "Give me the missive, and as soon as my lady is up and about, we will be off to deliver it."

Ian handed the packet to Sir Morris. "I cannot tell you how much I appreciate this," he said.

"Think nothing of it," Sir Morris said as he slipped the packet into his vest and went off in search of Edwina.

To his relief, his wife was not in the chamber they shared. He drew out the packet and opened it. The messages were addressed to the king, and to Griffith Beaufort. Sir Morris opened them and was able to decipher his own name amid the otherwise unintelligible wording.

He was certain the letter mentioned himself in most disparaging and uncomplimentary terms. It was best that it not reach anyone in the king's party.

Without another thought, he tossed both messages into the fireplace and watched as the flames consumed them. Then he replaced the packet beneath his vest, in case the fool messenger should surface from his lovemaking long enough to question its whereabouts.

Without further ado, Sir Morris rounded up his wife, and they left the Boar's Head Inn behind them. At the crossroads, they paused, and Ian would have been stunned at their duplicity, had he seen them continue on their journey by taking the road in the direction opposite Calais.

But Ian was oblivious of it all and took up residence with Gert in the suite the knight had vacated, never realizing that the message that had been entrusted to him lay in the ashes of the fireplace while he and Gert made love in the bed. And, although it took every farthing Ian had been given for his entire journey to pay Sir Morris's debt, he considered the money well spent, and never once doubted that someone as exalted as a knight of the realm would not keep his word.

Chapter Fourteen

The castle at Oatlands was a structure of ancient beauty. The walls, heavily covered with tapestries, were lush with color. The baron's departed wives had done well by it, and he had spared no expense in keeping it as one of the show-places of the realm, as he would have spared no expense on Bess, had she allowed it.

"You light up these old rooms like a thousand candles," he told her. "Is it such a wonder I wish to dress you in a manner befitting such brilliance?"

"I grow large and awkward, and were I to succumb to your request and procure a new wardrobe, I would soon outgrow it."

"Then take a few lengths of cloth and lace to make me happy."

Bess smiled. "Very well, my lord, if it pleases you."

There was little Bess could do for the old man who had given her so much. He demanded nothing, treating her with the respect and affection befitting a daughter of the house.

In return, Bess accepted the position of chatelaine, and was soon a favorite with the servants and the baron's friends alike. Although most of the guests who arrived at Oatlands were many years her senior, Bess treated them all with kindness, and they accepted and loved her.

With the threat of Sir Morris out of the way, Bess was free to relax and devote her time to readying herself for the expected babe. The baron never seemed to tire of watching her as she sat and stitched the tiny garments.

Indeed, he had done everything possible to keep her from any distress. Even when Ian returned without bringing an answer to her message, the baron had tried to make light of the situation, telling Bess it was likely Griffith himself would be coming to fetch her.

Ian felt a bit guilty about not personally delivering the note, but not guilty enough to admit his indiscretion. And, like Bess and the baron, Ian found himself watching each new arrival in the hope that one of them would bring some word that the message been received.

Henry had managed to keep a stern expression on his face as his cousin entered his apartments in Calais. It was toward the last days of his visit, and the servants were in a flux packing the royal belongings for transportation back to England.

"The marshal has agreed to our terms," Henry said without expression, "and, since he is satisfied that you are too old to insure the happiness of his infant daughter, he has agreed to another match. I take it this meets with your approval?"

Griffith could hardly hide his joy. From the moment he had left Bess, he had been haunted by the fertile beauty of her body, and he longed to be with her and watch her grow with the seed of his love.

"It does, Your Grace," he managed to say, choking on his happiness.

"Very well, then." Henry got to his feet and stomped across the floor. "I will order Wolsey to write up the necessary agreements and send to Rome for any dispensation they may care to make. Once the dispensation is received, you can marry your Bess, when and where you choose. And you may tell your lady that her king has, indeed, honored his vow to reward her for her efforts to save his life. The ban is lifted, as of this moment. You must return to England with me, but you may send word to Bess whenever you wish.''

Griffith made the smallest of bows and bolted from the room as the roar of Henry's laughter followed him through the halls.

Within the hour, Prigge had been apprised of the circumstances and entrusted to carry the message containing Griffith's joyous news to Bess. He left for Essex a full week before the ship bearing Henry and his cousin reached England.

As they approached the English shore, Griffith's eyes scanned the crowd. He had hardly thought that Bess would come, as she was well along in her pregnancy, yet he could not help but hope to see her shining face.

But his anxious gaze found only Prigge, who stood some distance apart from the crowd and looked decidedly unhappy. The man's demeanor did not improve as the smiling Griffith came hurrying toward him.

"How is my lady?" Griffith asked. "What message did she send? Did she laugh or cry when she read the missive? What ails you, man? Can you not speak?"

"Mistress Bess was not at Essex, my lord," Prigge said as he shifted his weight from one foot to the other. "She has been gone for well over a fortnight, with no trace. Lady Mary has been trying to get word of her, but no one seems to have any idea where she might be."

"She couldn't have disappeared into thin air." He took the man's arm and led him to a nearby inn, where they took a room for privacy. "Tell me all you know."

"Lady Mary went to court to serve the queen. Mistress Bess chose to stay in the dower house. There were the usual visitors, whether the lord and lady were in residence or not. The only people significant to Mistress Bess were her mother, the Lady Edwina, and the woman's husband."

"Damn!" Griffith let the word escape through clenched teeth. "She's gone off with the woman."

"I thought the same, my lord," Prigge said, "but it seems they know nothing of their daughter's whereabouts. They have been seen several times, in various parts of the countryside, and do not have the girl with them."

"If she has been harmed in any way...." The words escaped Griffith, though he tried to stop them.

"I doubt it, my lord, but I vow I questioned every servant on the Essex estate, and every peasant and villein in the area, and no one knows what happened to the lady. It is as though she simply walked out the door and disappeared into the mist."

"We will go back. Someone will know of her whereabouts. We will put out the word that Henry has given us permission to wed. She will come back to me as soon as she realizes all is well and our fondest dreams are about to become reality."

"Perhaps she has returned to the convent," Prigge suggested. "I did not think to check there, due to her... condition."

"Yes, we'll look there, too," Griffith agreed. "We'll find her, Prigge. Michaelmas is but a few weeks hence, and I want to make her my wife before the child is born."

Prigge followed Griffith, giving sincere thanks that his master did not see the expression on his face, for infants had a way of coming into the world in their own time, and Griffith's plans might easily be thwarted by the arrival of his child.

* * *

Henry watched as his cousin darted in and out of court like a man possessed. Finally he was unable to remain silent, and he stopped Griffith as he hurried from the audience chamber into the great hall.

"We must talk," Henry said as he took his cousin's arm and shoved him into an alcove overlooking the bailey. "What has happened, cousin? You insisted that I nullify your betrothal and give permission for you to marry your little Bess, and now you seem not to be able to locate the lady. What has happened?"

No one enjoyed a good mystery more than Henry, and Bess's disappearance intrigued him, though until this time he had kept his distance.

"I do not know, Your Grace," Griffith admitted. "She was to have awaited word from me at Essex. And, although I am the first to admit that I was overlong in sending word to her, she was well aware there might be difficulties. She had promised that she would wait, regardless of the outcome, but when I sent Prigge with my message, she was nowhere to be found. Beyond that, we have had no sign of her."

"Face it, man," Henry said. "She grew tired of waiting and ran off with some other man. From what you have told me, the poor girl had the very devil of a time because of her love for you from the beginning. You can't blame her for wanting a safe and respectable life. After all, had it not been for you, she would have been a nun. Take my advice. Stay out of her life. If she wants you, she will send word. You have given her enough misery. Do not compound it by adding disgrace. Leave her to her own devices, and let her rebuild her life."

"If she were able," Griffith spoke out boldly.

"What do you mean?"

"I fear she has come to harm. No one saw Bess leave, although several people said her mother had come to visit, sporting a new husband."

"Have you spoken to the woman?" Henry asked, trying to place the people.

"I have Prigge after them, and expect some word in a matter of days."

"I wish you the best of luck, cousin." Henry slapped him on the shoulder. "Why don't you come with me for a few days? I am going hunting."

"I appreciate your invitation," Griffith answered, "but I cannot leave until I know that Bess is alive and well."

Henry shrugged. "As you please. If you change your mind, I will be at Oatlands. I hear the game is exceptional there this season."

Griffith bowed to this king. "I will send a message if I learn of Bess's whereabouts," he said.

"I'm sure you will," Henry agreed halfheartedly as he watched his cousin hurry down the hall. It was too bad that Griffith had declined his invitation to join his party. Henry enjoyed his company, and would miss him sorely. Still, until Griffith found Bess, his company would hold a certain element of distraction. It was probably for the best that Griffith did not go along.

The Baron of Oatlands bustled across the floor and pulled his chair over next to Bess.

"You look like a cream-fed cat," she told him.

"And well I should, for I am that content." He patted her hand. "But I have reason to smile, and so shall you. I know how dull it has been here for you, but there will be some excitement soon. The king has announced he will be coming to Oatlands to hunt. He will be arriving within the week."

He smiled fondly at Bess. "Perhaps things won't be so boring for you with some young people around."

To the baron's horror, Bess's face went a dead white, and she would have fallen had he not caught her.

"What is it, child?" he demanded, his forehead creased with concern. "Surely your time cannot yet be upon you."

But Bess could only cling to him, her heart pounding wildly. If the king was coming, surely Griffith would be with him.

This must be Griffith's way of surprising her. He would arrive with king and court, and marry her before them all.

Her face brightened, and her heart sang with happiness and love.

The baron's sharp eyes caught more than Bess would have wished. It was clear to him that she expected the man who had fathered her child to be traveling with the king's entourage, and while he knew that he would miss her sorely when she had married and gone, it was for the best.

The Baron of Oatlands was old and tired. He wanted only to live out his life in peace and harmony, and while he cared very deeply for Bess, he worried daily that Sir Morris would return and take her from him by sheer force. He knew he was no longer a match for the younger man in feats of arms. The threat of trying to protect Bess and the child she carried weighed heavily on him, and he would be glad to relinquish it to a man who was equal to the task. A man such as Griffith Beaufort.

As for Bess, from the moment the baron told her that the king was coming, she flew into a flurry of cleaning and readying the house for guests. Maids and footmen hurried from one task to the next, hardly pausing for breath as she sent them again on their way.

Although her figure had thickened, Bess concealed her pregnancy in the voluminous folds of her gowns and proceeded to add panels to the dresses so that she would be comfortable in the presence of the court.

Her greatest pride was in the ivory gown, heavily encrusted with jewels, pearls, and the finest lace. The baron had insisted she have it, and had not allowed her to decline his offer.

"The last to wear it was my daughter," he had told her. "I thought the gown had outlived its usefulness, but now you shall wear it, and with my blessing."

"But, my lord, I cannot. I am not of your blood, and do not deserve the honor," Bess protested.

"There is naught of my blood left on this earth," he had told her. "And while you may not be of my blood, you are of my heart, and that in itself gives you the right to wear the gown."

Seeing that he would not be dissuaded, Bess had taken the gown to her rooms.

All was in readiness when the horns sounded, announcing that the hunting party had entered the grounds.

Bess, her heart aflutter, stood next to the baron as the horses pranced down the drive. How well she remembered the hunter's green that both Henry and Griffith had worn the day she had warned them of the plot on their lives.

Before the royal party reached the gates, a stag darted past them and ran toward the forest. Men and horses veered in their course and started after the unfortunate beast. As the sound of hoofbeats faded into the distance, the baron turned to Bess.

"I think it best if we wait inside," he said, taking her arm. "They will return when they have made their kill, and then we can give them our greeting."

He felt resentful toward the king and his kinsman when he saw tears like tiny stars on Bess's lashes. She hid her disappointment, but there was no doubt that she was hurt by the fact that Griffith had followed Henry to the hunt rather than come directly to her. For she did not learn for many hours that Griffith had not come at all.

At first, Bess was filled with disbelief. She sought out one of the king's servants whom she had never seen before and quizzed him.

"I heard the king traveled with his cousin Griffith, a mighty lord and skilled knight," Bess told the man as he sat before the fire in the servants' hall. "Which is he?"

"Lord Beaufort be not here," the boy replied. "The king has said he must wed, and he is out making things ready for his bride. In truth, we've seen little of him since we returned from Calais. I doubt not that we'll be celebrating his wedding in the near future."

The young man paid little mind to the plump woman. Her hair was covered, and she wore a wimple about her face. Her gown was clean, but the material was not nearly of the quality worn by the servants at the king's court. She did not seem to be putting on airs, and he liked that about her. Had she not been so much older than himself, with her thickened, middle-aged figure, he would have spent a great deal more time with her, for she was so interested in everything he had to say. It was only after he told her of the gossip concerning Lord Beaufort's wedding that she lost interest in his words and made her way slowly from the hall, as though the weight of the world were on her shoulders.

The Baron allowed Bess to keep to her rooms while the royal party was about. His heart ached for her, as several times he saw her gazing from the solar window to catch a glimpse of the hunt as it made its progress across the estate.

How could any man dare to hurt her so? Lashing out at everyone in his effort to find some way to ease her aching heart, the baron sought out Ian.

"I find it odd that you should sequester yourself away while the royal party is here," the old man said. "Surely you must have met some of the servants, or perhaps the squires, on your journey to Calais. Yet none seem to remember you, nor you them."

"I did not stay long enough to make any lasting friendships," Ian replied, improvising quickly. "Indeed, sire, I was so anxious to return that as soon as I was told there would be no reply I came back to England."

The baron regarded the man searchingly. "Even so. These are the same men who were with the king, and if you are to continue to bear messages for me, it would be in your interest to gain their favor."

Ian pulled his forelock. "Of course, my lord. I will go at once and see if there is anyone here I might have met in Calais."

He hurried off toward a group of servants, hoping the baron would not watch him too closely. He had no idea what he would say to them. They were total strangers, and looked at Ian with open curiosity. But there was one thing Ian needed to know, and what better time to ask it?

"Gentlemen." He bowed. "Is anyone here who served Lord Griffith Beaufort while he was in Calais?"

Two of the men nodded their heads. "Why do you ask?"

"It seems a message that should have been delivered to Sir Griffith may have been lost. I was wondering if any of you who were in Calais at the time might remember the arrival of a knight, rather shabbily attired. Not too tall, with dark hair and eyes, and a short, sharp beard."

The men looked at one another and shook their heads. "No man of that description came to Calais with a message for any member of the royal party," one said, and they all agreed.

"Would there have been a way he might have come and not been seen by any of you?" Ian persisted with a sinking heart.

"Never," they affirmed in one voice.

"That bastard!" Ian said under his breath. Then, aloud: "I thank you, gentlemen. You have been most kind in answering my question."

"Was the message of some political importance?" one of the men asked.

Ian winked. "More an affair of the heart," he confided, "and I fear that it has gone astray."

"It is sad," the man said in a commiserating tone, "but it seems to be the way of things, as Lord Beaufort also nurses his heart. It seems the lady of his choice has disappeared without a trace. Apparently she became tired of waiting for him to get the king's permission to wed with her."

Ian gave an understanding smile. "How like a woman to become impatient," he mused with outward calm, but inwardly he was filled with trepidation. The message he had carried was to have gone to Griffith Beaufort, and now he knew with certainty that it had never been delivered, despite the vows of the perfidious knight.

He felt sweat mist his brow as he left the group. The baron already suspected that something had gone awry. Would the man show mercy if Ian confessed his duplicity? Or would it be more prudent to take the chance that Griffith Beaufort would give up his search, in which case no one need know that Ian had shirked his duty. His silence smacked of deceit, but telling the truth could cost him his life, and he knew he would choose the lesser of the two evils.

Ian could only hope that the baron would not mention having sent a messenger for the remainder of the visit. It was with vast relief that he saw that the king's visit drew to a close without unpleasant repercussions. To be sure, the king was hardly aware that the baron's lady was not in evidence. Only his inherent courtesy made Henry ask to pay his respects to the baron's betrothed, but she sent word she was too ill to receive him. The royal party left the estate without giving a second thought to the woman who had made their stay a time of ease and comfort.

A tournament at Greenwich filled the castle to overflowing with knights who had come to participate. To their chagrin, the weather turned sour and, rather than risk life and limb sliding around on a muddy field, the men sought the warmth of the great hall of the castle.

Sir Morris of Bladacglen was especially disappointed, because he needed the money, having long since spent the allowance the baron had given him. He wandered aimlessly about the hall. He was looking for a game of dice or some other form of gambling that might allow him to win some money. Bearing that it mind, it was possible that one of the maids would be free with her favors. Edwina sat with the other women, her head nodding noticeably with the effects of the wine she had imbibed.

Sir Morris smiled at a serving wench, but she tossed her head, obviously looking for better game than a shabby knight. His search took him to the area where the king stood surrounded by several companions.

Henry was especially lighthearted these days, because the queen was again with child, and he felt certain his issue would survive. "The Baron of Oatlands was a good and generous host. I enjoyed hunting on his estates."

"*Good* and *generous* are not words I would use to describe the old miser." The words sprang from Sir Morris's lips before he could hold them back.

All eyes turned on the newcomer.

"Dare you contradict the king?" Walter Prigge inquired. He was bored, and anxious for any kind of action, be it only an argument.

"I only meant the king does not know the Baron of Oatlands as I do," Sir Morris said, temporizing.

"And how do you know him, sir?" It was Henry's voice that questioned now, and it was not to be ignored.

"I performed a service for the man, out of the kindness of my heart, and when I had fulfilled his wishes, he turned myself and my wife out, with only a pittance to show for my time and effort on his behalf."

"I've seen you at tournaments many times, Sir Morris," the king remarked, "and it seems strange to me a knight of your obvious ability would need to be supported by a man twice your age."

Thoroughly reprimanded, Sir Morris sought to steal away, but the king's voice halted him. "We had not heard of your marriage, Sir Morris. Who is the lucky woman?"

"The Lady Edwina Blummer, Your Grace." Sir Morris bowed low, hoping the matter would be dropped.

"Edwina Blummer," Henry frowned over the words. "I do not remember meeting her. Has she accompanied you to Greenwich?"

"Yes, Your Grace, she has." Sir Morris was praying that Henry would not ask to meet Edwina, but his prayers were not to be answered this night.

"You may present her to me," Henry said condescendingly. "I would meet this woman you have married." His eyes roamed over the room. It bothered him that he had heard the woman's name before and could not place it. It was unlike him to forget the slightest detail about any of his subjects. Perhaps seeing the woman would jar his memory.

Sir Morris fetched Edwina and led her forward. She made a wobbly curtsy and simpered up at the king. To Henry's disappointment, the woman's appearance meant nothing to him. He doubted he had ever laid eyes on her before, and he would be content never to do so again. It was a mystery to him why a man like Sir Morris would wed a matron so obviously his elder by several years. Especially one who evidently imbibed more than a ladylike amount.

"Your Grace," she said in greeting him as her husband helped her regain her feet. "It is such an honor to be presented to you. Of course, I have seen you from afar, and my daughter has spoken of you, but—"

"Do I know your daughter, then?" So, it was the daughter, not the mother, whom he knew.

"Oh, but certainly you know my dear daughter, Elizabeth," Lady Edwina gushed. "Why, until only recently she served as lady-in-waiting to the queen."

"Forgive me, lady," the king said in an offhand manner, "but there are many Elizabeths in my wife's retinue. It is impossible for me to remember them all." He had lost interest in the woman and the conversation, and was eager to dismiss her until her next words caught his ear.

"Ah, yes, Your Grace," Edwina agreed. "But how many of them have saved Your Grace's life?"

Henry's head snapped around in a manner that hardly befitted a king. Ever since their return from Calais, Griffith had mooned about, lost in a fit of pique that he could not find his beloved Bess. It had seemed that the woman had deserted him for another, and perhaps this was the case. Still, the very fact that Sir Morris was involved gave Henry reason to wonder at the fate of the girl, although the mother seemed pleased with the girl's situation in life, whatever that might be.

"Your daughter is Mistress Bess." It was a statement, not a question.

"But of course," Edwina simpered. "Can you not see the resemblance?" She turned her face and body from one side to the other so that her king could have a better view.

For the life of him, Henry could see no more resemblance between the drab little Edwina and the shining memory of Bess than he saw between himself and the squat figure of Sir Morris.

"Your daughter was never adequately repaid for her services to the crown. I wish to do her honor for saving my life, but alas, she has disappeared without a trace. Even now I have men out trying to learn of her whereabouts." It did not escape Henry that Sir Morris's fingers bit harshly into his wife's arm. "Surely, as Bess's mother, you would know where she has gone," Henry said smoothly.

But even his coaxing manner was no match for Sir Morris's determination. Without being formally dismissed, the man began pulling his wife away. "We have not seen Bess for eons," the man sputtered. "She is not a dutiful daughter, and gives little thought to her mother's sorrow in her absence. I will try to remember where it was we last heard from her, and come to you immediately with the location."

Edwina opened her mouth several times, but whether it was to speak, or from the pressure of her husband's hand, Henry did not know.

Sir Morris paused only long enough to suggest, "Since it is of such importance that you find Bess, I am sure there will be great recompense for the man who can tell you where she has gone."

Henry's eyes narrowed dangerously.

"I will see that the person who tells me how I may find Mistress Bess is rewarded according to his merit," he promised as he let the man drag his wife from the royal presence.

"Why did you not force Sir Morris to tell you of the girl's whereabouts?" Sir Charles Brandon asked. "It is not like you to let someone so crass demand a reward for information he should be happy to impart."

Henry tapped his fingers against the jewel-encrusted dagger at his waist. "I will learn all I need to know," he assured his friend. "But now it is imperative that Griffith return here in all haste. To that end, I assign you, Charles."

"So I am to miss all the fun," Charles complained good-naturedly.

"Only when Griffith returns will the true fun begin." Henry clapped the man on the shoulder as he sent him on his way.

It was through sheer luck that Sir Morris met his old acquaintance, Jasper. The man walked with a decided limp, a relic of the time Griffith had come to Bess's defense against Sir Morris and his cronies.

Jasper was not pleased to see Sir Morris, and did not pretend to be so, until Sir Morris apologized for his part in Jasper's disability and offered to try to make amends.

"I will be coming into some money quite soon," Sir Morris assured him.

"And how is that?" Jasper asked.

"The king is searching for my stepdaughter to repay her for saving his life. He will give me a fine reward when I tell him how to find her."

"So your life still revolves around the beauteous Bess," the man remarked.

"I have made her mother my wife." Sir Morris glanced toward the stairs, worried that Edwina might be sneaking down then, bent on *giving* information to the king that could more aptly be sold.

"I did not know the king searched for Mistress Bess, though it is common knowledge Lord Beaufort holds Mistress Bess most dear and has been searching for her untiringly."

"That hardly sounds likely, with his upcoming marriage," Sir Morris said, discounting the man's words.

"It is to Mistress Bess he would be wed," Jasper shot back, angered that his word should be questioned.

A smile tugged at the corners of Sir Morris's mouth, which he quickly suppressed. "It is hard to believe Lord Beaufort would still be interested in the welfare of a woman who carries another man's child."

Jasper blinked. "So that is the rub!" he said softly. "If Mistress Bess is pregnant, the child is most surely that of Griffith Beaufort. And should you be responsible for the girl being missing when he returned to Essex for her, I would leave England before I would face Beaufort, for his anger would be worth a man's life."

"But Griffith is not at Greenwich," Sir Morris reminded him. "And by the time he returns, I will be well gone, with my reward from the king's coffers. Come with me, my friend, and we will find some fine sport together."

The man shook his head. "The memory of your sport is far too painful," he said. "I fear I must decline your offer."

"Nonetheless, I would share my good fortune with you," Sir Morris told him benevolently.

"Do not bring my name into this, Morris of Bladacglen. I want no part of your schemes. They have brought me nothing but misfortune. I wish you luck, but I want no part of your reward, nor your punishment—whichever the king deigns to mete out.''

He limped off without looking back, leaving Sir Morris to wonder if Jasper knew more than he was willing to tell.

Chapter Fifteen

As Bess came closer to term, instead of becoming more placid and content, as do most women, she became nervous and agitated. She could not banish Griffith from her thoughts. She longed for the sound of his voice, the touch of his hand, the magic of his lips against her own.

During the day, she managed to hide her thoughts, but at night they became more and more prevalent, sending her into nightmares as she realized Griffith would not be there to see the birth of his son.

Thoughts assailed her like a swarm of angry bees, and she thrashed about in her bed, longing for sleep, even as she feared it. Finally, her overburdened body exhausted, she sank into troubled dreams. Dreams in which she was not in time to save Griffith from the outlaws who would have killed him. Dreams in which Sir Morris was carrying her away as he had threatened.

Sir Morris had spoken the truth! The baron was an old man and would not be there forever to protect her. Then Sir Morris would come, as was his right by his marriage to her mother. He would come and . . .

The screams built up inside her until they could no more be held silent.

There was only one man who could help her once the baron was gone, one man to whom she had pledged her life and her heart. And that man was Griffith!

The name burst from her throat, shattering the silence in the sleeping castle. But it was the baron who came to her that night, with Ian in his wake. The old man cradled her as though she were a frightened child.

"Is your time upon you?" he asked anxiously as her screams died away into great sobs.

"No, my lord, it was a nightmare. I dreamed I was alone and Sir Morris had come after me."

Ian stood just inside the door and said nothing. It was easy to put the pieces together. She had known true fear in her dream, and had called out the name of the only man who could save her. The man she loved. And that man's name was Griffith. But Griffith would not come to her, because the message had not been delivered.

He hung his head in shame. Shame, made all the worse by Bess's admission that she feared Sir Morris would come after her. Ian knew that Bess had refused to marry the baron, and that if she held to her refusal, Sir Morris would, indeed, come for her at the time of the baron's death.

The baron crooned soothing words and held Bess's hand until she slept again.

As he entered his own apartments, Ian fell on his knees before his master. "I beg mercy, sire," he said, groveling. "I must confess a most grievous offense, but I do so in the hope that it is not too late to make it right."

The baron was exhausted. It was the middle of the night. "Could this not wait until morning?" he asked impatiently.

"Nay, my lord. It cannot wait. I have lied about delivering the message to Calais."

The baron was suddenly wide awake. "What are you saying, man?"

"I stopped at the Boar's Head Inn, and met there a knight and his lady who were on their way to Calais. The man was somewhat in debt to the innkeeper, and offered to take the messages to the king if I would agree to pay his bill along with my own." Ian saw the dark scowl on his master's face and hurried on.

"A knight would much more easily reach the ear of the king, and he spoke intimately of his many meetings with the king and members of the court. I never thought a knight would break his word, once a bargain was struck.

"I gave him the packet and saw him ride out. After a few days, I returned here, certain the message had been delivered. But it had not, and the Lady Bess will surely die of heartbreak or fear. I realize now that the knight to whom I entrusted the packet was none other than the Sir Morris our lady fears.

"That Lord Beaufort is not here is my fault, and I beg you allow me to find him and right the wrong I have done, before you punish me."

The baron sank down by the table before the fireplace and stared at the flames. "Ian, I am very disappointed in you," he said. "But I will allow you to find Griffith Beaufort and tell him the truth of the situation."

Ian groveled again, kissing the hem of the baron's nightrobe. The older man jerked it away. "Make yourself ready to leave with the dawn. I will write a missive clarifying the situation to add credence to your explanation."

Ian bowed his way toward the door, thankful he had been given his life, at least for the time being. "Sire," he asked quietly, "where first shall I look? The king is no longer in Calais, and the Beaufort was not with him when he was here at Oatlands."

The baron banged his fist against the polished surface of the table, causing the writing materials to jump. "I don't care where you find him, but do so with all expediency, or your life is forfeit."

Ian opened his mouth to speak, then thought better of it and closed the door quickly behind himself. He must find Griffith Beaufort and convince him to return to Oatlands with him, for if he did not the baron would hunt Ian down to the ends of the earth.

Sir Morris knew that he should leave Greenwich before Griffith returned. It seemed the wisest course would be to take the reward the king offered and go on his way. Jasper was seldom wrong, and while Sir Morris had done many things that were ill-advised in his lifetime, he never willingly tempted death. To face Griffith Beaufort would surely be to do so.

So it was that Sir Morris found the king playing at bowls in the garden. The monarch was in a jolly mood, and Morris thought it favorable to his suit.

"Your Grace," Sir Morris began as he bowed deeply as he tried to keep out of the way of Henry's swinging arm, "I have given much thought to your request regarding Mistress Bess, and I believe I know where you can find her."

Henry stopped what he was doing and handed the ball to one of the squires. He wiped the sweat from his face and looked Sir Morris in the eye. "Is that so?"

"Yes, Your Grace. I am certain I can locate her, and I will be more than happy to deliver Bess's reward to her myself."

Henry shrewdly regarded the man through narrowed eyes. "Very well, Sir Morris, then just where is the lady?"

"You need not trouble yourself with her abode, Your Grace," Sir Morris assured him. "I will take her reward to her, and you need think no more about it."

"Is there some reason why you hesitate to tell me of her location?" Henry demanded.

"Never, Your Grace." Sir Morris denied the thought vehemently. "But you have so many important things on your mind, I am sure you don't care about a silly girl."

"I hardly call 'silly' the woman who put her own life in jeopardy to save mine," the king returned.

Sir Morris took the reprimand easily. "As you say, Your Grace. If I am correct, the girl may be residing with the Baron of Oatlands."

"We hunted there but a short time past," the king said, baiting him. "I saw no one even vaguely resembling the lady in question. Nevertheless, I will look into your information."

"Perhaps I am mistaken and she has gone, but I vow the old baron probably has her under lock and key." Sir Morris was troubled by the hard, piercing look in his king's eyes, and he started bowing out of the king's presence. Henry was too demanding in his quest to know of Bess's locale. It did not bode well for Sir Morris's plans.

Henry snapped his fingers, and one of the gentlemen handed him his coat. "Sir Morris," Henry called after the departing knight, "there is no need for you to wait around for remuneration, should your disclosure prove correct. Your wife, Lady Edwina, has already given me all the information I need, and any reward will be given in Edwina's name."

Color crept into Sir Morris's face. His eyes bulged in their sockets as though he were choking, and his fists clenched. He swung around, oblivious of the fact that he had turned his back on his king.

Henry laughed aloud at the man's obvious discomfort. "And, Sir Morris, I wouldn't do anything that might harm or anger Lady Edwina, because I have given her a small dwelling in which to live with whomever she may choose. It is an estate for life. Edwina's life. And the endowment will end with Edwina's last breath. Do you understand?"

Sir Morris did not turn around. He came to a complete stop, his shoulders slumped as he came to the realization of defeat. "Yes, Your Grace," he said through clenched teeth. "I understand perfectly."

A few minutes later, Sir Morris burst into the room he shared with his wife. Edwina ran to him, arms outstretched, oblivious of his anger.

"Did you hear the news, Morris? Did you hear what the king has done for us? He has given us our own home. Oh, my love, is it not wonderful? The culmination of all our dreams?" She threw her arms around her husband's neck and gazed, dewy-eyed, into his red face.

"I can see that you are as overcome as I was with our good fortune," she gushed. "But you need not worry. It is true. The king's man has just come with the deed itself. We can go to our new property as soon as I've finished packing."

Sir Morris struck his wife's hands away and found his voice. "Why did you tell him?" he demanded. "We could have held our information until he agreed to give us wealth! Riches! Power! And you sold it all for a moldering hut."

"But I thought you'd be pleased!" Edwina drew back, her hurt evident on her face. "He need not have given us anything. After all, it is a poor mother who would not know the whereabouts of her own child."

"God forbid that someone might think you have shirked in your duty to your daughter," he sniped, but his sarcasm was lost on Edwina, who had been reduced to tears in the face of his anger.

"I love Bess, and I always wish her the best," the woman declared between sniffles.

"You sold me out for a paltry endowment. I might have arranged an appointment at court. I could have lived in luxury for the rest of my life, with servants and fine clothes. I could have had everything I ever wanted!" Sir Morris shouted, but Edwina only stood small and silent before his wrath.

"But Morris," she said softly, "all I've ever wanted was you, even above the hope of bearing your child."

Sir Morris stared at Edwina.

The child!

Suppose Jasper had been correct.

The child of Bess and Griffith Beaufort.

A child with royal blood in its veins.

A child who carried a claim to the throne of a childless king.

The guardian of that child had a kingdom within his reach.

His countenance took on an evil smile as he wrapped Edwina in his arms.

"You are a good woman, Edwina," he assured her, "and there is no reason why you should not have all you wish."

"Oh, but Morris, in all our years together I have never been with child. I fear I cannot..." She hesitated over the words that declared her beyond childbearing age.

"Never fear, my love," Morris assured her with obvious glee. "If it is a child you want, then a child you shall have!" And with that, he kissed her soundly, and went to beg an audience with the queen, who would undoubtedly understand and sympathize with Edwina's plight.

* * *

It felt good to kneel and pray. Griffith rested his forehead against the cool stone of the prie-dieu. Perhaps Bess had knelt here, in this very place. The thought made him feel closer to her. How he wished she were here now. How he wished she would come through the silence of the chapel and pray beside him.

He could almost hear the rustle of her skirts behind him. If only his long search would end and he could take her in his arms. He cared not that she had left him, and cared even less for the reason. He wanted her back, in his arms and in his life. He was not complete without her, and would never be.

"Lord Beaufort," a woman's well-modulated voice said. "The postulant said you wished to see me."

Griffith got to his feet and looked into the careworn face of the mother superior.

"I came to ask if Mistress Elizabeth Blummer is here," he told her.

"You have sent messages asking after Bess several times, my lord, and each time I sent a message telling you I have not seen her since she left to save your life."

There was something in the woman's voice that led him to believe she did not think his life was truly worth saving, especially since Bess's soul had been forfeit in the bargain.

"I cannot find her, Reverend Mother," he admitted, his voice choked with unshed tears. "I have searched everywhere, but she has disappeared into the air. No one knows where she has gone."

"And so you come to me?"

"The convent is her refuge. I know that if she were in trouble she would come here, regardless of the penance she might suffer."

"And for what sin would she be given penance?" the woman asked, although one look at the handsome man before her told her more than she wanted to know. Her only feeling was one of surprise that Bess had not given in to her human passions far sooner.

"I have asked her to be my wife," Griffith said.

"And is this the reason she ran away?" The mother superior knew that Bess had fought her own devils while she was at the convent. She also realized that the young woman had been unable to commit her life to God and take the vows that would have shut her off from this man. It was God's will that Bess had overheard the conversation that sent her racing out into the world again. Just as it was God's will that she had reached her destination in time to save not only Griffith's life, but that of the king, as well.

"I cannot tell you where she may be found." She sighed, and gave in to the will of the Lord. "But I received a greeting from her on my saint's day, earlier this month, and the messenger wore the livery of a place called Oatlands."

Now it was Griffith's turn to sigh. "I thank you, Reverend Mother, but Bess cannot be at Oatlands. The king was there but a short while ago, and did not see her."

"Women need not be seen to be effective, my lord. It is possible she did not want to be seen. I do not care to guess her motives. I have told you all I know, and more than I should. I suggest we pray together before you continue on your way."

She indicated that Griffith should kneel beside her, and bowed her head in prayer.

The man was tall and blond of hair. He led his horse along the muddy road, paying little attention to the rain that soaked his cloak.

Ian slowed his horse as he came up beside him, unable to hope for a turn of good luck that might have allowed him to stumble on Griffith Beaufort. "M'lord," he ventured as he slid to the ground to keep from soiling the knight's cloak by spattering mud from the road. "Are you perchance Lord Griffith Beaufort?"

The man looked over quickly, his eyes hooded against the impertinent question. "Who asks? And for what reason?"

"I have a message to be delivered into the hands of none other than Lord Beaufort," Ian told him. "Are you he?"

The knight took in the man's horse and livery. "No, I am not. But why should a messenger from the Oatlands be looking for Beaufort? He did not even go to Oatlands for the hunting when last we went with the king."

"It is a message from my master, the Baron of Oatlands," Ian told him. "I am desperate to find Sir Griffith. If I do not, it is worth my life."

Charles Brandon laughed. "Surely not! I have known the baron all of my life, and have never known him to be of violent nature."

Ian fell into step beside the knight. "He has reason to distrust me, my lord," he admitted. "You see, I was to have delivered a message to Griffith Beaufort when he was in Calais. I entrusted it to another man, a knight, whom I believed would be true to his word. Lord Beaufort never received the message, and the Lady Bess is in dire straits because of my deception. As I said, it is worth my life if I don't find the Beaufort and give him the message."

"And what message is that?" Charles Brandon asked, as casually as he could manage.

"Lady Bess is at Oatlands, and her time is almost upon her. It was my lack of perception and my trust in the wrong man that caused her such grief." Ian wiped his nose on his sleeve and plodded on.

"So you search for Griffith Beaufort," Charles repeated. "What a piece of luck! For, you see, I am searching for Griffith myself. The king wishes him to return to Greenwich."

Ian stopped. "Oh, sire, you cannot tell him that. He will obey the king's order, and my lady will be in anguish without him."

Charles Brandon could not help but agree with the man. There was no need for the king to personally tell Griffith of Bess's whereabouts while the girl waited, wondering why Griffith did not return to her. Had Henry been more generous with his favors and prompt in his rewards, this would never have happened.

Brandon clapped the man on the shoulder. "Should either of us find Griffith, we will send him posthaste to Oatlands and Bess. What say you to that?"

"Oh, bless you, m'lord." Ian all but groveled in relief. "Bless you."

"Then 'tis done," Charles declared. "I shall keep in contact with the king, and will surely hear if you succeed. You must get your information directly from Oatlands, be it good or bad."

"With both of us searching, we cannot help but find him. The man could not have disappeared from the face of the earth." Ian smiled broadly as he made his pronouncement.

But finding Griffith would be more difficult than either of them could imagine, for neither would think to look inside the walls of a convent for a knight of the realm.

As the hours marched on, Ian's enthusiasm was lost. He was cold, wet and hungry as he led his lamed horse along the tree-lined road. He had found no sign of Griffith Beaufort. His feet dragged through the mud and his spirits were as low as his physical condition.

He dared not return to Oatlands without the man, for he knew it meant his life to do so. He paused at the crest of the hill. Below him he could see the buildings of a small religious community. His soul cried out for succor. If he must return to Oatlands and face his fate, he would at least know that God had forgiven him his sins. With this thought in mind, Ian started down the hill toward Saint Lawrence of Blackmore Priory.

Sir Morris restrained himself from pacing the floor as he awaited admittance to the queen's audience chamber. It was imperative that he see her without Henry's presence. Thank the Lord, Henry no longer made impromptu appearances during his wife's audiences. Henry no longer considered her advice mandatory, and preferred to ignore both Catherine and her advice as much as possible.

To his vast relief, he was finally ushered into the audience chamber. He bowed deeply, dropping to his knee before the queen.

"Your Grace, I come to beg your consideration of my petition." He gave her his most charming smile, the one Edwina had found most beguiling. "I ask your sympathy and your aid, for my appeal is not for myself, but for the welfare of a child."

Having lost her children to the grim hands of death, the queen looked into the tear-filled eyes of Sir Morris and regarded his words with the utmost sympathy. It did her soul good to have a man before her who showed such concern for a child.

"You may continue," she said in a soft voice.

"It is my daughter, Your Grace." Sir Morris lowered his eyes, as though in embarrassment at the words he must speak before his queen. "The girl is a beauty, and has attracted the attention of several men. It seems that she has given one of them her favor, and he, in turn, seduced her. Her mother and I have learned the girl is with child and will not, or cannot, name the father.''

The queen shook her head slowly back and forth, and Sir Morris quickly went on.

''It is not for the daughter I speak, Your Grace, but for the babe. My wife and I propose that the girl go to a nunnery to reflect on her sinful past, but the child is without guilt in this matter, and deserves better than to be turned out into the streets.''

''What is it you would do?'' the queen asked.

''My wife's childbearing years are past, but we are quite able to care for a child. I ask—nay, I beg—you to award guardianship of the child to me. I will take the babe and raise it on my own lands. The child will grow up as mine, without the stain of bastardy on its name.''

Again the queen's eyes softened. ''It is a noble and commendable thing you propose,'' she told him, ''but are you absolutely certain the father is unwilling to claim the child?'' It pained the woman to think of taking a child from its mother, as so many of her own children had been taken from her. The memory of her own loss was still fresh in her mind.

''I have explored every pathway to ensure a suitable life for this poor babe,'' Sir Morris assured her, ''and have come to the decision that there is nothing left for me other than to raise the child myself.''

It still did not sit right with the queen, but she could not doubt the knight's words. After all, he had in all probability been a knight of the realm since his youth, and was pledged by the vows of knighthood to protect women, children, and those weaker than himself. It was obvious that this was not a situation of political enhancement. The man had nothing to gain by taking in this fatherless child, other than added responsibility.

Still the queen hesitated. She wondered if God felt as she did now when he called her babes back to heaven. And she resented being put in such a position.

"Why do you not go to the king with your request?" she asked.

"Because with your kind and understanding heart, I felt that it was to you I should address my petition," Sir Morris lied smoothly.

"This is your daughter, you say?" There was an edge to the queen's voice as she postponed the moment when she would be forced to make some sort of decision and take a child from its mother, no matter how unworthy the woman might be.

"Yes, Your Grace." He bowed his head. "My daughter, Elizabeth."

Elizabeth was a well-used name. Half the women in court carried it, the queen mused silently. Aloud she said, "Elizabeth of Bladacglen. I do not know the girl."

"No, Your Grace," Sir Morris said, but did not raise his head lest she read the falseness in his expression. "My family has been living in Kew."

"Is this Elizabeth your only child?" the queen asked.

"She is, Your Grace, and her thoughtless actions have quite broken my lady wife's heart. I feel the only way for my wife to heal is to allow her to raise the child with guidance and love, as well as discipline. Instilling the strength to overcome the weakness of the flesh that may be inherent from the babe's mother."

The queen nodded sadly. "I can see that your heart is in the right place, Sir Morris," she said. "You and your wife will be made guardians of the child of Elizabeth, daughter of Morris and Edwina of Bladacglen. I will have the necessary papers drawn up immediate. There is only one thing I would ask in return."

"Anything, Your Grace," Sir Morris promised.

"If the young mother wishes to stay with her child, she is to be given that option. I cannot bear to think of a woman forced to give up her babe without recourse."

"But of course, Your Grace. I guarantee that your stipulation will be put before the child's mother, and she will be given the opportunity to make the decision as to whether to stay with the child or no." It was almost impossible for him to cover the glee in his voice. If all went well, he would have control of both Bess and her babe, and with the queen's blessing.

"Very well, then, Sir Morris, I will have the writ made up. You shall have it on the morrow. And good luck in your endeavor." With a wave of her hand, the queen dismissed him, watching with some anxiety as he bowed his way out of the room. She could find no flaw in his story. Still, there had been something in his telling of it that did not ring true. How she wished she could place this Elizabeth of Bladacglen, but the face eluded her.

Catherine was not as good at remembering faces as was Henry. But of course! That was the solution. She would ask Henry. No king knew more about his subjects than did Henry. She would bring it up when next they had a few minutes together. It would be satisfying to hear him praise her for her foresight and generosity in procuring a better life for one of their youngest subjects.

With a small smile on her thin lips, Catherine the queen gave the orders to her secretary to draw up the papers that would take Bess's child from her and legally place it in the hands of Sir Morris.

Chapter Sixteen

Lady Mary of Essex entered the queen's solar just as Sir Morris made his exit. For a moment, she did not recognize the man. He seemed familiar, but she could not place where she had seen him. Then his identity came to her, and she stopped and stared after him. His expression had differed from any other time she had seen him, in that his face had been wreathed in a smile.

It was unheard-of to question the queen as to her business with one of her subjects, but Mary determined to stay close to the queen and listen for any word as to what the man's business might have been. Mary had never forgotten Sir Morris and his uncontrollable affinity for Bess.

The day passed without any mention of Sir Morris's audience with the queen, and Mary began to believe that he might have been there to deliver a message for someone else.

It wasn't until the afternoon of the second day that information regarding Sir Morris's visit came to light. The king came to the queen's chambers quite unannounced and entirely unexpected. The ladies were all giggles as he complimented them before seating himself near the queen.

Catherine was obviously delighted with Henry's presence, as he had not given her an undue amount of attention over the past months other than his dutiful conjugal visits, which had ceased abruptly when she gave him the news that she was again pregnant. She simpered and smiled like an untried girl, blushing at Henry's compliments. And although Henry spoke to his wife, his eyes constantly roved over the ladies-in-waiting, and it was doubtful if he even heard Catherine's words.

Mary sat on a low stool with the light of the window at her back. Catherine had placed herself in the same proximity, since her eyesight was not as sharp as it had been. It was in Mary's mind that it might be prudent to relocate herself, but before she could gather up her sewing the queen's words stopped her.

"It is not only you, my husband, who is able to give surcease to the troubles that plague our subjects. Only recently I was able to reverse a terrible wrong and provide love and care for a poor unfortunate babe." She beamed proudly as she made her pronouncement, but Henry paid her little mind, his eyes and his smile still caressing the ladies of the court.

"And who is this most fortunate waif?" Henry asked.

"It is the child of the daughter of a knight from Bladacglen. Her name is Elizabeth, I believe. Elizabeth of Bladacglen," Catherine said with some satisfaction.

"I was unaware Bladacglen had a daughter," Henry remarked, vaguely recalling the old man who had supported Henry's father. One of the ladies bent forward to pick up a lute, and Henry completely lost his train of thought as he allowed himself to admire the proffered cleavage.

"But certainly he has a daughter. And a pregnant one, at that," Catherine assured him with unbridled satisfaction. "It is his daughter's child he wishes to care for as guardian, and after a long discussion we came to an agreement."

"I'm certain you were able to give fair judgment for all concerned," Henry said, motioning the young musician to sit on the bottom step of the low dais, just at his feet, where her every move would be seen, and fully appreciated, by her king.

"I suppose I may have been somewhat overgenerous with the woman, but I made him promise that he would keep and care for child and mother together, should she be willing to change her ways and learn to be a good and dedicated mother," the queen said with self-righteousness.

"The girl was seduced by a man somewhat above her in blood and rank. It is sad but true that it happens quite often, although it seldom comes to our attention. The child's father either could not, or would not, wed with her, and I can tell you I had quite a time talking the knight into taking both mother and child, should it be the young woman's wish. I simply could not bear to see a woman separated from her babe against her wishes."

"You have always had a good and generous heart, my love," Henry said absently as the maid-in-waiting bent over her lute and began to caress the strings with long, tapered fingers.

"Of course, I do not recall this Elizabeth of Bladacglen, but the knight said his wife and family had been residing at Kew for the past few years. I was sure you would know of whom I spoke. Your memory is so much better than mine, and your knowledge of your subjects is second to none." She smiled up at him awaiting some acknowledgment of her compliment.

It took Henry a moment to pull himself from the contemplation of the musician's bosom, but he finally managed to gain control of his mind long enough to consider the queen's words.

Henry stroked his chin and turned his full attention to his wife. "I know but one knight from Bladacglen, and I have never heard that he had managed to beget an heir, either male or female. For that matter, I cannot think that he has anything to give an heir, for in his own right he has nothing. Bladacglen is a title of origin, rather than ownership. It is his wife who has a small endowment, and that only for the remainder of her life." His laughter rang out above the music. "They would not have that, were it not for the wife's willingness to tell me that her daughter is residing as a guest of the Baron of Oatlands. Information for which I am certain my cousin Griffith will be very grateful."

Henry smiled his approval at the woman as she finished her little tune and placed the lute at his feet. He sensed, rather than saw, Catherine lean toward him, urging him to go on with his story. "You will remember the daughter," he continued in deference to his wife. "It is Mistress Bess. The girl who saved my life."

Catherine nodded, pleased that she again had her husband's full attention. "But of course. Mistress Bess asked leave to visit a friend. I thought she would have returned by now. But what has she to do with Sir Morris?"

Henry snapped around so quickly that the chair in which he sat threatened to overturn.

"Sir Morris? Are you telling me it was to Sir Morris you granted guardianship of this child?"

"But of course." The queen was taken aback by her husband's abrupt change of attitude. "I have been telling you for the past several minutes. But what has Bess to do with this?" she asked again.

"What has Bess to do with Sir Morris? Bess is his stepdaughter! Surely it was not her child you gave to Sir Morris to raise!" Suddenly he was on his feet, and the women shrank back in fear at his mounting rage.

The queen did not flinch, but her eyes shifted nervously as her moment of triumph evaporated.

"For the love of heaven, woman, do you know what you've done? You've given Griffith Beaufort's child to one of the most devious men in my kingdom. If Sir Morris gets his hands on that child, he will spirit it away and we won't see it until it is old enough and powerful enough to challenge our own children, through right of blood royal, for the throne of England!"

Catherine gasped and put her hand over her mouth. "It cannot be. The woman in my service was called Bess Blummer. I know my own ladies-in-waiting."

"But obviously not well enough to keep you from interfering where you should defer to me." Henry's chair clattered from the dais and tumbled to the marble floor. "You have put my throne in jeopardy, and threatened the very foundation of my kingdom, not to mention the welfare of the woman who risked her life to save mine. I have things to do other than to repair your mistakes, but now I will be forced to take time from my busy schedule to do so."

Henry marched toward the door as the ladies scattered like flower petals in the wake of a storm. He flung the doors open as he turned again to the queen. "From this time forward, I would appreciate it if you would restrain yourself from interfering in situations that are none of your affair." With that, he cursed roundly as he stomped back toward his own quarters.

Lady Mary sat stunned by what she had seen and heard. She now knew where Bess had gone, and realized her friend must be warned without delay of Sir Morris's plan to take her and Griffith's child.

Making her curtsy to the distraught queen, Mary went to summon a messenger to deliver her warning to Bess.

Bess accepted the baron's explanation of Ian's failure to deliver the message with quiet dignity, but the baron was aware that she carried an air of expectancy about her that had nothing to do with the upcoming birth of her child. Together they awaited word from Griffith, reassuring each other that the news, or the man himself, would surely come.

As the days dragged on, the baron saw Bess pale at the doubt that could not be kept at bay. "What if the rumors are true?" she burst out, unable to hold back her fears. "What if he is ordered to wed?"

The baron patted her hand. "What if the woman he is to wed is you, and he has been searching these past days, trying to find you?"

Bess sighed and rested her head on the old man's shoulder. "I pray that what you say is true, but in my heart there is great fear."

"I swear to you, I will protect and shelter you until my last breath, and beyond if the good Lord gives me the means to do so," he vowed. "Put your mind at rest, my child. Your anxiety cannot be good for the babe. All will be set to rights. I will see that it is so."

And while his words were brave and his voice was firm, the baron could only pray that he would live long enough to keep his promise, for without his living presence at her side, the baron knew, Sir Morris would be upon Bess in a heartbeat. He added his own prayers and supplications to hers as they both prayed that Griffith Beaufort would come to Bess's aid, and in all haste.

Bess had grown more lethargic as her time drew near. She rested more often and gave the orders for management of the household from her solar, rather than overseeing the servants herself, as she had done when she had first arrived at Oatlands. The servants loved and respected her and did not shirk in their duties, whether she was there to watch them or not. They took pride in their work and gladly went about their tasks according to her specifications.

As she rested, Bess allowed her thoughts to wander back to the days she and Griffith had spent together. She remembered so clearly the love in his eyes when he had come to her. The light of anticipation and desire as he had taken her in his arms. His words of love and adulation over the softness and the whiteness of her skin. His compliments as he had told her how he loved to look at her lithe body and rounded limbs.

What would he think if he saw her now? She had been in the bloom of pregnancy when last they met. It would no doubt be a shock should he come upon her and behold her in her last stages, her belly filled to overflowing with his babe.

And there was no doubt that the child would be of good size and health, for it kicked mightily, causing even the skirts of her gowns to bounce. The baron watched for any movement of the babe, and chortled with delight each time the child actively expressed himself.

"Sometimes I almost wish Griffith would not come until after the child is born," Bess confided to the baron. "I am so ungainly. I do not wish him to see me this way."

"You are beautiful, and do not think otherwise. Remember, your ungainliness is brought about by his child, and he will rejoice," the baron assured her. And for a time Bess's fears were assuaged.

The sun was warm and the weather fair. The baron asked Bess to walk with him along the battlements. "The heat feels good against these old bones," he commented as they moved slowly along. His age and her condition made them a perfect match in pace and endurance, for they stopped often and looked out over the countryside.

It was during one of these periods of rest that they spied the horseman riding just beyond the copse of trees that surrounded the castle.

Bess reached out and took the baron's arm. "Look! There! A rider, just through the trees!"

The baron did not see the man at once, but the horse moved at such a pace that he was soon well within easy view.

"I do not recognize the colors," the baron mused. "Bess, do you know them?" He turned to where she had been standing, only to see her hurrying toward the tower door to greet the messenger in the courtyard when he arrived. "Is it Griffith?" the baron called, following as quickly as his age allowed.

Bess was in the courtyard when the man rode through the open gates and into the bailey.

The baron could see the disappointment on her face as she realized it was not Griffith Beaufort riding toward her. Panting for breath he reached her side to be nearby, whatever news the man might bring.

The baron was certain that this man must be Beaufort's forerunner, come to tell Bess to prepare herself to leave. It saddened him, but he knew it must be done.

Her love for Griffith was such that it could not be denied and would not dim with time or distance. The baron would miss her bright presence, but he would never begrudge her the happiness she could find only with the man she loved. He only hoped that they would wait at Oatlands until after the babe was born, for it would do no good for mother or child to leave with Bess's time so close upon her.

He would make the offer, but he knew that the final decision was out of his hands.

The man dismounted and bowed before them. "I bring a message of the utmost import," he announced. "It is to be given to no one but Mistress Elizabeth Blummer. Are you she?" He bowed again, somewhat agape at the shining countenance of the beautiful young woman standing before him.

"I am Elizabeth Blummer," Bess said, fighting to control her voice and keep from snatching the missive.

Without further ado, he placed the letter in her hands. She stared at it, unseeing, knowing she could not trust herself to open it for yet a moment. Somewhere in the vast recesses of her mind she heard the baron's voice.

"You have ridden hard and long. Whence did you come?"

"I rode direct and with all haste from Greenwich, where the king and queen are in residence."

"You do not wear the royal livery," the baron observed.

"Oh, I do not come from the king." The man laughed easily. "I serve the house of Essex. It was the Lady Mary who sent me, insisting that I give the note to no one but Mistress Bess. I was also instructed to stay at the lady's disposal should there be a need."

The baron's brow furrowed. So the man was not from Griffith—but perhaps he brought news of him. Bess had mentioned Lady Mary often, and with great affection. Indeed, it was at Essex that the Baron had first seen Bess, and hers had been a place of honor and friendship in that household, as it was in his own.

"There is refreshment within," he told the messenger, deftly moving him toward the door to give Bess the privacy she might need in reading her letter.

Bess stepped away a bit and broke the seal. As the men reached the door, she gave a little cry. The nimble young messenger leaped past his older counterpart and caught her in his arms as she collapsed, the letter clutched tightly in her hand.

They carried her through the hall and into the library, where the young man placed her on a couch.

The housekeeper waved burned feathers under Bess's nose until her eyelids fluttered. Once she regained consciousness, the baron sent both the messenger and the somewhat indignant housekeeper away.

"What is it that has upset you so?" he asked as Bess opened her eyes. "Has your friend sent unpleasant news regarding your young man?"

Bess struggled to a sitting position. "Unpleasant, most definitely, but it has nothing to do with Griffith," she told him, fear and anxiety creeping into her voice.

"Can you tell me what has happened to upset you so?" he persisted.

Bess drew in a ragged breath. "It is Sir Morris," she managed. "Mary is in waiting to the queen, and has learned that Catherine has appointed Sir Morris guardian of my unborn child."

At first, the baron could not comprehend her words. Then his hand slammed against the mantel. "It cannot be so! How could the woman do such a thing?"

"Apparently he petitioned for guardianship, labeling me as unworthy to be a mother because I am not married."

"Then you shall be married. I will marry you, without delay. Morris of Bladacglen will have neither you nor your babe. I swear it on my hope of heaven."

Tears streamed down Bess's cheeks. "But I cannot! You said yourself that Griffith did not receive my original message telling him I was at Oatlands, and Ian has hardly had time to find Griffith and tell him where I am. I cannot marry you, when Griffith might arrive at any moment."

"Would you let that toad, Sir Morris, snatch your child from your breast?" the old man asked, losing patience as the possibility of having to fight Sir Morris became more imminent.

"You would not let Sir Morris snatch the babe. You have sworn..."

The baron sat beside her and took her hands in his. "Bess, Sir Morris may come with an army. He knows I will fight him. But he knows I am an old man, no longer prepared for war, and in all likelihood, I will lose. Unless I can protect you by giving you my name as my wife, I do not know how I can keep him from ultimately taking your child. We can only hope that Griffith comes in time to intervene."

"I will leave here. I will go away where Sir Morris will never find me," she said, struggling to her feet, only to have her knees buckle beneath her. Her pain-filled eyes met the baron's, and she crushed his hands against the pain. "Call the midwife. I think my time is upon me."

It was a long, miserable ride, and Griffith arrived at Oatlands red-eyed and unshaven. He had not known sleep from the moment he had been accosted by Ian, the messenger from Oatlands, who had discovered Griffith at the convent and all but fallen on him in his joy as he tearfully recited his somewhat garbled message regarding Bess's plight. The mention of Sir Morris had been enough to send Griffith racing to her, leaving the little messenger far behind, dragging his lame horse and loudly giving thanks to his Maker that the lost Griffith had been found.

The gates of Oatlands were open, although it was very early in the morning and servants bustled back and forth between the castle and the village below.

"Is this a day of celebration?" Griffith asked the sentry.

"Nay, my lord. But, God willing, it soon will be! Our fine lady has taken to term, and even now we await news of the birth." The man glanced up at the solar wall. "'Tis only that it seems an overlong time. O'course, 'tis different for a lady, I'll warrant. Why, my wife hardly had time to get inside the house before our first child was born. And a fine, healthy lad he was, at that." He beamed at the thought of his first-born and dutifully held the knight's horse.

Griffith clutched the man's arm. "Is it Lady Bess who lies in labor within?"

The man nodded, giving Griffith a split-toothed grin. "That be our lady," he agreed.

Griffith buried his face in his hands. "I wish to see the baron," he told the steward as he dismounted. "I am Griffith Beaufort."

The Baron of Oatlands stood before the huge fireplace, his coat of arms bravely displayed above, Griffith noted as he entered the room. Even with his many years, the man was an imposing figure.

Warily the two men eyed each other.

The baron spoke first. "Why did you not wed with Bess when she told you she was to have your babe?"

Griffith, though taken aback, could not stop the truth that sprang from his lips. "I had no idea she would leave Essex. I thought she loved me as I did her."

"Leave! She was drugged and kidnapped by Morris of Bladacglen and brought here under the pretext of my taking her child as my heir in payment for Sir Morris's debts. I did not know that it was Bess's child of which he spoke, and when I saw it was she, I took her into my house and ordered him from my property, ignoring his wrath. But the man is evil and seeks revenge." The old knight clapped the younger one on the shoulder. "Thank God you have come in time."

The look on Griffith's face was one of such utter confusion, the baron knew his words had taken the man completely unawares.

This was the father of the child Bess now labored to bear. He prayed the man would prove his love for Bess by giving her his name and his protection.

Griffith strode across the floor, running his fingers through his thick hair.

"I was overthrown when I returned from Calais to find Bess gone. It was as though she had disappeared from this earth. No one knew where she had gone. The Lady Mary was as clueless as myself, and the servants at Essex knew nothing. She seemed to have vanished without a trace. It wasn't until I met Ian that I knew she had tried in vain to reach me, and waited anxiously for me, as I searched unceasingly for her."

"You acknowledge the child is yours?" the baron challenged.

Beaufort threw caution to the winds. "Bess has known no man other than myself. On that I would stake my life."

"And so it is to this day. You have been and shall always be her only and dearest love," the baron told him. "She needs you far more than you realize. She has been in labor for a great many hours—far too long, in my opinion—but the child will not be born. I fear for them both."

There was a rapping at the door. Both men turned as an old woman appeared. At the baron's silent question, she shook her head. The hopelessness in the woman's face echoed in the baron's voice.

"If you would see Bess alive, go to her now. I have protected her from the world to the best of my ability. I cannot protect her from the will of God."

Wordlessly Griffith clasped the old man's hand before following the woman from the room.

Bess lay white-faced and still against the pillows. Her labor had ceased, and still the babe would not be born. The women wept for their mistress, but there was little else they could do.

Griffith knelt at her side, stroking her hair and whispering her name, but there was no response. He turned to the woman who had brought him to the room.

"Surely something more can be done!"

"No, my lord, there is nothing more to do, except pray. Had the baron demanded it, we would have taken the babe from her body earlier, when we were sure it still lived, though it might well have cost the life of the mother, but he would not hear of it. Now our lady has not the strength to deliver, and the child has not the strength to be born. I fear it is all over. We have sent for the priest."

Realizing Griffith might only have moments in which to be alone with Bess, the midwife sent her companions into the outer chamber.

Griffith turned to the bed, taking Bess's hands in his. A thousand thoughts flew through his mind. Bess, as she had looked the first time he saw her, in the chapel at Pembroke. Bess, as she had laughed and danced in the gypsy camp. Bess, as she had defied every social law by coming to his tent to tend his wounds. Bess, her eyes filled with love and desire for him, always, only for him. He could not bear to lose her, when he had only now found her again. He could not bear to live without her, for without her the world was filled with emptiness.

Without realizing what he did, Griffith had spoken his thoughts aloud. Bess's eyelids fluttered and opened slowly to focus on his face.

"Griffith..." she whispered. "Is it truly you? How came you here?"

"I came to see the birth of our son, but I was delayed by a misdelivered note, and you, my beloved, always thoughtful of my wishes, have waited for my arrival."

A soft smile played about the corners of her lips. "He is a strong and lusty son. I thought he must have come, though I did not hear him cry, yet I have no more pain. Just a sense of peace that has come with your presence. I am thankful for the respite, although my dearest wish has been to have you near when our child is born. Was it so with you, my lord?"

"I wished for nothing but you, my love. I feared the worst. Beaufort wives have always had trouble birthing their babes."

Bess's eyes misted. "Our son is strong and healthy. He kicks mightily. I have longed to have you feel his strength."

Bess took Griffith's hand and laid it against the mound of her stomach.

"Poor little mite," Bess said dreamily. "After such a long, fruitless struggle, he must be sleeping."

Griffith placed both hands against her belly, bowing his head until his forehead touched between them. "Aye—" the tears in his voice were muffled "—assuredly, he sleeps now, our little son." And so shall he sleep...forever, Griffith thought, as the last remnants of hope left him.

If only he had not gone with Henry to Calais. The child might have come into the world amid joy and happiness, rather than being trapped inside his mother's body, where he would perish along with Bess's and with Griffith's hearts.

He thought he had prayed with sincerity when he searched for Bess, but to find her and lose her in the same hour was more than he could bear.

"Oh, Bess, Bess, I love thee...and I will love thee forever," he whispered.

Suddenly Bess stiffened beneath his hands. A cry was wrung from her lips. Griffith's head jerked up as Bess grasped his hands in a grip that bespoke both pain and renewed strength.

As the pain subsided, he brushed the hair from her forehead, pressing his lips against the smooth skin as he murmured words of encouragement and hope. Hope that was born in his heart as he bent to kiss the hands that clung to his.

With each pain, his hope was renewed. Perhaps the child had regained his strength and would now enter the world alive and strong.

But regardless of the strength of the child or the severity of the pains, Bess grew weaker as the moments passed.

"If she loses consciousness before the babe is born, it is all over for them both," the midwife confided as she gave him a damp cloth with which to wipe Bess's forehead.

"Look at me, my love." Griffith called Bess back from the edge of consciousness. "Look at me, and fight to give our son his life." He sought to keep the tears of despair from his eyes and his voice. "Remember how brave you were when you traveled across England to save my life and Henry's. You did not give up then until your mission was accomplished, and you must not now. You must stay with me and see our child well born into this world and stay with him until he grows to be a man, for I vow I cannot live without you, any more than can he."

He buried his lips in the palm of her hand. Through her pain, Bess remembered the first time he had done so. Remembered the thrill that had run through her body, settling in its core, leaving her legs too weak to hold her.

For one split second, she relaxed against the pain. The tightly held muscles gave way to the remembrance of their love as Griffith held her in the embrace of his eyes and his arms until she moaned, arching against him, and he threw the covers aside in time to ease his child from her body.

Griffith's shouts, and the cries of the newborn babe, brought the women rushing into the room to finish the delivery, but Griffith refused to relinquish the child.

"Our son, Bess," he said as he laid the child across her stomach.

"Our son..." she repeated as she touched the tiny hand before slipping quietly into a peaceful sleep.

Chapter Seventeen

Bess slept long and dreamlessly while her tired body regained its strength. In their euphoria over the birth of the healthy babe and the near-escape from the jaws of death of both mother and child, the baron and Griffith toasted each other over and over as relief and joy obliterated all other consideration.

Shortly before dawn, the baron went to his room, but Griffith returned to Bess's side, watching while she slept. The baby fussed, cared for by the wet-nurse, who asked Griffith if he wanted to hold the child. As he held the warm, sweet-smelling babe, a drowsy sense of well-being overcame him. He was starting to his feet to put the baby back in his cradle when he saw Bess's eyes upon him.

Silently she held out her arms and took the child, but when he would have returned to his chair, she stopped him.

"Stay here with us," she begged.

Sliding gently atop the quilt, Griffith took Bess and his son in his arms, and with a newly discovered sense of peace the little family slept, wrapped in the embrace of love.

Their rest was disturbed at the first light of dawning as the castle was awakened by an insistent pounding on the gates of the bailey.

Bleary-eyed guards stumbled forward to ascertain what the problem might be.

"Open the gates," a knight shouted up at them. "Open the gates in the name of the queen."

The men blinked in confusion, their minds befuddled by their own celebration of the previous day's events. And while they did not wish to wake the baron at such an hour, they knew they stood to receive just punishment if this man's clatter disturbed their lady. The men had begun lifting the heavy crossbar that held the massive gates closed when Lady Mary's messenger ran up to them.

"Do not open the gates until you receive the order from your master," he warned them. "I fear it is the men who wait without that I came to warn you against. Awaken the baron, or you will rue the day."

The guards looked at each other, and then at the man with whom they had been celebrating the night before.

"We will do as you say," they told him, "but should you be wrong in your assessment of the situation, it is you who will rue the day."

With that, one of the men went to the keep, while the other sought to silence the insolent knight who raised such a commotion outside the walls.

The baron himself awakened Griffith. When the man was not in the bed assigned to him, the baron went to Bess's chambers and spirited Griffith, still groggy from sleep, into the hallway.

"You must come quickly," the old man said. "Sir Morris has come to take your child, and he swears he has a writ from the queen herself giving him permission to do so."

Griffith tried to clear his mind from the remnants of the first decent sleep he had known in over a week. His head throbbed and his body ached as though he had given birth to the babe himself, but the Baron's words were not to be ignored. Especially words that were prefaced with the name Sir Morris.

"What are you saying?" he asked, wondering if the old man had been pushed over the edge of sanity from the strain of the previous day.

A repeated pounding sounded in the distance and echoed through the castle like the footsteps of doom as Griffith struggled to clothe himself.

"A messenger came from Bess's friend, Lady Mary," the baron said as he tried to help Griffith garb himself. "The man said that Sir Morris had obtained papers from the queen giving him guardianship of Bess's child. Before we could investigate, Bess went into labor, and I became so concerned with her condition, I vow I forgot all about Sir Morris and the threat he posed."

Griffith stared at the man in disbelief. "We will go down now and read these papers Sir Morris claims to have obtained," he said, and fled from the room with the baron hurrying in his wake.

The sky lightened to reveal a small army of men, which Sir Morris had brought to strengthen his claim. Griffith went with one of the guards to inspect the weapons stored in the armory, while the baron stood firm on the battlements, ordering Sir Morris from his land. Sir Morris held to his premise and demanded that he be allowed to take the child since he had already ascertained from conversation with the guards that Bess's child had been born.

"I will not leave without Bess's child," Sir Morris declared. "If you do not give me the child, prepare for a siege."

The baron almost laughed. It was unimaginable that at his age he should be threatened by this upstart, and with something as damaging and time-consuming as a siege. Yet from the size of the army and the number of war machines they possessed, a siege looked to be very possible.

"I demand to see this order from the queen," he called, challenging the knight. "I do not believe you speak true."

"I have the paper, old man," Sir Morris boasted, "and I will show it to you, or your representative, but only on my terms. It does not leave my hands, for I trust you no more than you trust me."

"Very well," the baron decided. "We will meet on either side of the portcullis and each of us will hold on to the paper through the iron grillwork, so that it may be read by myself and any representative I chose."

"Agreed." Sir Morris gave a wicked snort, for he knew that his writ came from the queen and must be obeyed.

Sir Morris did not take the time to wonder at the tall, hooded guard who stood beside the baron and read the document over his shoulder. He was secure in his rights, and felt certain the baron was powerless to do anything more than offer token objection. He knew Bess would never marry the baron while Griffith Beaufort lived, and as long as she refused to wed, she fell under his dominion as his wife's daughter.

The thought of Edwina irritated him. The woman failed to see the advantages of taking Bess's child and asked—nay, begged him— to reconsider. He could not help but wonder if she did so in consideration of her daughter's feelings, or because she did not wish to rear another child. It was impossible for him to tell, and in truth, he did not care. It was enough that the child would be his, and if Bess refused to relinquish the babe to him, Bess would be his, also.

"Enough!" he said as he jerked the paper from the baron's hand. "You have read enough to know that what I say is true. You can see the signature and seal of the queen. By law, you must relinquish the child to me, and at once."

The hooded guard bent toward his master, as though to support him against Sir Morris's verbal onslaught. It pleased Morris to think that his very words were deemed so powerful that the baron must have assistance to sustain himself against them.

But when the old man looked at Sir Morris through the bars of the portcullis, his eyes were hard and unforgiving. "The document you have is worthless, Sir Morris," he said. "There is no Elizabeth of Bladacglen on my lands or in my house. And no woman of that name has borne a child, to my knowledge. Now, be off with you. You have no business here."

Sir Morris's eyes narrowed. He looked at the document and tried to decipher the words. He could write his name, or sign for the amount of a debt, but having no inordinate knowledge of the written word, Sir Morris assumed that his contemporaries, as well as his peers, were no better off than himself. Indeed, he could not read the document, and was stunned that the baron could do so.

"I see no discrepancy," he blustered. "The girl is of my house and identified as being of Bladacglen. She is unmarried, and while you may keep her here if you so choose, her bastard child is mine to do with as I please. I will take the child, with or without the mother."

"You will take nothing," the baron declared. "Nothing except yourself and your men off my lands."

"They will not be your lands when I report to the queen the injustice and disrespect you have shown her authority," Sir Morris threatened.

"I cannot give what I do not have," the baron returned. "There is no Elizabeth of Bladacglen in my household."

"She is here! She is here!" Morris raged. "I will have her if I must starve every man, woman and child from this place." He beat against the bars in frustration. "You have no recourse but to give the child to me. The queen will have your head for this! Henry will destroy your house and all inside for disrespect to the wishes of his wife."

He hammered on the grillwork as the men continued to walk away. "Come back here! Come back, I say! By the queen's command! Come back!"

But they did not so much as look back as they disappeared into the castle and the guard secured the gate for a siege.

"The man is right, you know," the baron admitted to Griffith. He paced back and forth beneath his coat of arms in the great hall. "Oatlands is not prepared for war of any kind, let alone a siege. And I have no doubt the man will fight. He is obsessed with the idea of having Bess, and he knows if he takes her child she will go also."

"The man has no grounds. The writ was obviously acquired under false pretenses. He dared not even identify Bess by her true name. It is a farce, and should be treated as such," Griffith scoffed.

"But it is a farce signed and sealed by the queen of England and, therefore, cannot be taken lightly," the baron pointed out.

Griffith brushed the situation aside. "There is no cause for alarm. By the time he can mount his siege, Bess and I will be man and wife. He cannot take the legitimate son of the king's cousin, regardless of the paper he holds."

But the baron shook his head. "It is not so simple," he said. "With Sir Morris outside the walls, I doubt there is any chance we will be able to smuggle the priest into the castle."

Griffith opened his mouth to protest, but his words were cut off by the sound of a catapult slicing through the summer morn.

* * *

Ian was more than glad to be returning to his home, knowing that his misadventure had been assuaged and his misdeed, forgiven. He was proud that he had found Griffith Beaufort and, after confessing his part in the fiasco, sent the knight on to Oatlands, where he had no doubt been reunited with Mistress Bess.

As his horse plodded through the copse of trees that surrounded the estate, he wondered if the child had already been born. It was only when he was within sight of the castle itself that he realized there was undue activity in the area.

Curiosity piqued, he dismounted and moved silently toward the castle. Could it be a festival honoring the birth of the child? Or was it a saint's day he had somehow forgotten?

He stopped at the edge of the trees, his mouth dropping open in astonishment mixed with horror. His home, his Oatlands, was being attacked, and from all indications, the attacker was preparing for siege.

He ducked back into the wood and almost tripped over an old woman. "What do you here, good mother?" he asked, recognizing one of the elders of the village.

"I was not quick enough to get inside the castle walls, and am destined to hide within the safety of the wood until the siege is over," she told him.

"But who has taken such action against our lord?" Ian asked in bewilderment.

"Some dastardly coward known as Sir Morris of Bladacglen. He has come to take Lady Bess's babe, but the baron and the knight, Lord Beaufort, have vowed to fight to the death to protect her," the woman expounded.

"Then Lord Beaufort is here?" Ian demanded.

"Inside the castle walls," the woman told him.

"And the child has been born?"

"A fine, healthy boy," she said.

"But what claim can Sir Morris possibly have on the child of Lady Bess and Griffith Beaufort?" he asked, almost to himself.

"Hah!" the woman's laugh was mirthless. "I'll tell you what claim. The claim of guardianship. Signed by the queen of England herself. And he will take the child, or raze the castle trying. And there be no one inside to even baptize the poor little mite, for the priest came back from ministering to the sick and found himself trapped here in the woods with me!"

Ian looked at the castle and at his tired horse. He knew what he must do, and there was no time to waste.

"Thank you for your information, good mother," he said as he swung into the saddle. "And keep yourself hidden until I return."

He touched his heels to his mount and galloped off the way he had come.

Ian knew there was little hope of his getting an audience with the king, but he also knew he had no choice. The baron had given him a second chance, even though Ian knew he didn't deserve it. He was certain Bess had interceded for him, and that it had been her prayers, as well as his, that led him to the convent where Griffith had stopped.

His indiscretion had been such that he could have been put to death on the spot, and with justification, yet his liege had spared his life and allowed him to make amends. Now it was Ian's turn to save the life of his master. Somehow he would make the king listen to his plea.

Ian had seen the royal standard flying from the turret of Richmond Castle and knew the king had gone to Yorkshire. Now he rode desperately for that destination, in the hope he would not be too late.

It was with great relief that he saw the standard still flying. He climbed stiffly from his horse and started forward, only to find crossed halberds blocking his way.

Just then Henry walked across the lawns surrounded by his court.

"Your Grace!" Ian shouted. "Your Grace! A boon! A boon!" He dodged and shifted, trying to catch the attention of his king.

"Stay back, you fool," the guard growled, thrusting him aside.

"You must hear me, Your Grace!" Ian's voice rose in desperation.

"He'll hear you, and order you silenced forever if you don't stop your caterwauling. Petition the gentlemen of the bedchamber for an audience, if you must have the king's ear."

"Your Grace! Please, hear me!" Ian persisted as the guards pushed him back, until finally in utter desperation, Ian realized that he would not be allowed to speak to the king until it was too late for Mistress Bess, for Griffith, for the baron, and for Ian's beloved Oatlands.

"Your Majesty!" he shouted as the guards lifted him from his feet. "Sir Morris lays siege to Lady Bess!"

The king stopped and turned toward the disturbance. "Hear you what he said?" Henry asked.

"He said Sir Morris has laid siege to a lady," one of the men chortled before bursting into full laughter, in which Henry joined.

"So it is Sir Morris again, is it?" Henry mused. He had given orders that Sir Morris be arrested and relieved of his ill-gained writ regarding Griffith's child. Apparently the man had managed to evade the king's men.

"Bring that man to me," Henry ordered with a snap of his fingers.

The guards dumped Ian unceremoniously at Henry's feet. Ian scrambled to his knees, glanced up to make certain the king was paying attention, and launched into his story.

He had given no more than the briefest details when Henry flew into a rage, muttering curses against interfering women, lecherous knights, inept soldiers, and queens who should concentrate on bearing healthy children rather than trying to take babes from their parents. Henry blasted his way through lords and ladies, and paused in his advance and his tirade only long enough to say that he would see to this matter himself. His men must be ready to ride within the hour. When they arrived, all would know what it meant to thwart the wishes of the king.

Though weak from childbirth, Bess climbed from her bed as the first sound of the projectiles from the catapult hit the courtyard. She watched from the window of the solar until the men and women of Oatlands had fought off the attack with projectiles and arrows of their own. It was only after Sir Morris had gone back to lick his wounds that Bess made her way down to the great hall, where Griffith and the Baron discussed further defenses.

Through the huge doors, Bess could see the damaged walls being shored up by the men. She caught the glimmer of tears in the baron's eyes before he could turn away.

"My lords, you must help me to escape with my babe. If I am not here, Sir Morris will have no cause to destroy Oatlands."

"It is too late to safely smuggle you out," the baron told her with a shake of his head. "And I would not take the chance, had I the opportunity. You are far too weak to survive such a trip, even with Griffith at your side."

"We have no choice but to fight," Griffith admitted. "I would it were otherwise, but there is nothing more we can do. Sir Morris has the advantage, and the armed, trained men. If we could send a message to the king, we might be saved."

"We can send one of the men from Oatlands. Although that has not always been the most suitable choice, either," he added, remembering the fiasco of Ian's supposed delivery.

"We will send a man out just after nightfall," Griffith proposed. "In the meantime, you, Bess, will go back to your bed." He lifted her in his arms and carried her up the stairs.

"I should stay down here and manage the household," she protested. "The siege may be lengthy and the servants will need someone to keep order and distribute the supplies."

Griffith realized the wisdom of her words. "Perhaps you could have a couch placed near the hearth in the great hall. You can give your orders from there, but I will not have you running from buttery to battlement until you have regained your strength. Without you, I have nothing to fight for, nothing to live for, nothing to love," he murmured against her neck.

"Ah, but you have," she reminded him gently. "You have our son."

"And I love him dearly," Griffith agreed, "but he is not you."

Bess relaxed in his arms and let him place her on her bed, knowing she had gained a great concession in being able to run the household from the hall, as well as having heard the assurance of Griffith's love for her. But love mattered little if Sir Morris broke through the meager barriers and won the day, for even the greatest love meant little when life was taken away.

Her first thought was to pray, but there was too much to be done. Her prayer would be one of action, and she knew

God would look on them with mercy and understanding, in that they stood and fought against evil, rather than knelt and waited for evil to overtake them.

She called to her women and gave orders for them to make her a cot in the hall. Then she sent for the steward and went over the supplies and staples stored inside the castle walls and tried to get an estimate of how many people must be cared for. And, although the numbers were not reassuring, Bess knew that, somehow, she and Griffith would surmount this dilemma and survive. Together, they would win out, against all odds.

Chapter Eighteen

By the end of the third day, the people of Oatlands knew they could not hold out against Sir Morris and his mercenaries. The men he had with him were professional soldiers, hired out for pay. They were assured of reward by the queen's seal on the document Sir Morris showed them. It was to their benefit that they work with all haste to carry out the queen's wishes, take the payment Sir Morris had promised them and be off to work for another knight who would pay for their services. They fought tirelessly to finish the job they had set out to accomplish.

Bess had established herself in the great hall of the castle, and ran the household from there. Each day there were many mouths to feed, and wounds to care for, as well as fires to be put out and damage to assess. Reports were brought to her by the servants, Griffith and the baron himself.

It pained the baron to see his beloved home torn asunder, and it pained Bess to see him hurt; still, he would not allow her to take the chance to escape, although her strength had returned in good stead. It was all either man could do to keep her on her cot near the fire. Many times they entered the hall to find her on her feet, ordering her women around with an inordinate amount of energy.

"I have sent another messenger," Griffith said as they sat before the hearth to partake of the evening meal. Noble and servant alike ate of the simple fare in an effort to conserve the food they had. "I doubt the others made it to their destination. Indeed, one of the men was run down by Sir Morris's mercenaries as we watched from the battlements."

The baron's eyes were filled with worry. If a swift young man could not get through the lines, how could they hope to flee unnoticed with Bess and her babe?

The older man and Griffith had an unspoken agreement that they would protect Bess and the child at all costs, but Sir Morris was driven by greed, and payment would come soon.

Bess brought her babe down with her and placed him in a basket beside the hearth. As long as he was with her, she felt secure regarding his safety. The wet-nurse watched over both the little lordling and her own infant as they slept in the warm shadows near the hearth. Bess's eyes swept over them often. She was glad when her baby awakened and she could hold his sweet softness.

He gurgled and waved his fist, and Bess relinquished him to his wet-nurse to be fed. Sensing the lordling was receiving nourishment, the little son of the wet-nurse began to fuss, and Bess picked him up.

The wet-nurse looked at her gratefully. "Thank you, m'lady, for showing such concern for my babe," the woman said. "He almost seems to know that he is being passed over, for I vow, even I put the welfare of our little master above all else."

Bess looked at the fine, fair son of the peasant woman. He was a lovely babe, and it seemed unjust even to her that he should be placed second, but such was the way of the nobility.

The wet-nurse sighed. "It seems so strange that an army would fight for one child, while another is all but forgotten. I worry for him." Her eyes rested on the child on Bess's lap.

"There is little need to worry," Bess told her. "As William's wet-nurse, your child will be raised in my household, and be given far more opportunities than the other children of the castle. How else would it be?"

"It could only be as you say, m'lady," the woman agreed, without meeting Bess's eyes, for the women could not help but wonder if either child would leave Oatlands alive.

That night, Griffith escorted Bess to her room while the baron walked the battlements, watching for signs of attack.

"We expect nothing before first light," Griffith told her. "But, from what we can see, it looks as though Sir Morris is regrouping for a final attack. He is making ready to breach the walls, and we can only try to fight him off. But even then, it will only be a matter of time. We cannot hold out forever, and since he has the writ from the queen, the men have not deserted him as we had hoped they would."

"Could we not leave now, under cover of night?" Bess said, clutching his linen shirt. It was soft and warm beneath her fingers. "Surely we could slip away unnoticed."

But Griffith shook his head. "We have not been able to get even a swift messenger through the lines. I would have taken you and William away with me had there been even a remote chance that it could be done without dire risk. Sir Morris is mad with his lust for power. He will not rest until he has our son. Furthermore, we have not been able to get the priest into the castle to perform the wedding ceremony."

"But Sir Morris does not even know you are here, does he?" Bess asked.

"I have tried to keep out of sight," Griffith admitted. "None of the villeins would tell."

"If we were to say the baron had been wounded, or fallen ill, surely Sir Morris would allow the priest to come in to give him the last rites."

"And probably come in with him," Griffith observed gloomily. "Although I doubt the man would know the difference between extreme unction and high Mass, if it came to that."

Their eyes locked, and the joy of a shared secret sent a smile to their lips.

"Do you think the baron would agree?" Griffith asked.

"Absolutely!" Bess reached up and kissed him soundly. "We have fooled Sir Morris before," she said gleefully, and proceeded to tell Griffith of the sham betrothal.

"I will go to find him now, and we will put the plan into motion," Griffith told her.

But Bess's hand still lingered against his chest. "I know it is of utmost importance, but must you go now? After all, if the attack is not until the morn, we have the whole night. And although culmination is not possible, there is still a great deal of love that can be shared."

"Just holding you in my arms throughout the night is the culmination of all my prayers," he said as he took her into his arms.

"And so it is with me," she whispered against his neck. "Sometimes I have felt more a part of you during these moments of rest than when we are soaring through the stars of passion."

"We will know passion again, my love," he assured her, "but tonight we will know peace." And he doffed his clothing and lay down on the bed, taking her in his arms.

* * *

He left her before the first light of dawn, but his body was rested and his mind sharp. With great resolve, he went to find the baron.

The old man leaned on the parapet and looked out over the land he loved. In his own mind, he felt he must lose it all, and although he was not ready to do so, he could not doubt that it would ultimately be so.

He turned tired eyes to Griffith, who came rushing up to him with a smile on his face.

"Sire, you look tired," Griffith said.

"I have watched all night." The baron could not understand the younger man's demeanor. A castle under siege was a serious business, even if it was another man's castle.

"You must come inside and lie down. You look sick unto death." This time Griffith raised his voice and winked at the baron.

Realizing that the younger man's voice carried outside the castle walls through the morning silence, the baron was about to deny any weakness, but then he realized Griffith had an ulterior intent. In response to the younger man's whispered explanation, the baron said, in as loud a voice as he could muster and still sound weak, "You will have to help me, my son."

"I fear for you, my lord," Griffith replied, again in stentorian tones. "We must have a priest. The siege has been too much for you."

And as the sun broke through the shadows of night, Sir Morris and his men were able to see a guard carry the old baron from the battlements and into the castle.

Bess, herself, went to the portcullis to plead with Sir Morris.

"You must allow the priest to come within the walls," she called from the relative safety of the enclosure. "You cannot deny an old man the salvation of his immortal soul."

"And if I allow the priest to come in, will you send the child out with him?"

"Never!" Bess threw back at him.

"Then no bargain can be struck," he told her.

"The queen will hear of this, and devout woman that she is, she will take her support from you without hesitation when she learns you have denied an old, dying man his last chance to make his peace with God."

The mercenaries began mumbling. It was well-known that the queen spent many hours each day on her knees in prayer. They had no doubt that she would, indeed, look with disfavor on everything they had achieved, should she hear that one of her subjects had been denied the last rites.

Sir Morris would have ignored Bess's pleas and gone on with his planned attack, but the men balked, and he was forced to reconsider.

"Very well," he agreed hesitantly. "But I shall come with the priest, and stay with him every moment. You'll not smuggle the child out under my nose."

"Thank you, my lord." Bess managed to control the smile in her voice as she climbed from the stool on which she had stood and gave the baron's hand a little squeeze.

The baron lay on his bed. His face was noticeably pale, and his hand trembled slightly as he struggled unevenly for breath.

The priest hurried to him, obvious concern in his face and his voice. "Sire, what has befallen you? Are you wounded?'

"It is my age and the excitement," the baron told him. "I fear my life on this earth is at an end. I wish you to hear my confession, for time grows short."

"Of course." The priest took his place beside the bed, but the baron looked over the holy man's shoulder.

"I wish to confess the sins of a lifetime," he said. "My words are for your ears alone. I do not want my enemy to be party to my revelations."

The priest turned to Sir Morris. "Please, could you not stand outside the door?"

"I will stand *inside* the door," Sir Morris said. "I will not let any of you out of my sight." His eyes were on Bess, and he paid little attention to the bowed footman who obviously served the baron as personal valet.

"You will have to bend down to hear me," the baron told the priest. "I do not wish Sir Morris to know of my dying repentance."

The two men glared at each other past the flustered priest. The holy man bent down, his face a mask of confusion and disbelief at the words the old man spoke.

It seemed they took an inordinately long time, but then, the sins of a lifetime would take some time to relate, especially for so old a man, Sir Morris temporized.

The priest straightened up and glanced at Bess and the footman, who stood on the opposite side of the room. "Would you all gather round the bed, and I will...continue with the rites I have been summoned to perform?"

Sir Morris stood next to the priest on one side of the bed, while Bess and the footman knelt on the other.

Without further hesitation, the priest began praying in Latin. His words were garbled and run together, and Sir Morris was bored, although he watched with some greed as the baron pulled a ring from his little finger and passed it to his footman to give to Bess. Apparently the man had been as taken with the girl as had Sir Morris himself.

But Sir Morris wouldn't begrudge Bess the ring, for in the end he would have her son, and there was nothing, as an unmarried woman under his jurisdiction, that she could do about it.

The priest said more prayers in Latin, which Bess and the footman answered in the same language. Sir Morris had never paid any attention to the religious aspects of life, and had no idea how much longer the rites would continue. He could only hope they were at an end, for he was anxious to be away.

The priest smiled benignly as he made the sign of the cross over the bed. Bess gave the man a dazzling smile, but he held up his hand for discretion.

"I wish to have you sign the Bible, that you have witnessed this ceremony. Because the castle is under siege, I want it known that all was done right and proper and according to God's law," the priest intoned.

With that he brought over the huge book, handwritten by monks. Sir Morris made his mark beneath the date, and the baron followed suit.

"Now—" Sir Morris swaggered across the room "—before I leave, I will have the child, as is my right by law, or I shall bring this building down around your heads."

"May I see the document giving you this authority?" Bess asked.

Sir Morris brought it from his sleeve and gave it to her. "Do not think you can deter me by destroying it. The queen knows what she has signed."

"But this says that you have authority to take the child of an unwed woman, one Elizabeth of Bladacglen, whom we both know does not exist."

"It matters not," Sir Morris insisted. "The child is that of an unmarried woman of my house and under my authority. The child will be taken and raised under my guardianship."

"You have no authority to take the child of a woman wed," Bess pointed out.

"But you are not wed, and your child is a bastard." Sir Morris threw the words at her.

"That is not true," Bess said with great dignity. "I am wed to Griffith Beaufort."

"Griffith Beaufort cannot be found to validate your claim," Sir Morris told her, his tone derisive, "therefore it is void."

"My husband is easily found," Bess said, smiling. "He stands beside me."

Without a word, Griffith allowed the hood he had been wearing to drop from his head, and Sir Morris gasped in surprise and anger.

"Griffith Beaufort may be present, but he is not your husband. Show me proof that you are wed." The smile on Sir Morris's face was smug, as well as evil. He knew they had had no access to a priest since the siege began, and had they been wed when he came, they would have declared it so at that time and saved all a lot of grief.

Griffith took the Bible from the priest. "Here is proof in your own mark, where you have signed as witness to the marriage of Bess Blummer and Griffith Beaufort this day."

Sir Morris stared at the book. He longed to dash it from the man's hands. "It cannot be!" he protested. "It is not legal! I was tricked! I didn't know what I was signing!"

"It matters little," the priest said bluntly. "You did, in fact, witness the ceremony, along with the baron. Lady Bess and Sir Griffith are, indeed, husband and wife before God, and their child is the legitimate issue of that union."

Anything else Griffith would have said was cut short by the sound of horns, accompanied by the rumble of galloping horses. They all rushed to the battlements, the baron, having made a remarkable recovery, leading the way. From their vantage point, they could see the royal standard fluttering boldly in the morning breeze as Henry and his knights rode up before the castle, attacking anything that moved and carried arms.

Griffith handed Sir Morris the document from the queen. "Take your paper and be gone, or you will answer to the king."

Sir Morris dashed the paper to the floor and ran from the battlements, back into the castle.

As he rushed down the stairs from the tower to the hall, he spied a woman nursing an infant next to the fireplace. He skidded to a stop in front of her and peered at the golden head of the babe against her breast.

"You are the wet-nurse for the child of Mistress Bess?" he demanded.

The woman nodded her head, unable to utter a sound when confronted by this harried knight, who grabbed her arm and pushed her from the room. Without giving her a chance to do more than plead for mercy, he set her on the horse the priest had ridden into the castle and led the animal away at a gallop, woman and babe in tow.

The mercenaries, taken off guard by the king's forces, fought for their lives outside the barbican gates. Sir Morris, however, slipped through the postern gate and rode off, leaving his hirelings to fend for themselves against the king's men and the king's anger. He chuckled to himself then, wondering what Bess and Griffith would say when they learned he had stolen their child and his wet-nurse while they congratulated themselves for their cleverness in outsmarting him with their spurious marriage.

"But, my lord," the woman said as they paused on a hillock some distance from the castle so that Sir Morris could see whether or not they were being pursued, "the child is..."

"You keep your mouth shut about what the child is or is not. From now on, he is son of Sir Morris of Bladacglen and his lady, Edwina. You are his wet-nurse, and you will feed him and care for him until he is grown enough to be sent into some fine noble house, where he will serve as a page, a squire, and then someday become a knight."

"A knight?" the woman gasped.

"You have only to keep your mouth shut, and no one will be the wiser as to where he came from, or that he was ever the child of Bess and Griffith Beaufort."

The woman opened her mouth to correct his mistaken concept, but thought better of it. After all, who was she to question a knight of the realm, especially one who had taken her from a besieged castle where she had thought she faced certain death? She drew her son closer to her bosom and decided to take the man's advice. For it was worth her life and that of the child, and, indeed, who was to know?

Back at the castle, the whimpers of discomfort turned to loud cries of hunger as the second babe awoke amid the blankets in his cradle near the hearth. Suddenly he was lifted into warm, loving arms as questions were bandied about him. Then he felt a new and unfamiliar nipple against his pink mouth and took it hungrily as Bess suckled her little son, William Beaufort, and wondered where the wet-nurse could have gone.

Amid loud protestations, the mercenaries were taken prisoner by the king's men. It mattered little to Henry that they swore they had thought they served the queen and car-

ried out her wishes. Prisoners they were, and prisoners they
would remain.

It did not take long for them to convince Henry that they
knew nothing as to the whereabouts of Sir Morris. The man
had disappeared and left them to fend for themselves against
the wrath of the king.

"I came as quickly as possible," Henry told his cousin.
"It was young Ian here who gave me warning, and he will
be nicely rewarded, too, I'll vow. I have decided to take him
into my service, with your permission, of course." The king
acquiesced in form to the baron, but both men knew it was
not a request but a command, with which the baron gladly
complied.

The king's guard reported that they had sighted a man
they thought to be Sir Morris, but he had escaped.

"It seems as though he had with him a woman and
child," Henry said. "Could this account for the disappearance of your wet-nurse?"

"The child of the wet-nurse was a fine, fair boy. Perhaps
he mistook the babe for Bess's child and abducted him,"
Griffith mused.

"The son of the wet-nurse?" Henry's laughter echoed
through the hall. "Morris of Bladacglen has taken the son
of a peasant wet-nurse to raise?" He held his sides in mirth.
"It is more than I could have hoped. Let him raise the boy,
then. It is of no concern to me. We will see that it is docu-
mented as such in the official records, and Sir Morris need
never know, unless he tries to claim that the boy is someone
other than who he is—a peasant lad under the guardianship of Sir Morris and his wife."

"But surely Sir Morris will hear of his mistake and take
out his wrath on the hapless boy and his mother," Bess
worried aloud.

Henry gave her fears but a moment's thought before declaring, "There is little hope of such coming to pass. I have issued a decree that should Sir Morris leave English soil he will be banished and not allowed to return, on pain of death.

"According to my men, Sir Morris is bound for the border and Scotland," Henry said gleefully. "You see, the land I gave your mother, the Lady Edwina, is in Scotland. It is conquered land, and it behooved me to have English residents living there. Nonetheless, it lies in Scotland, and once there, Sir Morris will not be allowed to return to England, in punishment for the trouble he has caused me." Again Henry burst into a fit of laughter. He wiped his eyes and turned to Bess and Griffith. "And what of this fair son of England?" he asked. "Has the boy been christened?"

"Not as yet, Your Grace," Bess said. "The siege began before we were able to get the priest into the castle."

"Very well, then, I shall stand godfather to the boy myself," Henry volunteered, well aware of the honor he imparted. But as he received the thanks of the parents, he saw Bess and the baron exchange a quick look. Always perceptive of the feelings of his subjects, Henry interpreted the look with almost intuitive insight. The baron had been asked to be godfather to the babe, and Bess's quick look had been her apology to him that the honor would not be his.

"Have you chosen a second godparent?" the king asked.

"I had thought my friend, the Lady Mary..." Bess said. "But she is not here."

"Then this boy shall have two godfathers to see that he lives a good life and reaches the rewards of heaven," Henry declared, "for I'm sure the baron will also stand as the child's sponsor. Do you agree?" the king asked.

A smile lit the old man's face. "With all my heart," he said as he smiled at Bess and her child. "I am an old man and have but few years before me, but while I am on this earth I will do my best to see to the spiritual welfare of this child. And when I am gone, I will watch over him from the other side, be the good Lord willing."

"So be it," Henry intoned as he turned to Bess and Griffith. "Now tell me of this extreme unction wedding ceremony that caused Sir Morris to become the witness to the one act that would thwart his plan."

Bess signaled for more wine to be brought as she and Griffith related the story of their impromptu wedding for the edification and unbounded enjoyment of the king.

The morning was kissed with sunlight as Bess, Griffith and the king took their leave of the baron and began their journey toward Griffith's estates.

As they reached a fork in the road, Bess drew her palfrey to a halt and turned to look back at the castle standing sentinel behind her.

"Are you sorry to leave?" Griffith's voice asked gently.

"I found kindness and respect within those walls," Bess told him. "The baron was more than good to me. I pray he lives long enough that little William will know him. He is a fine man. William could not ask for a finer grandsire."

"Nor a finer mother than yourself." Griffith reached over and touched her lips with his.

"I would mother many sons for you, my lord," she murmured, looking down in pretty confusion at her bold admission.

A frown crossed his brow. The memory of her brush with death was still there. Bess saw it clearly.

"It is said the first is the hardest to bear," she told him. "Surely you would not deny me the right to see if it is true."

He did not speak, nor did he move. She rested her hand upon his, waiting until his troubled eyes met hers.

"Would you make a bargain with me, my lord? You see, I also have fears. I fear you will be wounded or killed each time you ride into battle with our king." Bess crossed herself hurriedly to defray the effect of her words. "I know my fear is as great as yours. Would you strike a bargain that if I bear no more children, you will forgo the pleasures of the tournament and any battles that do not specifically threaten your land?"

"I cannot do such a thing! I would be the laughingstock of the court... the country!"

"And would I be less a laughingstock if I were barren for the rest of our marriage?"

Griffith laughed aloud. "God save me! My wife is a convincing woman. A veritable doctor of persuasion!" His laughter ceased, and he leaned toward her. "Very well, we will consider having one more child. But only one! Does that suit you?"

"It suits me very well, my lord husband." She reached up to receive his kiss. "Very well, indeed."

Bess urged her horse forward, her eyes sparkling like frost on an autumn morn. After all, she thought happily, she intended to have only one child... at a time....

* * * * *

MORE ROMANCE, MORE PASSION,
MORE ADVENTURE...MORE PAGES!

Bigger books from Harlequin Historicals. Pick one up today and see the difference a Harlequin Historical can make.

White Gold by Curtiss Ann Matlock—January 1995—A young widow partners up with a sheep rancher in this exciting Western.

Sweet Surrender by Julie Tetel—February 1995—An unlikely couple discover hidden treasure in the next *Northpoint* book.

All That Matters by Elizabeth Mayne—March 1995—A medieval about the magic between a young woman and her Highland rescuer.

The Heart's Wager by Gayle Wilson—April 1995—An ex-soldier and a member of the demi-monde unite to rescue an abducted duke.

Longer stories by some of your favorite authors. Watch for them in 1995 wherever Harlequin Historicals are sold.

HHBB95-1

Take 4 bestselling love stories FREE

Plus get a FREE surprise gift!

Harlequin®
Historical

Why is March the best time to try
Harlequin Historicals for the first time?
We've got four reasons:

All That Matters by Elizabeth Mayne—A medieval woman is freed from her ivory tower by a Highlander's impetuous proposal.

Embrace the Dawn by Jackie Summers—Striking a scandalous bargain, a highwayman joins forces with a meddlesome young woman.

Fearless Hearts by Linda Castle—A grouchy deputy puts up a fight when his Eastern-bred tutor tries to teach him a lesson.

Love's Wild Wager by Taylor Ryan—A young woman becomes the talk of London when she wagers her hand on the outcome of a horse race.

It's that time of year again—that March Madness time of year—when Harlequin Historicals picks the best and brightest new stars in historical romance and brings them to you in one exciting month!

Four exciting books by four promising new authors that are certain to become your favorites. Look for them wherever Harlequin Historicals are sold.

On the most romantic day of the year, capture the thrill of falling in love all over again—with

Harlequin's

Bachelors

They're three sexy and *very single* men who run very special personal ads to find the women of their fantasies by Valentine's Day. These exciting, passion-filled stories are written by bestselling Harlequin authors.

Your Heart's Desire by Elise Title
Mr. Romance by Pamela Bauer
Sleepless in St. Louis by Tiffany White

Be sure not to miss Harlequin's Valentine Bachelors, available in February wherever Harlequin books are sold.

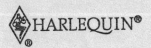 HARLEQUIN®